young,
gifted&dead

LUCY CARVER

MACMILLAN

First published 2013 by Macmillan Children's Books
a division of Macmillan Publishers Limited
20 New Wharf Road, London N1 9RR
Basingstoke and Oxford
Associated companies throughout the world
www.panmacmillan.com

ISBN 978-1-4472-3576-7

1 3 5 7 9 8 6 4 2

A CIP catalogue record for this book is available from
the British Library.

Typeset by Ellipses Digital Limited, Glasgow
Printed and bound by CPI Group (UK) Ltd, Croydon CR0 4YY

chapter one

Nihil sed optimus.

It's Latin for 'nothing but the best'. OK, so quoting a dead language might not seem like a cool way to begin, but it's our school motto and I thought you should know that right from the start.

Anyway, the truth is you can't get through the ancient oak doors of St Jude's Academy unless you have a brain the size of a planet and your parents appear five years running in the *Sunday Times* Rich List.

Nihil sed optimus, like I said.

My brain's a pea compared with my gifted, hyper-intelligent, living-in-a-bubble fellow students. Oh, and I don't have rich parents either, so I have no clue why they ever let me in. The only thing that's special about me is that I have perfect recall: a photographic memory. It's useful for passing exams, but it's not always a blessing – sometimes I have no control over what I remember and the things I'd rather forget – my memory catapults back to a time or a place and it's like living it all over again. And when you see something so awful you want to bury it deep in your mind and never think about it ever again a memory like mine is a cruel thing to have.

Here's the thing about this school – you can wear the

uniform, you can board in a Jacobean mansion in rolling Cotswold countryside with all the protection and privilege in the world, but you can still end up on a mortuary slab four weeks before Christmas, hours after they've dragged your body from the lake.

The body I'm talking about belonged to Lily Earle. She was my roommate and the very first student I met here at St Jude's. She was happy on that first day of term, and that's how I most like to remember her.

'Hey, I'm Lily,' she called across the quad as I lifted suitcases out of the boot of Aunt Olivia's car. 'You must be the new girl, Alyssa.'

I nodded and blushed. *This girl is mega confident. She's a breath of fresh air, no hang-ups to drag her down.*

Boy was I wrong.

I mean Lily dazzled right from the get-go. Her smile was big and broad, her voice low with a husky edge. On that first day her tousled rock-chick hair and black eyeliner set her aside from the uniformed crowd, not to mention the breathtakingly short skirt and the legs that went on forever. I remember every detail.

'You want to meet some of the gang?' she offered. I had no chance to refuse because Lily was as irrepressible as a can of shaken-up Coke – open, hiss and stand back. 'Luke, come over here. Luke Pearson – Alyssa . . . ? Sorry, I forgot your last name.'

'Stephens.'

'Alyssa Stephens. Luke's a maths genius – yuck! And would you believe – his dad drove Formula One racing cars.'

I said hi to a kid who made it clear he couldn't have cared less about meeting little newbie me.

'Gotta go,' he muttered, hitching his bag further on to his shoulder and staring off into the middle distance.

Lily laughed at him. 'Gotta go where? Paige isn't here yet.'

'Who says I'm looking for Paige?'

'Yeah, but you are,' Lily insisted before she dragged me off to meet Zara and Harry.

'Don't let the long blonde locks fool you,' was all Lily said about Zara Maxwell Stirling, who did at least manage a smile when introduced. 'She understands quantum physics.'

'Hey,' Zara said with a backwards swish of the shampoo-ad hair and a half-interested glance in my direction.

'Whereas with Harry what you see is pretty much what you get,' Lily explained.

What I saw was a tall, thickset, muscular guy who could have stepped straight off the rugby field. His hair was short and blond, and he'd probably had his nose flattened in pursuit of an odd-shaped oval ball. I expected him to grunt a greeting and wasn't disappointed.

'You're new,' he said. Not a question but a blindingly obvious statement.

'Thanks, Captain Obvious!' Lily grinned, then dragged me on across the quad, pointing out other students and teachers: 'Jack Hooper – we call him Hooper. He's kind of shy. That's Guy Simons – head of sport, yuck!'

'Sport's not your thing?' I ventured.

'There's only one kind of physical activity that I enjoy!' she answered with innuendo so heavy that it made me laugh out loud.

'Exactly!' she giggled. 'So tell me, Alyssa – have you ever been in lurve?'

'Whoa!' What could I say to this sudden change of gear except a flat 'no'?

'It's amazing – just you wait!' she sighed.

From which I gathered she was happy. She had someone she loved and who loved her – lucky girl.

I'd been at St Jude's for less than a term when, through our first-storey, stone-mullioned window, Paige and I watched them pull Lily Earle's corpse from the freezing water. Even from a distance of two hundred metres I recognized Lily's long dark hair and the black leather jacket she'd been wearing when we said goodbye.

'Are you sure it's her?' Paige had asked, wanting it not to be true.

'It's her.'

Like I said, I have to force my mind back to the last time I saw Lily alive in late November– it never goes there willingly. But I make myself because maybe I'll remember something else that will give me a clue. I'm looking for something that happened during those lost four days between her scramble to pack her bag before she dashed from the dorm and the day they found her body.

'So why the big rush – did your family business go belly-

up?' Paige asked. *We quizzed Lily while she frantically stuffed clothes into an overnight bag. Lily did everything at breakneck speed – talking, packing, texting her brother to say she was on her way. That's how she was, multitasking, hurtling through life until she hit the final obstacle.*

'No.'

'*Does your dad want to make you the youngest ever MD of the digital media section of his multinational news corporation?*' I asked.

'Give me a break, Alyssa,' Lily said, *stuffing frayed jeans and her favourite silver sequinned top into an overnight bag.*

'*Sorry, but we're only trying to find out why you're freaking out.*'

No reply.

End of flashback.

So it's not that I didn't care that Lily was leaving St Jude's before the end of term and I didn't know where she was going or for how long. But I pictured her on a train heading for Paddington station, not tangled in pond weed and gasping her last breath within sight of my bedroom window.

I mean, how do you not feel sick when you think of that? How do you not have nightmares?

After Lily left that day, Paige and I immediately felt the quietness of our room without her and her rock-chick music constantly blasting out. The painting she'd been working on was propped on its easel, stinking the place out with the smell of turpentine and oils. It was her usual riot of reds, yellows and oranges, a happy abstract mess. Tubes of paint without their tops lay squidged out of shape on her desk; her brushes stood in a jar.

Weird – Lily left a trail of destruction wherever she went (paint-smeared jeans strewn over the bed, knickers and bras under it, phone charger always flung into some dark corner and lost), but boy did she take good care of those sable brushes.

Paige stinks in a different way – of horses and horse manure, hoof oil and liniment. But people don't notice their own smells, I guess.

I go the other way – I spray and spritz every personal surface, nook and cranny, maybe to an OCD extent. I just don't want to walk into a room and see Harry or Zara or Jack's nose start to scrunch. If I'm honest, especially not Jack's.

You're going to think I'm totally heartless for thinking about a boy at a time like this, but my stupid memory is kind of inappropriate sometimes. So let's pause the action again, press Rewind back to Day 1 then zoom in on Jack Cavendish and my first sight of him.

I guess it's the eyes – clear honey brown, heavy lidded with dark, straight brows. Or maybe the bod – six foot three with tennis players' biceps, triceps, six pack and thighs. And you know those sporty little muscles just above the knee? Every time I see Jack in shorts and tennis shoes I can't take my eyes off them. I'm weird that way, but only with Jack – I should make that clear.

And need I say he's also exceptionally intelligent, even

for St Jude's? He does things with numbers that a maths PhD student can't do, and this is according to our Oxford graduate head of department, who's taken on hundreds of gifted students and seen them through their baccalaureate. She says that even she is amazed by Jack's genius.

You'd have to hate him if he wasn't also laid back, gregarious and above all funny. Killer combination.

And the second Lily had stopped dragging me around and introducing me to the St Jude's gang I noticed him. There in the main quadrangle where families were still dropping off their sons and daughters, and porters were carrying luggage through narrow arched doorways, up stone staircases along low corridors to students' living quarters, I saw this vision step out of his dad's red Maserati Gran Cabrio. See – every detail is imprinted in my brain.

There was a glow about Jack as he stood in a shaft of sunlight, shaking his father's hand and walking away. He moved slowly and gracefully into the shadow cast by the dorm's weathered stone walls, creating the effect of him walking on water.

'Alyssa?' a voice said, and it took me a while to realize it was my Aunt Olivia trying to catch my attention. 'I have to leave now if I want to make my meeting in London.'

'Cool,' I said.

'You're sure you can manage to find your room without my help? According to the details the school sent us, it's room twenty-seven.'

I'd managed trickier situations, starting at a very young age, so I nodded.

'Then I'll say goodbye.' Aunt Olivia, bless her undemonstrative heart, was ready to deposit me in the quad like a parcel neatly tied up and delivered. I had my matching M&S cases at my feet, my whole future ahead of me. Her task was complete.

Quick job description. Aunt Olivia is my closest living relative since my parents died in a plane crash when I was three years old. She's my mother's older sister, childless and career focused, named in the will as my guardian in the event of Mum and Dad's early death – you have to wonder if maybe a spooky premonition came into play here.

To tell you the truth, there wasn't much family money and, anyway, it's held in trust until I reach twenty-one.

My aunt obviously loved my mother, but she doesn't love me. Couldn't, actually, and this is because I remind her too much of the sister she's lost – the same long, flame-red hair and pale skin, the green eyes.

I know this mostly from family photos, since even my miraculous power of recall doesn't go back into babyhood and to actual, living memories of my flame-haired mother. No, what I do remember is the endless procession of nannies (Helens and Joannes and Brigittes) employed to allow my aunt to pursue her career. I lived in a big house without siblings, where there were birthday visits to the ballet, and Christmases minus any attempt to con me into believing that Santa Claus did exist. Which is how come I grew up the way I did – feeling like the odd one out, a serious, literal-minded kid with not much in her life to laugh about.

Aunt Olivia, to give her credit, was the one who'd done

her research and found out I could sit a scholarship exam for St Jude's. 'It turns out you're an exceptional pupil,' she'd said in a who'd-have-thought-it way, at the same time digesting my clutch of ten A*s at GCSE. 'So we need to find you a sixth-form college where you won't stick out like a sore thumb.'

That's me – all my life, a sore thumb. Thanks, Aunty Ol.

'Bye,' I said on the day she deposited me in the quad. No backward glances, no kisses, no regrets on either side.

I was still thinking about Jack Cavendish and the way he seemed to glow.

'Alyssa?' A girl with fair, wavy hair broke my bubble. She rushed up behind me on the narrow stone staircase leading to Room 27, grabbed one of my suitcases and bumped it unceremoniously up the steps. 'I'm Paige Kelly. We're roommates.'

Roommate number one – Lily Earle – hyper, artistic and in love. Roommate number two – Paige Kelly – horse-mad and easily surpassing me in the sarcasm stakes, as you'll see.

Fast forward through one week of being the shy newbie, getting used to my 'exceptionally gifted' fellow students, when Jack Cavendish ran up in full tennis gear and talked to me. Miracle.

'You're Alyssa Stephens – right?'

I nodded, glanced down and caught sight of those little knee muscles that I mentioned earlier. Quads. *Quadriceps femoris* – 'four-headed muscle forming a large, fleshy mass which covers the front and sides of the femur'. I looked it up on Wikipedia.

'You're rooming with Paige and Lily?'

Another nod and a tragic sense that my pale cheeks had turned the colour of boiled lobster and my tongue was suddenly three times too big for my mouth. Open it to speak and the uncontrollable organ would slobber out over my bottom lip like some ancient, panting bulldog.

'Can you give Paige a message from Luke?' Jack asked, then took one look at my broiled cheeks and crazed attempt to keep on breathing, and quickly changed his mind. 'Hey, on second thoughts I'll pass it on myself. Any idea where she is?'

'Stables,' I mumbled, only it came out 'stubbullz' or 'stblz' with a kind of horsey cough hanging off the end. I mean, I totally mangled the vowels and came out with a sound that didn't in any way resemble human speech.

Jack frowned – a tiny crease appeared between those beautiful eyebrows. 'Oh yeah, Paige is inseparable from that horse. I should've known where to look.'

Idiot. You'd never think that my great-aunt, Lady Caroline Stephens, was a code breaker at Bletchley Park (she had the photographic memory thing going on too). With her attention to detail, she'd proved herself to be one of the best female brains of the Second World War. Or that my great-great-grandmother wrote seminal feminist pamphlets and went to prison with the Pankhursts. I come from a long line of super-intelligent women, for Christ's sakes.

'But anyway,' Jack continued, 'there's something else I want to ask you.'

'Fire away,' I mumbled. From coughing horse to a fair imitation of Her Majesty the Queen in a nano second. *Fire away, yah. Shoot me right between the eyes like a sick horse; put me out of my misery and make it quick.*

Jack grinned. (Whoa, that grin!) 'It's nothing bad. At least, I hope not.'

'Oh.' Gulp. How much worse could I be handling this, my first conversation with Jack Cavendish? I say 'conversation', but you have to have two participants to hold one of those, and so far my contribution was nil.

'You can say no if you like. I promise not to fall apart.'

'No to what?' God, my blushes had spread through my entire body, and I was leaking from every pore.

'A kid from the local comp is holding a party in the village this Saturday.'

'He is?'

'We'd need special passes.'

'We would?'

'Yeah, Cinders. Otherwise we'd have to be back before the clock strikes twelve.'

'What are you saying?' The 'we' was confusing me, plus the chimes of midnight reference. I clearly wasn't following Jack's train of thought.

Significant pause on his part, then, 'Come to the party with me?'

My mouth fell open. Literally. Major slobbery-dog moment. 'With you?' I echoed.

'Why not? No, listen, forget it. Harry Embsay probably already asked you and you said yes.' Jack was hanging his head, turning away, jogging across the quad towards the archway that led to the stable block.

'He didn't, I didn't!' I called after him. I took a deep breath, swallowed hard, ran a few steps to catch up. 'And yes, I'll come. I'd like to. That's so cool. Thanks for asking me. Wow!'

'Jack?' Lily did the jaw-drop thing, just like me. 'Jack *Cavendish* asked you to Tom's party?'

'He did.'

'You're sure it wasn't Jack Hooper?'

'I'm sure.'

'Jack Hooper's the one with googly eyes and the big Adam's apple. He's a nice guy, but Jack Cavendish is sex on legs.'

'I know.'

'Wow!' Lily seemed impressed. She sat cross-legged on her bed with her hair twisted up and piled on top of her head, surrounded by debris – empty paint tubes, sweet wrappers, broken Kindle. 'Until Luke came along, Paige fancied Jack Cavendish forever – all through Years Nine to Eleven when we were in main school. In fact, she admits to creepily stalking him, don't you, Paige?'

'I wasn't the only one.' Busy polishing something to do with Mistral, her equine Olympic hopeful, Paige sat at the window with her back stubbornly turned.

'Honest to God, she did,' Lily insisted. 'Any time Paige

wasn't jumping cross-country fences or doing dressage, whatever the hell that is, she was sneaking down the boys' corridor and listening at Jack's door or watching him out on the tennis courts with her binoculars trained on his butt . . .'

'Bollocks,' Paige muttered through clenched teeth.

'Oh, sorry – not his butt but his bollocks,' Lily laughed. 'Alyssa, believe me – if you steal Jack from her, she'll never speak to you again.'

'Look who's talking,' Paige remarked without elaborating.

At this stage – seven days into my first term at St Jude's – Paige didn't speak to me much anyway, not once she'd realized that I didn't know a horse's fetlock from its withers. She'd made it crystal clear that non-horsey people were low life, ranked alongside plankton.

'I didn't know I was stealing him from anyone,' I pointed out.

'You're not,' Paige cut in, expertly applying the metal polish. 'Not from me, at least. Actually I'm going to Tom's party with Luke. You know – Luke Pearson, son of the Formula One racing supremo and big-time property developer.' More polish and a whole lot of rubbing. Then she attached pieces of bit to bridle, fastened buckles and slung the whole thing over her shoulder. 'Who are *you* going to the party with, Lily?' she asked pointedly as she strode out of the room.

Lily reacted as if she'd been slapped in the face.

'You OK?' I checked. I think now of how vulnerable she was – up one minute and down, down, down the next –

the type of car-crash personality you quickly learn to look out for. I remember the startled hurt in her eyes and how I wanted to smooth it away and make everything all right.

She nodded then pasted on a fake smile.

'So you'll be going to the party with your special guy – the one you mentioned the first time we talked?'

Lily shook her head. 'No. Actually, Paige was referring to the fact that my beloved boyfriend just dumped me,' she confessed quietly. 'Anyway, I guess I deserve whatever she throws my way.' Then she was up off the bed and playing loud music, preparing her brushes, squeezing paint, mixing colours while I found Jack C on Facebook.

'What exactly are you looking for?' Lily asked, leaving her canvas to glance over my shoulder and managing to dribble red acrylic on to my white top. 'Do you want to know how many girls he's slept with? Whether his current status is single, and, if so, how the hell that happened, even for a nanosecond?'

'Why he even asked me to the party in the first place,' I added, rubbing at the paint with my fingertips and making even more of a mess, plus revealing to Lily the fact that in the sphere of boys and relationships my self-confidence is zero.

Her jaw dropped again and more paint dribbled. 'You're not serious?'

'Yes, I'm serious.'

With her free hand, Lily marched me to a mirror and made me stare into it. 'That's why,' she told me with her wide, beautiful grin.

chapter two

Jack got two late passes from the bursar's office and we went to Tom's party in Chartsey Bottom. I kid you not and don't laugh because it's childish and not cool – this is the name of an actual village.

You can't quite see the Bottoms, as locals call it, from St Jude's – there are acres of lawn, the lake and an ancient oak forest in the way. Then a small, fast-running river with an old water mill perched on its bank, a few farmers' fields and finally you come to a row of limestone cottages forming one main street with a tea shop called the Squinting Cat (I don't know, don't ask), a specialist greengrocer's selling organic veg, a florist's, the Church of St Michael's and All Angels, and the Bridge Inn. Behind the village is a gentle swell of green hills, then more woodland, then Upper Chartsey, even smaller than the Bottoms.

It's all chocolate-boxy beautiful and you have to be brain dead to want to live there. This is how Tom explained it to me when I first met him at his party the following Saturday.

Tom, by the way, is tall and bony with corn-stubbly fair hair.

'So how come you know Jack and the other St Jude's students?'

'We play them at five-a-side soccer,' he told me.

'And how come you ended up living here?' I asked, one eye on Jack who was talking to a boy who'd barged in between us and hauled Jack off into a corner to discuss something important.

'Ask my parents,' Tom grumbled. 'Except you can't because they're in Islington visiting my grandparents, which is where we used to live until Mum made us move out and buy this house in la-la land.'

'I take it you don't like it?' I stated the obvious to keep Tom talking so that I could leave spare brain capacity to try and guess what was so urgent between Jack and barge-boy.

'What's to like? You see one field, you've seen them all. The same goes for cows and sheep – four legs and rancid smell, end of.'

'I guess.' There was a small pause then curiosity won out. I said, 'Who's that talking to Jack?'

'What? Oh, that's Jayden. He goes to my school. He and his mates crashed the party.'

I had to admit that Jayden did look like a gate-crasher, even though I hate to stereotype. He had a lean, prowling look, hunched forward and peering out from under his projecting brow with grey eyes that darted everywhere and didn't rest on the person he was talking to. Feral is the word that comes to mind, like a tomcat or a big, bruising male fox.

'Will you throw them out?' I asked Tom, who seemed not to care that every lowlife kid in the Bottoms might now follow Jayden's lead. I did a quick head count, picking out

Paige and Luke, Harry, Zara, Lily and Jack among the dozen or so invitees from St Jude's.

Out of uniform, the girls looked stunning – Paige not the least bit horsey in sky-high heels and a red dress with peplum waist, Zara the Hollywood babe in slinky, side-boob-flashing halter-neck and Lily doing her tousled rock-chick thing. But there were about the same number of guests who I didn't recognize and didn't feel so comfortable with – Tom's friends from Ainslee Comp, ten miles down the main road towards Gloucester.

This is a lot of people and place names to throw into the mix all at once. I felt that myself at the time – kind of overwhelmed by new faces and, feebly, ashamedly wishing that Jack would break away from wild-boy Jayden and come back to me.

Great-great-aunt Caroline the code-breaker and my great-great-grandmother the suffragette must have been spinning in their graves.

'So why do you call this la-la land?' I asked, wrenching my attention away from Jack and Jayden.

But Lily broke up our conversation before Tom had time to answer.

'There you are!' she cried, sliding an arm round his waist and standing on tiptoe for a full-on lip kiss. Her eyes were staring, her pupils dilated. 'It's ages since I saw you – at least ten whole minutes. Tell me you missed me.'

Tom looked embarrassed. Lily surged on, swishing her hair back from her face and swamping him with another octopus embrace.

'Cool party,' she sighed, batting her eyelashes before kissing him again. 'You play the best music. C'mon, let's dance.'

He wrestled himself free and kind of thrust Lily into my arms. 'Don't give her any more of anything,' he warned. 'I don't know what she's had, but she definitely can't take any more of whatever it is.'

Out came Lily's bottom lip. 'Awww!'

'I mean it,' Tom insisted, walking off.

'He's right,' I tried to tell her. Her off-the-shoulder sequinned top was sliding dangerously low down her left boob, threatening a serious wardrobe malfunction, and her long hair hung lank over one mascara-smudged eye.

'Party pooper,' she muttered, hitching the top straight and falling off balance at the same time. Giggling, she clutched at me for support. 'Hey, Jayden!' she cried, spying Tom's gate-crasher. She tottered across to join him and Jack, except that Paige and Luke got in her way just as her thin legs did that wobbly-spaghetti thing and she finally collapsed in a heap in the middle of the dance floor.

Next thing I knew, Luke had pulled her on to her feet, Paige was dragging her to the downstairs cloakroom and Jack was at my side.

'Does Lily do this a lot?' I wanted to know. I hadn't drunk enough myself to just shrug it off and carry on partying with the best-looking guy in the room.

'Lily has a few issues,' was all Jack would say. He seemed to be on guard after his conversation with Jayden and only relaxed after he saw him leaving through the French

18

windows of the grand eighteenth-century house. Exit gate-crasher with two of his Uppers' mates.

'Glad you came?' Jack asked me when the drama was over.

I nodded, scared that if I attempted actual sounds I would re-create the slobbery-dog effect.

Boldly he put his arm round my waist and sidled me up against the wall. 'Glad you came with me?'

Willingly cornered, I told him yes – a whole, recognizable word.

'Me too. This is cool.'

Loud music, dim lights, a crush of people and the warmth of Jack's hunky body next to mine – this definitely qualified as cool. Concentrating on the hunky bod, I smiled at him then sighed.

'Do you like this track?' Jack asked when a new album started.

The lights were low, the music slow and smooth. I nodded.

It was a girl singer belting out a number about being in love for the first time. The song was her Number 1 hit – 'You're the One for Me' – about the precise moment when you know in your heart that your life has changed forever. Sober, I pour scorn on stuff like this. After two glasses of Sauvignon and staring into Jack's beautiful golden-brown eyes, it was a different story.

'Dance?' he asked.

'Love is a window that opens up your heart,' she sang. 'I hear you tell me that we'll never part.'

*

19

'Typical Lily.' Paige shrugged when I tried to quiz her about our roommate's alcohol-assisted meltdown. I'd finished slow dancing with Jack, and Paige and I had joined the queue for Tom's upstairs bathroom.

'It wasn't anything we said or did?' I needed to be sure I hadn't offended my hyper-sensitive roommate – easy to do by accident with someone whose skin is paper-thin.

'What? Oh no. I love Lily to bits but she's hard work sometimes.' Paige informed me that Harry was at that very minute making sure that Lily got back home to St Jude's in one piece. 'Talking of Jack . . .'

'Were we?'

'Yeah. Well, we are now. Have you two – you know?' Nudge, nudge.

Paige's question shocked romantic little me. In fact, it straight away made me think of bloodlines and thoroughbred stallions. 'Hey, slow down, this is our first date, remember.'

'So? We're talking about a six-bedroomed house here.'

I made a face as if I'd tasted something nasty. I didn't want to discuss my oh-so-limited sexual experience – not there, not then, not any time.

Paige came over all innocent. 'What? You're telling me you wouldn't if he asked you?'

Luckily the bathroom door opened and Luke emerged, cool as a cucumber. Cool as in looks – tall, lean, designer-label boy – and cool as in manner. He told Paige in an offhand way that he, Jack Hooper and Zara were moving on from Tom's party to another in Upper Chartsey.

'Can I come?'

'It depends. We're leaving right now.'

'I'm ready.' Abandoning her place in the queue, she winked at me again and wished me luck, the way she did when she was speaking to a fellow three-day eventer – hearty and insincere at the same time. The last I saw of her as I glanced from the landing down to the hallway below, she was draped around Luke as he, Zara and the other Jack exited through the front door.

My Jack – I call him that just to keep things clear – was waiting for me downstairs in the room with the French windows. He could see I wasn't totally into Tom's party and all the new faces, writhing bodies and drunkenness happening around me.

'You want to leave?' he suggested.

Which is how I found myself walking through an oak forest at 12.30 a.m. with the hottest boy on the planet.

'What's that?' I squeaked when something whoo-whooed above our heads.

'Owl. Watch where you put your feet.' Jack pointed to a big root jutting out across our path, then he took my hand to help me jump across a tiny stream.

'Where are the street lamps?' I quipped. Give me pavements and green-man crossings any day of the week. Except tonight I found I was enjoying the mulchy silence as Jack and I walked hand in hand.

I smiled to myself. Aunt Olivia had sent me to St Jude's to learn literature and languages, history and biology, little thinking that learning in more fascinating, non-academic areas might also occur.

'Why the smile?' he asked.

'Oh, nothing.'

He slowed down until we almost came to a halt, leaned against me and whispered, 'Yeah – something.'

'Nothing. I'm just happy, that's all.'

'Then I'll tell *you* something,' he said, under the gnarled branches with glimpses of moonlight overhead. 'You were easily the most beautiful girl at the party.'

'No way,' I contradicted, just that tad too fast. It's my usual saddo way of batting back compliments and I think it stopped him from doing what he'd been about to do, which was to kiss me.

'For sure,' he insisted. 'Harry and Tom thought so too because they told me so. You weren't comfortable, though, and I'm wondering why not.'

'I guess I was worried about Lily.'

'She was hyper,' he agreed. 'Totally into showing us she didn't care that Jayden dumped her.'

'Jayden?' This was the first I'd heard about Lily and the foxy, feral gate-crasher, obviously.

'Just after term started. She told everybody he did it by text. Major drama. You two room together so I'm surprised you didn't know about it.'

'She mentioned her boyfriend ditched her, but she didn't say who it was. Anyway, the text thing – not nice!' Maybe the rejection explained why Lily's moods typically plunged far down to a place where nobody could seem to reach her. 'Is that what you two were talking about, back at the party?'

Jack shrugged as we emerged from the forest and caught

our first view of St Jude's. 'And other stuff.' Feeling in his back pocket, he faked surprise.

'What's wrong?' I asked.

'The late passes – I lost them.'

'You didn't!'

'I did. No, I didn't.' He was laughing, shaking his head, enjoying the look on my face. 'Actually, I never had them.'

'Really?'

'Really. I would have got a straight no from D'Arblay.'

'The bursar? Why would he do that?'

'I was grounded at the end of last term. D'Arblay's an elephant – he never forgets.'

A bit like me, then.

'I don't believe you did that!' I wailed. I didn't want to be in this much trouble within two weeks of starting at my new school.

'Believe it,' he laughed, running across the field, dragging me with him. 'There's a way to get back in without being seen, but we need to climb the wall behind the stables. Are you up for it?'

I was going to do the girly 'not in this dress' thing, but then I thought, Sod it, why not?

I ran ahead until we came to the wall.

'You first, he said.

'Stop laughing. This isn't funny.'

'OK, me first,' he decided. His athletic vault on to the top of the high wall scored a perfect ten with this judge, I can tell you. Then he leaned down to offer me his hand.

'I can do it,' I insisted. My legs were almost as long as his, and I was no slouch in the gymnastics department either. So I hitched my floaty skirt over one shoulder and joined him on top of the wall.

Hand in hand we jumped.

My skirt billowed around me, and my hair fell forward across my cheek.

We landed in the stable yard. Jack pushed my hair from my face.

We were so close that his features turned blurry and I could feel his breath. Too close, too fast, too soon. I pulled away.

'Sorry,' he mumbled.

What was wrong with me? I liked – I *loved* the feel of his fingers pushing my hair from my face and the nearness of his lips. So why was I giving him the opposite signals?

'No, it's me – I'm sorry.'

Jack jerked his head towards the main building. 'So, shall we?'

Shall we go back to the dorms – him to the boys', me to the girls' – and turn the lights out on what had been the best evening of my entire life?

'Not yet,' I whispered with my heart in my mouth.

It was enough – I may have given off mixed signals, but this was the trigger – I didn't need to say anything else to make Jack smile, lean in again and kiss me.

Yes, he kissed me.

Mistral, Paige's grey horse, poked his head over a stable door and snickered.

I kissed Jack Cavendish back. Sweet, sweet moment that I'll always treasure.

The memory kept me awake Saturday night and lasted all through Sunday.

'So?' The minute she woke up the morning after the party Paige demanded the down-and-dirty, horsey details.

'So nothing.' Love is a window that opens up your heart, I thought. My life had changed forever, but I didn't feel ready to share with Paige.

'Alyssa, you cannot be serious!' she squealed. 'You don't go to Tom's party with Jack Cavendish then go coy on us. It's against the rules.'

'Whose rules?'

'Mine. C'mon, c'mon – give!'

'OK, so we walked back together.'

'You walked . . . !'

'. . . Together. We talked.'

'Talked!'

'Don't snort. It makes you sound like a horse. Yeah, "talked".'

'And?'

'OK, then – we kissed.'

'Better! Ooh, Alyssa, you kissed Jack Cavendish – for how long?'

'I didn't look at my watch.' You know you don't count the minutes in this situation. 'Let's just say we were the last ones back from Tom's party.' All the lights were out in the dorm corridors and when I crept back into the room I shared with Paige and Lily, sleep was the last thing on my mind.

Luckily a still-miserable Lily interrupted Paige's inquisition. Speaking from under her duvet, she was hungover, deep down in the mire: 'Who did Jayden end up with?'

'I have no idea,' Paige lied. She'd gone on with Luke and Zara to the party in Upper Chartsey (Uppers as opposed to Bottoms, mostly down to the drugs available at parties held there, I was told) and she must have been clued in to our feral friend's every midnight move.

'Anyway, don't tell me.' Lily groaned and pulled the duvet further over her head. 'I don't want to know. And, anyway, whose idea was it to send me home with Harry Embsay?'

There are certain things so shocking that even I don't retain them at the time. They explode in my head and scramble my brain and even when my thoughts knit back together in some kind of order, that one gruesome thing doesn't reappear until much later. It was like that with Lily. But I have to remember it, even if I don't want to. I owe it to Lily.

Paige and I had come out of a maths lesson with Shirley Welford. We had the afternoon free so we went up to our room to change out of our uniforms into jeans and sweaters. It was Paige who'd looked out of the window and seen the emergency-service vehicles surrounding the lake – two police cars and one ambulance.

'What are they doing there?' She sounded irritated.

'Look – they've put tape across the lawn. There's a no-go area.'

'So?' I joined her at the window.

'It's blocking off the lake and the woods – just where I was planning to ride Mistral.'

'Must be serious.' Besides the vehicles I counted five police officers, two paramedics and three divers in black wetsuits.

Looking back, I'm disappointed by how long it took for Paige and I to get our brains into gear.

The divers slid into the lake and disappeared below the surface. A police officer saw D'Arblay walk across the lawn and warned him not to go beyond the blue-striped plastic tape. And still I didn't do the simple two-plus-two arithmetic.

'What are they looking for?' I wondered.

D'Arblay seemed to argue with the policeman. A diver resurfaced empty-handed. The grey light of a November afternoon turned everything monochrome.

The diver took off his breathing apparatus and said something to the paramedics. A second diver reappeared and held up an object that seemed to be of interest. A shoe. A female police officer took it and placed it in a plastic bag as evidence.

'Definitely serious,' Paige agreed.

It could have been any sodden, dripping shoe, and yet it looked familiar. Even from a distance I could make out rows of silver studs against the black leather. But no – I still wouldn't let the idea into my head.

The two divers slipped back into the water like seals. Minutes went by.

'That shoe . . .' Paige began.

I shook my head.

'It looked like Lily's.' It was Paige – she was the one to open Pandora's box and let the nightmare truth fly out. 'They think she's in the lake.'

Yes, they were looking for Lily, diving down into the murky depths, searching among the weeds and the mud. I held my breath, unable even to think.

D'Arblay remonstrated with the cops. The two paramedics went right to the water's edge. A diver came up with a heavy, limp, human-shaped form in his arms. He staggered out of the water and put his burden down. The body wore Lily's leather jacket and its long black hair dripped muddy water. Both feet were bare.

The truth was out and battering its way into my brain.

Saint Sam (I'll explain the nickname in a moment) strode across the lawn to join the bursar while the paramedics went into the ambulance and brought out a body bag.

So now we're back to the present, and still wondering what happened to Lily. Everyone is saying that she killed herself, but I don't believe it. I spent a lot of time with her in classes, plus socially in the evenings. I shared a room with her, for God's sake. Surely I would have picked up on it if she had been feeling suicidal. There must be more to it, something that I'm not seeing.

As I remarked earlier, Adam Earle didn't rush to St Jude's

when they found his sister's body. Neither did her father, Robert, who, it turned out, was doing important business in Chicago. Her mother, Anna, eventually deputized her oldest son to show up at the scene and deal with possible press fallout. There were satellite vans, reporters and cameramen flashing and clicking at the gate when Adam drove by, straining for a picture to make the next day's front page. *High-profile media family falls prey to tabloid frenzy.* Don't we just love the irony?

Adam talked with Saint Sam and Terence D'Arblay, plus a couple of Lily's teachers, spending the most time with Bryony Phillips who was halfway through teaching *King Lear* to me, Zara, Harry and Lily, among others. 'How sharper than a serpent's tooth' and all that. It was in Bryony's classes that I learned how much Lily hated every member of her family and especially her filthy rich father (or 'the tyrant', as she called him). She was definitely a one hundred per cent thankless child.

Then, at 4.30 in the afternoon of Adam's second visit, Saint Sam called for me and Paige to join them in his study.

'This is a difficult time,' Dr Webb began, elbows on desk, manicured hands clasped. The bursar stood to attention behind him; Adam Earle sat in one of the studded leather armchairs by the long, leaded window with the ancient coat of arms.

Adam looks nothing like Lily, by the way. His hair was already taking leave of his skull, but what was left of it was fair and wavy. He had none of her energy, none of her neediness – at least that was my first impression as he sat sober-suited and quiet in the red armchair.

'Paige, you've been friends with Lily for some time now. Alyssa, I realize that your acquaintance was shorter, but when you room with someone you do get close very quickly.'

We stood and waited. We were still in shock over Lily and neither of us had anything to say.

'We're here to listen whenever you need to share your concerns.' Saint Sam's nickname suited him, obviously. He talked quietly, he looked you in the eye, has the stuffy air of a bishop, the calm, considered frankness of a counsellor, and always with the best interests of St Jude's closest to his heart.

Behind him, sentry D'Arblay gave a slight nod of agreement. *Nihil sed* blah blah. Nothing but the best. We'll give you two fellow students all the professional help you might need to deal with this trauma.

'Lily's brother, Adam, would like to ask you a few questions.'

'If you don't mind,' Adam added. Like politeness has to be observed even when your kid sister has just been found dead.

'Don't worry – none of this will go beyond these four walls,' Saint Sam assured us. 'Whatever you tell us will remain completely confidential.'

As if we cared. All that mattered to us right then was how Lily had ended up in the lake.

Adam stood up from his chair, stared out of the arched,

gothic windows across the lawn to the lake beyond. 'Did Lily say anything to either of you?' he asked without turning round.

Late autumn leaves swirled in eddies across the grass; the sky was leaden.

'In what way?' Paige countered.

I felt uneasy, with a building suspicion that the grey suits were hiding something.

'Did she tell you why she packed her bag and went?'

'Yes.' I don't need to tell you that I remembered the conversation word for word. That's the thing with us eidetics (look it up or I'll tell you later) – our recall sometimes covers all five senses, not just the visual. 'She said it was a family crisis.'

It was then that Adam Earle turned his full attention on me and Paige, and his gaze grew more focused. 'Anything else?'

'Nothing,' Paige insisted.

No, but she flung jeans and a sequinned top into her bag in reaction to an email from you, I thought. She was definitely going somewhere in a mad, bee-stung rush.

'How did she . . . seem?' Adam asked.

'Hyper,' Paige told him flatly. 'Just like always.'

Not quite always. I remembered the few days after Tom's party when Lily could hardly get out of bed. And the time in Bryony's English lesson when Lily had been the only one to get the *King Lear* bit about not heaving your heart into your mouth just to please your father. She'd written an A* essay about it and read the whole thing out to the class,

31

how you have to stay true to yourself and not do things just for greed or profit, how money and power will make you corrupt. I was impressed.

But then, yeah, there was her fizzy creative energy with body and brain in overdrive, slapping paint around, slashing and ruining her own work after a last meeting with Adam and Saint Sam, her losing things, getting drunk and throwing herself at boys – all that stuff.

'You know Lily was bipolar,' big bro Adam saw fit to tell us now. 'That's the reason her behaviour was sometimes a little . . . bizarre.'

Oh well that's OK, then. Stick a label on her, give it a medical framework. I shook my head and bit my lip. So, Adam, don't whatever you do let the grief get to you. Don't break down and say that she was your kid sister and you miss her like hell.

'Her illness could be a problem sometimes,' he acknowledged. 'Especially if she didn't take her medication.'

So here's the solution – tuck her away out of sight in an obscenely expensive Cotswolds sixth-form college where she could be bipolar and exceptional in private. A sore thumb among other sore thumbs, just like me. Good thinking. I couldn't help frowning as Adam talked on.

'On the day she left – did she seem . . . preoccupied?' he asked.

I hated his habit of mulling over words until he came up with the one that fitted best.

'Not so you'd notice,' Paige said as she backed towards the door. I could see she wanted to be galloping Mistral over cross-country jumps, not dealing with questions she couldn't answer.

'And she didn't say – anything? Anything personal?'

'Jesus!' Paige was halfway to the door. 'Why is he asking us all this stuff?' she asked D'Arblay.

Saint Sam stood up and came out from behind his desk. 'Adam thinks you have a right to know this,' he confided gently. 'It seems Lily was pregnant.'

That stopped us dead in our tracks. Paige gasped. I stared while the principal drew a folded piece of paper from his inside jacket pocket.

'She sent this email,' he added. 'Telling us exactly why she killed herself.'

chapter three

The first question you ask when you get news like this – well, me anyway – is, 'So who's the father?'

It cut through the stunned silence and thudded into my chest like an arrow. Who got Lily pregnant?

The second thing that occurred to me was, 'Am I the only one who didn't know about this?' But no – a quick glance in Paige's direction told me it was as new to her as it was to me.

'This is a printout of an email from Lily – the police have another,' Adam said, taking over from where Saint Sam left off. From the way red blotches had formed on his neck I could see he was struggling to stay calm and was actually doing a pretty good job. 'She doesn't give any details about the pregnancy, but the preliminary forensic report confirms her . . . condition.'

'How pregnant was she?' Paige wanted to know. Like me she was obviously working out the paternity issue.

Think about it. As far as we knew, Lily hadn't had a boyfriend since Jayden did the dirty and dumped her in the first week of term. Sure she'd been seriously slutty at Tom's party, but she'd gone home alone (or at least with Harry as her bodyguard-cum-chaperone and that definitely didn't count). We were now early December.

'They think about thirteen weeks,' Adam told us.

It had to be Jayden, then.

Unless Lily had been with someone else during the summer break. I imagined a different scenario – a holiday fling in Greece, Italy, the Bahamas – wherever the Earles hung out *en famille*. A sexy local guy with a tanned and ripped torso, too much wine, a starlit sky, a walk along the beach with Lily in one of her manic, daredevil phases . . .

I was still working it out when Paige had her meltdown. She was halfway out of the room, remember, when Saint Sam dropped his pregnancy bombshell, and she stayed fixed to the spot. She kept shaking her head then she let out a small, soft groan. More head shaking until finally she hugged herself and bent double then started to sob.

'Don't!' I begged. Meltdowns are infectious. I couldn't bear the sound of Paige crying and I was scared I was about to go the same way. Anyway, there were hot tears in my eyes and I was shaking like a leaf, thinking of Lily almost halfway through a pregnancy and locked in a lonely, dark night of the soul.

'Why didn't she tell us?' Paige said over and over as the bursar tried to help her.

'She didn't tell anybody at St Jude's,' Adam explained. 'We don't think she even saw a doctor.'

'So that wasn't the reason you came to visit four weeks after term started?' I had to keep on asking questions, otherwise I'd have been with Paige in total collapse, and D'Arblay only had one pair of hands.

Adam shook his head, obviously ill at ease, possibly lying.

'She was upset,' I told him. 'She came back to the room and wrecked one of her paintings.'

My razor-sharp memory replayed the scene and I give it to you again, with added details, in case the extra info turns out to be crucial:

Lily took a knife and slashed through the reds and oranges. Stab, stab, stab, then slashed right across the diagonal, like she was killing a part of herself.

'I hate all this,' she'd cried.

'What do you mean?' I'd asked. 'What do you hate?'

'Everything.'

(The trouble is when someone is as OTT as Lily was you tend not to take them seriously.)

'What do you mean, *everything*?' I'd moved in to stop her cutting the canvas, though it was too late – the painting was already ruined.

She raised the knife and turned on me with a wild look. 'What do you know, Alyssa?' she yelled. 'You've only just got here. What could you possibly know?'

'Lily, cut it out,' Paige said, sensible and determined. She came and grabbed Lily's wrist. The knife dropped to the floor, the crazy look faded from Lily's eyes and suddenly it was over. We never mentioned the slashing incident again.

'Lily may not have told anyone at St Jude's that she was pregnant, but she actually did discuss it with our mother,'

Adam went on. 'We know that she used an over-the-counter pregnancy test.'

And the family did nothing? I shook my head over and over. What's with that?

Adam cleared his throat. 'Anyway, Lily's email is a form of suicide note. It makes it clear that she was well aware how far on she was and how upset she was about it.'

If you close your eyes to steady yourself, it sometimes makes you even more dizzy. I found this out during the conversation I was having with Adam Earle. When I opened my eyes again, the room swam. The lions and unicorns in the coats of arms in the leaded windows danced. It turned out my brain had gone to mush and I'd run out of questions too.

'Worse than upset, actually.' Adam obviously wanted to be more precise. 'The pregnancy must have plunged Lily into unrelieved depression.'

'No.' Paige was back on her feet, breaking away from D'Arblay's ministrations. She shoved the bursar aside and advanced towards Adam. 'Alyssa and I were with Lily all this term and I personally didn't see any massive difference. Up and down – just the same old, same old.'

'Believe me.' There was steel in Adam's voice now. 'I knew my sister better than you did. The mood swings, the silences, the deliberate staying away from family.'

'No.' Faintly I backed up Paige's refusal to agree with the official version. Remember Lily's contribution to the *King Lear* debate about ungrateful daughters? Spend a moment:

Lily's voice rang clear in my head. Her eyes flashed with rage;
she was totally intense: 'I have no idea why Cordelia would even
want to stay loyal to that nasty old perv.'

Our group of English literature baccalaureate students sat in
a sunny classroom overlooking the lake, amazed that she felt so
strongly. Jack Hooper, who is a sensitive soul, actually edged his
chair away from where she sat.

'I would have got the hell out,' Lily insisted. 'The old man's
a fool for trusting the other two daughters. He gets what he
deserves.'

'But that's the point,' Bryony explained. 'The king is a fool
and he has to literally go mad and get through to the other side
before he sees the truth.'

'I still say she should have ditched the tyrant straight off,'
Lily muttered.

'Tyrant' – that's the way she talked about her own father,
as you know. 'The tyrant has bought another TV network,
yawn, yawn', 'The tyrant is flying out to Chicago in his
private jet. How green is that?' 'Jesus Christ, not again – the
tyrant wants to see me!'

Yeah – these were her last words as she hurtled out of
our room with her hastily packed bag; 'The tyrant wants to
see me. I'm out of here!'

'It was definitely Jayden's baby.' Afterwards Paige and I
both fixated on this one point.

We were back in our room, beds unmade. Paige's horse
tack hung from the back of her chair ready for cleaning.

Adam's car was still in the visitors' car park under the glare of bright security lights.

'Adam focused on the fact that Lily didn't mention a name,' I reminded her. 'Why couldn't it have been somebody she met on holiday?'

Paige shook her head. 'Lily wasn't like that. She didn't do one-night stands.'

'No? Didn't you see her coming on to Tom at his party?'

'Only because she knew Jayden was watching her. She wanted to make him jealous.'

'OK.' It only took me a few seconds to realize that Paige was probably right.

'Anyway, Lily didn't go on holiday this year.'

'She didn't?' No luxury yacht in Monaco, no penthouse suite in Nassau. Bang went one of my theories.

'No. She was in the UK, drifting, doing her own thing, staying away from her dad.'

'The tyrant.'

'Yeah. She came to see me ride in the Burghley Horse Trials. That was late August. Harry Embsay and Guy Simons were there too.'

'Guy?' I echoed.

'Yeah. He's mad about three-day eventing – didn't you know?'

Funny – I hadn't pictured Guy Simons in dressage gear. Like Harry, he was more the rugby type, with muscles but without the flattened nose.

'Anyway, Lily, Harry and Guy – they all stayed with us for a few days.'

'And then?'

Paige shrugged. 'Lily went into one of her moods over something Harry said. She told me she was heading off to her mother's cousin's estate in the Highlands for the last week of the holidays. I didn't believe her, though.'

'Didn't her mother check up on her? How come she just let her sixteen-year-old daughter float around the country?'

'You haven't met her mother,' Paige pointed out, which struck me as vague though I didn't follow it up. 'Anyway, I reckon she never made it to Scotland.'

'Which would give her free time to hook up with Jayden.'

Paige nodded. We thought for a while.

So here it is – my new theory.

Lily finishes her GCSEs. She has a whole summer ahead and she's in a state of rebellion. No one's going to tell her what to do or where to be. She lies to her parents, says she's fixing to visit friends and distant family then deliberately strays from her plans in order to spend time with lean and hungry Jayden. She probably has him marked out as some kind of Heathcliff figure – wild and dangerous, origins unknown.

Guess the rest.

She loves Jayden, is totally into him mind, body and soul, but he just uses her. When term is about to begin and she tells him she's pregnant, he acts like a total shit.

Goodbye, he tells her. Be seeing you. *Adios.*

Doesn't it make you sick to your stomach? Wouldn't you just like to kneecap him or strike him dead the next chance you get?

*

'Who did she send the suicide note to?'

Word of Lily's suicide message had spread beyond the honeyed walls and arches of St Jude's, across the rolling hills to Chartsey Bottom.

It was two days later and Paige, Jack Hooper, Harry Embsay and I had met up in the Squinting Cat cafe with Tom from the Old Vicarage and his Ainslee Comp mate, Alex Driffield. Alex was the one who asked the question.

'Email actually,' Paige told him.

'So who did she send it to?' Tom added.

Paige and I shook our heads. The silence was thick with emotion – mainly shock/horror, even forty-eight hours after Adam's visit.

'Lucky for the family that there *was* an email,' Alex said, knocking back the remains of his Coke as the waitress scooped up our empties. 'Otherwise the filth would've been all over this.'

'Filth,' Paige mocked. 'Did I hear you say that, or did I imagine it?' That's what she does – she shows contempt every chance she gets. But it's a cover and we all tolerate it.

'He's right,' Jack Hooper pointed out.

The other Jack – my Jack – is nowhere on the scene, notice. Where is he? Where the hell's he been since the suicide news broke?

In fact, where's he been all term? You're bound to be asking this. After our romantic first date, you might think we'd have been joined at the hip. I wish.

He'd called me the most beautiful girl at the party and

we'd kissed in the stable yard. My heart was singing: 'Love is a window that opens up your heart.'

The Sunday after the party it was strange – I thought about Jack all day but didn't run into him. I quickly got to thinking . . . Was he deliberately avoiding me, and, if so, why?

'Stop pissing about, Alyssa. Go find him.' Lily broke through her own misery long enough to offer me advice.

Paige backed her up. 'Yeah, you go, girl.'

But I didn't want to risk coming out into the open, showing Jack how smitten I was and making a fool of myself. That's pride, you see – a kind of Achilles' heel of mine. I dress it up as shyness but it's definitely part pride too.

Anyway, on Monday morning I was summoned to the bursar's office before lessons.

'You're new here, Alyssa,' were Terence D'Arblay's ominous opening words. 'And that's the only excuse I can think of for Saturday night.'

I swallowed hard.

'Saturday night,' he repeated patiently then waited.

Whoa, did he think I would roll over and confess I'd gone out without a late pass? Well, think again, *Mein Herr*.

Picture the money man's smooth expression, slicked-back hair, expensive suit, a hint of seedy cabaret host, total grasp of detail. Get it?

'There's no point your denying it,' D'Arblay broke the silence. 'You were seen climbing back into school grounds with Jack Cavendish. In fact, we caught you on our security camera.'

Shit. I shrugged and kept my mouth tight closed.

'It's very disappointing,' D'Arblay went on.

'Disappointing' is a killer. It's the teacher word, the parent or guardian word when you let them down and they dump a load of guilt on your shoulders.

'All you had to do was come and knock on my door and ask for an official pass,' he said in his high, clipped voice, his hooded eyes dark as currants. 'There would have been no argument about my granting you one. It was only Jack who'd been grounded.'

I met his gaze, didn't grovel.

'So I can only surmise that you didn't quite grasp the rules, Alyssa, or that you assumed, wrongly as it turned out, that Jack had secured passes for both of you.'

No comment.

'And for that reason I'm prepared to give you the benefit of the doubt,' D'Arblay concluded.

Which rock did this out-of-touch guy crawl out from under? What was he doing on the staff at St Jude's, which Aunt Olivia had chosen for me precisely because it was supposed to 'foster each student's exceptional talent and individuality'? That's what it says in the prospectus. Somebody ought to tell that to this crusty dinosaur who was currently giving me the benefit of his doubt.

Anyway, the result was that D'Arblay issued a warning, but didn't ground me.

'The guy's a wanker,' was Paige's verdict when she heard that the bursar had grounded Jack for a further week.

'A shit-head,' Lily muttered.

I did run into Jack at dinner that evening – saw him from behind, broad-shouldered and slim-hipped, standing in line at the serving hatch.

'Grounded for another week,' I said with a sympathetic tut. 'Sorry.'

'It was worth it,' he grinned. 'D'Arblay told me I was a bad influence.'

'You are.' I grinned back.

'I have to be a good boy, otherwise he might not let me fly out to California on Saturday – I've got a placement in a special tennis academy over there, where I get coached by two ex-Grand Slam players.'

'This Saturday?' I echoed. Selfish me – I straight away felt my heart sink like a stone. 'How long for?'

'Three weeks.'

'Three weeks?' That took us to half term. It was an absolute age, a whole era. The Earth's crust might even shift.

'Will you miss me?' he asked, too flippantly for my liking.

'No!' I lied. Yes, yes, yes! But what was he thinking, kissing me and not telling me he'd be away for three weeks? Why had he taken me to Tom's party and made me fall in love with him then thrown me into this abyss? OK, I'm totally overreacting.

The force of my one small negative seemed to throw Jack. He shuffled off with his tray of pasta and salad and went to sit with Luke and Harry. No more smiles, no more special looks, not even eye contact.

The light went out. Panic set in. What about our slow dance, our walk through the woods, our kiss?

'Hey,' he said to me the next day and the next, obviously waiting for a thaw in my demeanour.

Outside I was frosty, inside I was burning up. What did Jack want me to say, do, feel? I didn't know so I acted like a rabbit caught in headlights – not a squeak of protest, not one single move to save myself.

By Thursday I couldn't take any more. 'What about your trip?' I asked him in the quad after lessons had finished. I ran into him in his tennis gear – nothing deliberate. 'Will D'Arblay let you go?'

He nodded. 'I thought you weren't talking to me.'

I blushed. 'Funny – I had it the other way round.'

The puzzled frown came back. 'Alyssa – what happened? What did I do wrong?'

And this shows you how clunky and immature I am, how I just couldn't handle the tsunami of emotions and hormones that had swept over me the previous Saturday night.

'You didn't do anything wrong,' I told Jack Cavendish coolly in our last conversation before he set off for California to join all those toned tennis babes and west coast surfer girls. I spoke as if I didn't give a damn. 'Bye, Jack. Have fun,' I said.

I slammed the love window shut. I convinced myself I'd been blinded by his quads, fallen into lust and got it all wrong. Sorry, my mistake.

He'd go to be coached in California and he'd come

back with a tan. In the meantime, in my own mind I dug a division between us that was the depth of the Grand Canyon. I guess it might have been to protect myself from any deeper hurt, but then I'm not a trained shrink.

'He's right,' Jack Hooper said. We're back in the Squinting Cat, discussing Lily. 'Much better for Lily's relatives if the coroner's verdict is suicide.'

'Or an open verdict.' Like I said – Alex was into TV crime and Sky Sports, not much else. Girls didn't feature in his world. I guess he was saving them until he got to uni and could more freely expand his horizons. 'That's where there's not enough evidence to prove that the victim killed herself. It spares the family the guilt of not having done anything to help.'

'Nope. There was an email.' Suicide – case closed, according to Tom, who looked at his watch. 'Hey, what time does the five-a-side match start?' he asked Jack.

Hooper rolled his eyes. 'Do I look like I would know?'

He'd never kicked a ball in his life or raised a bat or a racket in anger because he's more the cerebral type, following in his family tradition (mother a society photographer snapping the Duchess of This and the Earl of That, father a bestselling author). And Jack's already had three short stories and one novella published in online literary magazines. He's sweet, shy and vulnerable – all that stuff.

'Five thirty.' Alex supplied the answer. He picked up his sports bag and made a move towards the door.

'Who's playing for your team?' Realizing that her 'filth' comment had left a bad taste, Paige made an unconvincing attempt to show an interest in the indoor football match between Ainslee Comp and St Jude's.

'Me, Alex, Micky, Sammy and Jayden,' Tom told her. 'Sorry, got to go. We're late.'

St Jude's Sports Centre is huge and state of the art. It's well set back from the Jacobean part of the campus, hidden behind copper beech trees in summer but in winter exposed to the strong west wind that blows down the valley and robs the trees of their canopy of dark red leaves. There's a car park to one side, and further over to the right another shiny building that houses the new school library and a ton of IT equipment.

'I take it you're not going to watch the match?' I asked Paige as we stepped off the bus outside the school gates and made our way up the drive.

This late in the year it was already dark and the gothic windows and arches were lit up from within. A wind was blowing sleet into our faces.

'Duh – no!' Paige laughed.

'Luke's playing,' I reminded her. Since Tom's party, she and Luke had limped along. Their on-off relationship wasn't good for her nerves, but at least they were on for part of the time, which is more than Jack and I were.

You might have already gathered that I don't like Luke. His family's filthy rich and he's hot in an R-Patz way, but he knows it. He looks in the mirror too much and he treats

Paige like dirt. I kept trying to convince her that tall, blond Tom Walsingham, party-giver and streetwise football player, was much better boyfriend material.

She tutted and threw back her head. 'It's Wednesday. I have dressage with my trainer in the indoor arena.'

'Sorry – I got your priorities all wrong.' We'd passed under the main arch into the quad and were ready to go our separate ways.

'If you insist on watching the match, keep an eye on Jack,' she told me. 'He'll be playing against Jayden. That should be interesting.'

It wasn't a football match, more a gladiatorial contest between Jack and Jayden, with a supporting cast of eight other players.

Guy Simons was the referee. He showed five yellow cards and used his whistle a lot.

Whistle – foul tackle by Jayden. Whistle – hand ball by Jack. Whistle – Jayden forgot about the ball and scythed Jack's legs from under him. Whistle for half time with the score at 1–0 to Ainslee, with Jayden the scorer.

The teams gathered in two huddles at opposite ends of the pitch, the Ainslee players grinning and cock-a-hoop, our team forming a circle and locking arms, heads down to discuss tactics for the second half.

'Harsh,' Zara muttered as the ref pocketed his whistle and took a breather.

I turned to my neighbour on the St Jude's supporters' bench. 'You're talking about Guy?'

She nodded. 'He's definitely the type who could abuse his authority.'

'Maybe power goes to his head.'

We paused for a while and considered Guy Simons. I reckoned he was mid thirties, a typical sports fanatic with too much brawn and not enough brain. If he hadn't trained as a teacher, I could see him joining the army and running around deserts, camouflaged and carrying a weapon.

'They call this a classless society,' Zara sighed.

After almost a term at St Jude's, I was at last getting to know her. It had taken some time because Zara wasn't a girls' girl and she seemed to spend most of her time effortlessly seducing boys. I mean, if you look like a combination of Scarlett Johanssen in her perfume ad and Kate Winslett in *Titanic*, what chance the rest of us?

'What do you mean?' Finding it hard to take my eyes off Jack in the centre of our huddle, I didn't pay much attention.

'It's war out there,' she explained. 'Comprehensives versus fee-payers. Them against us.'

'Things did heat up towards the end of the half,' I agreed. Sammy had kicked Luke in the left shin and been shown a yellow card, then Jayden had hacked Jack's feet from under him again as Jack made a run for goal. Guy Simons didn't see it and the St Jude's appeal for a penalty had been turned down. Zara and I had shown our disgust. 'But if you ask me, it's more personal than simple class warfare would suggest.'

'So who wants to kill whom?' Zara wanted to know. ('Whom' – dative form of 'who' and grammatically correct. You don't often hear that in anyone under fifty.)

'Jayden hates Jack and vice versa.' ('Vice versa' – phrase of Latin origin. Wow, we're sophisticated!)

Zara and I sat for a while watching the teams take up position for the second half. Jack and Jayden stood in the centre spot, eyeballing each other with pure rage while waiting for the whistle.

'That figures,' Zara agreed. 'Jack never forgave Jayden for stealing Lily from him.'

My jaw dropped as the whistle went and Jack booted the ball out on to the left wing.

'Didn't you know?' she said sweetly. 'Jack and Lily were an item all through Year Eleven, until Jayden got his hooks into her. Of course, that was long before you arrived on the scene.'

'I never knew that!' My voice had come out as a dry croak, as if someone had punched me in the throat. 'Lily and Jack – are you sure?'

My secret, start-of-term obsession with Jack had hardly registered on Zara's radar so she didn't think to spare my feelings. 'Sure I'm sure. Jack adored Lily. We all did.'

The match ended and I left the sports centre to wander in the grounds alone. It was still sleeting.

'You'll get wet,' Guy warned en route to the teachers' quarters. He's not exactly the caring sort – too extreme-sport for that – but even he could see that walking in the December dark without the proper gear wasn't good for a girl's health.

'I need a breath of air,' I told him.

He gave me a strange look and yomped on.

It was quiet by the lake, you might say deathly quiet. Truthfully, I hadn't been down here since they'd found Lily and I wasn't conscious of where I was heading until I reached the bank and gazed out across the black water. I felt my feet squelch through mud and my legs brush against tall, coarse grass. These must have been Lily's last sensations – squelching and brushing – as she waded to her death. I shuddered. Tears and raindrops blinded me; I felt I had no one in the world to turn to.

So what was new and how could I ever have been expecting it to be any different? I'd arrived at St Jude's as an outsider, not expecting to fit in, maybe not even wanting to. After all, it had been Aunt Olivia's idea for me to sit the scholarship exam and I just happened to have the type of brain that takes in facts and regurgitates them on demand.

Eidetic – OK, it's a term that still needs some explaining. 'Eidos' – Greek for 'seen', but actually any of the five senses can kick-start me into reliving an event – it can be visual, but it can also be a sound, a touch, a taste, a smell even. And – *whoosh* – I'm back in the original moment. In other words, I remember things with uncanny precision, which, I'll remind you (because your memory probably isn't as good as mine – yeah, hate me now!), is how I passed the entrance test for St Jude's.

'You'll love it, Alyssa.' Aunt Olivia didn't ask me – she *told* me – in the weeks and months before she dumped me in the quad with my M&S bags.

I hadn't been convinced, but Lily had welcomed me

with open arms, then I'd caught sight of wonder boy Jack stepping out of his dad's Maserati and for a few brief, very brief, days I had hoped that my aunt was right – slow-dancing at Tom's party, walking through the forest, running across the stubble field, falling into Jack's arms.

Then tragedy – he'd flown out to the Californian tennis academy and while he was away masochistic me had convinced myself that he didn't care, had no feelings for me, was totally indifferent to how I might feel in return.

'You're weird,' Paige had said flatly when she finally picked up my negative, self-destructive vibes. This would be about two weeks into Jack's sabbatical. 'How could he not be into you?'

'Yeah, Alyssa,' Lily had agreed. 'How could he not? I've already told you – just look at you, girl!'

I told her I'd looked and didn't like what I saw.

You're thinking, *Grow up, Alyssa! Just be nice to Jack when he gets back. Start over.* But, hey, I didn't have the confidence.

He came back with the tan and the look of a guy who wasn't interested any more. Let it be.

Alone and cold by the lake, reflecting on my failings and weaknesses, I stared at the oil-black water. There was no moon, no stars, only sleet driving against my face.

'Don't stand so close to the edge,' a voice warned.

I didn't look round. I knew his voice, felt his presence, and it sent a tingling sensation down my spine.

'Alyssa, step back,' Jack said as he took my hand.

I pulled away from his grasp.

He let go and waited for me to be ready to talk. 'I saw you walk down this way.'

I stared at the water, dark and deep.

'I'm sorry,' he said.

I turned. 'What for?'

'Being a loser. Not knowing how to act.'

'When?'

'All the time I'm around you. I've been a total tosser.'

'No.' Yes, actually. I remembered the cool and distant 'heys' as he passed by in the days after he'd told me about California. But then that had been down to me and my immature overreaction. 'No really – it's OK.'

'I had a lot on my mind – getting ready for the trip, other things.'

'It's OK,' I said again. 'I understand.'

'I just want you to know one thing – at Tom's party I was genuine. I wasn't just using you.'

'To get back at Lily?' I said baldly. 'It's OK – Zara just told me you two were an item.'

Jack nodded. Like me he was wet through, his hair sticking to his scalp, rain running down his face. 'I guess I should have mentioned it. But I was over her – in that way. I was moving on.'

'So why did you two finish?'

Jack thought for a while before he spoke. 'It just happened. My dad knows Lily's mum – they're both on some kind of committee at the National Opera – so we've hung around together since we were little kids. Then suddenly for a few months we were an item.'

'You adored her?' That's the way Zara had described it and the word was like an itch I had to scratch.

He frowned and half turned away. '*Everyone* adored Lily.'

And wanted to look after her and admired her and was scared of her mood swings. Again I kind of understood.

'I miss her,' I confessed.

'I adored her, but we just wore out,' was how he finally described it. 'We were into different things – me with my sport, her with her painting. And life with Lily was intense. I'm more of a laid-back guy.'

'It's OK, you don't have to explain if you don't want to.' Adam had told Paige and me in confidence about Lily's bipolar disorder and I tried to figure out if Jack also knew about the diagnosis. From the look on his face when he searched for the word, 'intense', I guessed that he did.

Again he took my hand and this time we stepped back from the water's edge together. 'Lily and I had stopped dating months before she went with Jayden. I want you to know that.'

'Does it make any difference?' I wondered out loud.

'You think I was still jealous of Jayden?' Jack didn't need to have things spelled out – for a guy he was sensitive to these emotional issues. 'I wasn't, but at the same time I knew he wasn't right for Lily.'

'So what was wrong with him?'

Jack shrugged. 'You've seen him.'

I thought of Jayden, reluctant daddy and feral gate-crasher with his Upper Chartsey mates. 'Hey, Jayden!' a newly pregnant Lily had cried as she tottered towards him fuelled by alcohol and everything else she'd been able to lay her hands on, before she'd wobbled and collapsed and been carried off by Luke and Paige.

I could smell her Lola perfume mixed in with the alcohol, could see again the red-wine stains on her sequinned top. And I read cruelty in Jayden's hooded eyes as Lily sank on to the Turkish rug – his top lip curled to show his teeth as he turned away and made his exit through Tom's French windows.

'I can totally see you'd be worried about her,' I told Jack.

His angst suddenly burst through. 'And I didn't do anything to help.'

I said I didn't think it would have made any difference, that Lily had a self-destruct button that even an outsider like me had spotted early on. 'So don't feel guilty.'

'I do. I will.' Turning, he walked me away from the lake, squelching up the slope out of the swamp. 'Always, especially now. Maybe if I'd talked her out of going with Jayden, she'd still be alive.'

'You think she killed herself because he dumped her?' I voiced the most obvious theory. 'You know she sent an email?'

Jack stopped short, halfway between the lake and the main house. 'Sure – I was the one she sent it to,' he confessed quietly.

'Say that again.'

'She sent me the email from her iPhone – probably the last thing she did before . . .'

'She told you what she was planning to do? What did she say?'

'Here,' he said, pulling a piece of folded paper from his pocket and handing it to me with a trembling hand. 'I printed it out, gave two copies to Dr Webb and kept one for myself.'

'It'll get wet,' I warned, putting on a burst of speed until we reached the stone archway leading into the quad where we stood under an ornate wrought-iron lamp. 'Here, now wait while I read it.'

Hey, Jack.

Lily's suicide note began like an everyday digital message, but it soon plunged off course.

Hope you're cool with me sending you this email but I couldn't think of anyone else I wanted to say bye to as much as you. You can pass it on to anyone else who might miss me. I know *you* will miss me a bit, Jack, because we go way back. I'm sober by the way, not pissed like you might think.

I stopped reading to shake my head and get a grip.

'I know,' Jack groaned. 'It hurts like hell.'

So I have something huge to tell you and you can pass this on too if you like. I'm pregnant, Jack. Big breath. Read again: I'm pregnant. This is not a lie – I did the test twice and both times it came up positive. Careless, huh? You'd have expected better of a smart St Jude's girl like me.

I closed my eyes and tried to get my breathing back to normal. It was a while before I could go on reading to the end.

So at first I didn't tell anyone what I'd done except the baby's father who of course didn't want to know – why should he? And I'm telling you now, giving you the reason why I'm going – it's because I don't want to go on living the out-of-control way I've been living these last few weeks that I'm out of here and won't be back (too shitty and painful and head-fuckingly awful, and anyway what kind of mother would I be?).

So sorry to dump this on you, Jack. And tell Paige and Alyssa hey and sorry to them too. We had fun sometimes, didn't we, girls?

I cried. The sobs just came. Jack held me and hugged me and we didn't say another word.

chapter four

'So Mistral's basic transition from trot to canter still needs work,' Paige sighed as she made us both hot chocolate before bed. 'Georgie, my trainer, said it needed to be smoother, but Mistral was tired tonight – he acted like he didn't want to know.'

I took the mug and cradled it. My eyes felt hot and sore from all the crying in Jack's arms.

'Usually those basic transitions aren't a problem. When he has his head screwed on, you can't fault him. But in a way I know Georgie's right – Mistral has to be perfect one hundred per cent of the time, tired or not.'

'Paige,' I interrupted.

'I mean, at the standard we're aiming for, which is Olympic dressage level, no one can afford to have off-days.'

'Paige!'

'What? Oh sorry, did I put in too much sugar? I forgot.'

'No. Paige, listen to me – Jack and I are talking again.'

'My God, what took you so long?'

'Yeah, I know. I'm an idiot.'

Paige didn't disagree. 'So when you say "talking" . . . ?'

'I said sorry.'

'And? Are you two an item again? You kissed and made

up and don't tell me no because if you do I might have to bang your stupid heads together.'

'Later,' I pleaded. 'No, the thing is, Paige – I read Lily's email.'

She frowned and I could see her brain change gear. 'The one Adam told us about?' she asked falteringly.

'Yes. Jack was the one Lily sent it to. He just told me.'

'Oh God!' All the breath went out of her and she slumped on the bed beside me. 'And I'm burbling on about horses.'

'The email makes it seem more real. And it was gut-wrenching, the way Lily blamed herself, saying how stupid she'd been.'

'Lily wasn't stupid,' Paige argued. 'That was the last thing she was. It was that shit-face Jayden.'

'We think.'

'We *know*!'

'She said she didn't want to go on living the way she'd been living these last few weeks. She said to say bye to me and you.' I began to cry all over again, joined this time by Paige.

'I can't believe it,' she sobbed. 'I still think she'll be back, chucking stuff over the floor, stinking us out with her paints. To tell you the truth, I steer clear of this room and spend as much time as I can with Mistral because I know every time I look at her empty bed I do this – I break down.'

This was hearty, cynical, horse-obsessed Paige's confession and, what do you know, her distress broke down my defences and I relived it all over again.

They pulled Lily's body from the lake – three divers in black wetsuits. Her hair streamed back from her face. Her travel bag and one of her shoes were missing. It was a clear, cold day, with a touch of frost.

'Jack plans to contact Adam Earle,' I told Paige through my tears. 'He wants to know about Lily's funeral arrangements.'

Adam Earle's staff blocked all Jack's calls and emails for the rest of the week, but Adam himself showed up at school again on the Saturday morning. This time Lily's mother, Anna, came along, dressed all in black.

We saw her from our bedroom window, stepping out of her son's car – tall, beautiful and fragile, as if a strong wind would blow her over. Her eyes were hollow, the corners of her mouth turned down and her skin was deathly pale.

'What do *they* want?' Paige's tone was hostile.

A rapid knock soon told us the answer.

Zara poked her head round the door. 'Hey, you two. D'Arblay says can you make yourselves scarce? The mother and brother want to come in and collect Lily's things.'

'Where are we supposed to go?' Paige objected, ready to stay right where she was.

'Stables?' Zara made the obvious suggestion as she vanished again.

Mule-headed Paige decided to take her time, but I made a quick exit – I didn't feel up to facing Lily's brother and her grieving mum. So I sped along the corridor and down the stone stairway into the quad where, unluckily, I ran into Mrs Earle, who was standing at the narrow entrance to the boys' staircase, deep in conversation with Jack.

He spotted me and called for me to join them.

It was obvious he needed rescuing so I took a sharp, shallow breath then steeled myself for the conversation I was about to have, the questions I would have to answer. This wasn't about me, I reminded myself. Hold back the tears, be dignified and do it for Lily – all of that.

'Mrs Earle, Alyssa. Alyssa, Lily's mum.' Jack eyed me nervously as we shook hands.

I saw echoes of Lily in Anna, in the long, dark hair and eyes, the curve of her eyebrows.

'The funeral's fixed for next Wednesday. It's going to be at St Michael's.' Now Jack set up a background commentary while Lily's mum and I simply stared at the ground. 'Everyone believes that Lily would have wanted it to be in Chartsey because it's where she felt she belonged. Adam's arranging the details with Dr Webb.'

I would have nodded and walked on, away from Mrs Earle's silent agony, if Adam hadn't suddenly opened the long, lead-paned window of the principal's study and called my name. 'Alyssa, have you got a moment?' he asked.

You didn't say no to someone like Adam Earle.

'Wait there. I'll come out,' he said.

The window closed, and while we waited Anna Earle's manner seemed to change from silent and grief-stricken to edgy and afraid.

'I should have come here sooner,' she explained to Jack in a sudden, breathless rush. 'I wanted to be here, believe me, just to see for myself.'

'We were all shocked. And we're so sorry.' He was two

sentences ahead of me at expressing how we felt and I could tell he was trying to protect me. I was tongue-tied, not doing well at all.

'Adam said it would be better if I stayed away until the police . . .'

A couple of students crossed the quad, coming towards us – Harry Embsay and Jack Hooper. They sensed the tension and veered off under the main archway.

'Until the police finished doing whatever they had to do. That's terrible, isn't it?' At this point Anna's voice cracked.

I nodded. *Get a grip – you will not cry!* went in a loop through my brain.

'We heard the news over the Atlantic. It came through on the pilot's radio. Robert wasn't with us. He'd stayed behind in Chicago. Adam and I landed at Heathrow. He took me home, made sure I was in good hands then came up to St Jude's as soon as he could.'

People in shock need to tell you the mundane details – I read that somewhere. They turn the whole thing into a plain, simple story, which they repeat over and over, word for word. It gives the pain a framework they can deal with, some kind of defence against an otherwise unbearable avalanche of emotion.

By this time Adam had appeared, shadowed by Saint Sam who hovered in the background. Anna Earle's flow of information dried up immediately. She seemed to hold her breath and fade elegantly into the background.

'Alyssa,' Adam began. He ignored his mother and Jack. 'I'm glad I caught you. I was just arranging funeral details with the principal – which students will represent the school, who will speak the eulogy, which hymns and so on. Dr Webb thinks it will be appropriate for you and Paige to speak during the service.'

I noticed Anna's reaction – little shudders on words like 'funeral', 'eulogy' and 'hymns', as if sharp darts were piercing her pale skin. Her face was an open book, emotions all on the surface, just like Lily's. Like mother, like daughter, I realized.

'What would I have to say?' I asked.

'Oh, it needn't be a long speech. Maybe you could focus on what Lily was like as a roommate – any good, recent memories you might want to share. I'll get Paige to cover the pre-sixth form stuff.'

I nodded and muttered that I would try to write something down.

'Great, thanks. The police have accepted the coroner's initial report.' Adam went on without missing a beat. 'There's no sign of a struggle or any suggestion at this stage that anyone else was involved. And of course we have Lily's email.'

Was this man a machine? I glanced at Jack, who stood with narrowed eyes and clenched fists.

'Which frees us to go ahead with the funeral next week. We're fending off press interest by insisting that it's a private family occasion, and that's one of the reasons why we're holding it out here in the Cotswolds, away from the full media glare. Although of course there can't be a complete news blackout, given my father's international profile.'

OK, enough! Really – I had to put some distance between myself and Adam Automaton Earle. Jack obviously felt the same so we mumbled our goodbyes and got out of there together.

'How are you doing?' he asked.

'Terrible, thanks.'

'Thought so.' We walked together under the archway on to the front drive. That part felt good, at least. 'What do you say we get out of here?'

I nodded and let him steer me towards the sports centre and new library.

'Now we know why Lily hated her family and stayed away as much as she bloody well could,' Jack said as we grabbed a couple of mountain bikes from the bike shed next to the sports centre. St Jude's provides them for the school community to use as and when – a bit like Boris Bikes in central London. It makes it easier for students to get into Chartsey.

Jack and I rode there mostly in silence, sharing the misery of Anna Earle's situation.

'What about Lily's mum,' I asked as we hit the top of Main Street. 'She seems different.'

'Like she might even care,' Jack agreed.

'Look what I snuck out of Lily's box of oil paints!' Paige crowed. She'd texted me and found out that Jack and I were at the Squinting Cat, holding hands across the table and busily avoiding Anna Earle and the automaton. She joined us now, slapping a small notebook down on the table. 'Her diary!'

I recognized it straight away – the pale blue cover scrawled all over with Lily's intricate designs, dog eared and paint spattered.

'You stole it!' I yelped.

Jack trapped it with his hand, as if it might have legs and walk away unaided.

Paige came over all innocent. 'I wouldn't say "stole". I was just tidying stuff, ready for Adam and Mrs Earle to pack up and take away. The diary kind of fell out of the box into my hand.'

'You stole it,' Jack confirmed.

'Did you get a chance to read it?' I asked.

'Parts of it.'

'Does she come across as – you know, depressed?'

'Enough to throw herself in the lake?' Paige shook her head. 'No, like we said – she's up and down, the way she always was. And she doesn't mention being pregnant either, unless these little marks above the date mean something.' Sliding the page-a-day diary away from Jack, Paige opened it at random and pointed to small shapes that Lily had drawn. They reminded me of Egyptian hieroglyphs – part geometric, part pictorial. One was a square with four legs, one a stickman, along with other twiddles, triangles and swirls.

'Could they be Lily's version of writing in code?' Jack wondered.

'But why would she?' I wondered. 'I mean, who did she think was going to read her private diary?'

'Paige?' Jack's question in answer to my question came quick as a flash, but Paige didn't even blush.

'I'm not sorry I took it before Adam could get his mitts on it,' she insisted as she turned the page and stabbed at an entry with her finger. 'There's stuff here that Lily would never have wanted her family to read.'

Saturday, April 5th. Big fight with the tyrant.

Followed by a clever Lily-style caricature of Robert Earle, instantly recognizable. Bald head and scrawny neck, deep-set eyes with dark circles like a meerkat.

Will not, repeat WILL NOT play his game.

Paige flicked to a later entry.

Monday, July 4th. Called Mum to ask how she was. Tyrant came in and grabbed phone from her. HATE HIM!!! Met J after school. LOVE HIM!!!

Then a row of tiny hearts in red felt tip, linked by capital letters spelling out Jayden's name.

Am thinking of getting tattoo around ankle, with J's name linking chain of hearts, as above.

'Good job she didn't,' Paige commented. 'You can get chucked out of St Jude's for less than that. They don't regard getting a tattoo as part of expressing your individuality.'

I took the diary and flicked through until the start of September. 'You were right about her not going to stay with her cousin,' I found out. 'It says here she was with Jayden in Upper Chartsey.

September 5th. House was all ours, I read. J's mum and kid bro staying in caravan in N Wales. J and I lived on chips, pizza and LURVE!!!

More hearts followed and a rectangle with legs – maybe a bed? And at the top of the entry I noticed new hieroglyphs – a circle with a dot followed by a question mark, a smiley face which didn't need a super intellect to interpret and the stick man walking what looked like a stick dog.

'Wasn't your aunt a famous spy or something?' Paige mentioned. 'Come on, Alyssa, didn't you inherit the family code-breaking gene?'

'Great-great-aunt,' I told her. Then, 'Give me chance.'

'So what else do we learn?' Snatching the diary back and knocking it against her cup of coffee ('Oops!'), Paige studied more entries. 'We know she loved Jayden and stayed with him while his mum was away – sorry, Jack.'

'No, Lily was doing her own thing. We'd moved on.' He looked steadily at me as he said this, as if saying, Now do you believe me?

I do. I believe you!

'We also know that within a couple of weeks of being loved-up in Upper Chartsey, Jayden had dumped her and Lily's life sucked,' Paige reminded us. 'And listen to this.'

'Wednesday October 3rd,' she read. 'A. came here after big fight with the T on the phone. Won't take any more meds, just in case. ⊙ Didn't explain why. Hate him. Don't want to end up

67

like M. Took it out on work in progress. A and P tried to stop me. Swear I'll never paint again.'

'Remember that?' Paige asked me excitedly. 'Come on, you're Memory Girl. Give us an action replay.'

Wednesday, October 3rd. A date is enough to plunge me once again into total recall:

I was sitting on my bed when Lily stormed in and started flinging things around the room. She wasn't crying but she kept on grunting as though someone was using her as a punch bag.

'I'm sixteen. They can't tell me what to do.' Tearing clothes out of her drawer and throwing them on the floor, she seemed to be looking for something she couldn't find. 'Has anyone seen my phone?'

'It's on your bed,' Paige told her.

'Not that phone – my secret phone!'

'Sorry, I don't know anything about it, and that's probably because it's a secret.' Paige pointed out the Catch 22. Lily ignored her.

Instead she turned on me. 'Alyssa, have you seen it?'

'Is it the one in the black case?'

'No, that's my normal phone. I mean the red one without a case.' There was a heap of T-shirts and sweaters on the floor, which Lily was burrowing into. 'Jesus, I hate all this!'

'What do you mean?' I asked, getting up to help her look. 'What do you hate?'

By this time Lily was crying and she'd left off looking for

her phone and throwing things and picked up the palette knife instead. 'Everything.'

Paige and I tried to stop her from wrecking her canvas. Lily held the knife like a dagger and slashed into the abstract painting. It was very Gerhard Richter – controlled chaos, bright red circle and sweep of yellow across the diagonal, with paint laid on in thick layers, which were scraped back in some places to show areas of black underneath.

'What do you mean – everything?' I grabbed her wrist, but she broke free and made more slashes with the knife.

'What do you know, Alyssa? You've only just got here. What could you possibly know?'

Paige was stronger than me and she stepped in briskly to take the knife from Lily. 'Breathe,' she told her. 'Calm down and we'll help you find your phone.'

'They won't even let me speak to him and anyway he's not answering my texts,' Lily sobbed. 'I wish I'd never told my mother. Or him, or anybody!'

She collapsed forward and we could hardly tell what she was saying, too focused on stopping her from turning the knife on herself to really listen or to ask who 'he' was.

Only now I got what I hadn't got at the time. When Lily stabbed the canvas and it seemed to me she was trying to kill part of herself – that was the baby, the secret that she'd dared to share with her mother.

'You see this circle with the dot?' I said to Jack and Paige as we studied the stolen diary. 'I reckon that's a symbol for the baby. And I think the stick man with the dog is Jayden.'

69

Jack rocked back on his chair while Paige flicked through the book.

'Yeah,' she said. 'That must be right.'

You're thinking, What if Jayden doesn't have a dog, Alyssa? What if it turns out you're crap at breaking secret codes, despite your great-great-aunt Caroline?

'I'm sorry, I have to go,' Jack decided after two cups of coffee in the Squinting Cat. 'I don't want to. I'd rather stay and help you two work this out, but I have study group in fifteen.'

We do this on Saturdays at St Jude's – it's a non-uniform day, but not a non-work day. We still get together for informal study groups that are meant to help with a big project in say science or French. Yeah, I agree – it sucks not to have the whole weekend free.

'See you later, Alyssa.' Jack stood up then leaned over and kissed me on the lips. Our first PDA – nothing major, but still a big step forward for both of us. And the brush of his lips against mine was a totally pleasurable sensation that I longed to repeat.

'Me too – I have to go.' Paige pretended not to notice, but she gave me a secret wink as she stood up. 'Are you coming, Alyssa?'

'No, I'll stay. Leave the diary with me.'

'You're sure?'

I nodded and told them I wanted to be certain that the automaton was clear of the school premises before I ventured back. 'I'll see you both later.'

This left me alone with my third caffeine kick and time

on my hands to study Lily's entries. I reread all the way through September and into late October, where the circle with the dot appeared every day, sometimes with a smiley face but more often with a sad one. By this time there was no stick man and dog. On October 20th she'd devoted the whole page to headlines from the business sections of national newspapers, which she'd first photocopied, reduced in size then cut out and haphazardly pasted on to the page. *Comco Buys Talk TV*, *Earle in Fresh Takeover Battle*, *Comco Leads Campaign to Expose International Fascist Cells*. In the middle of the jumble of newsprint Lily had drawn her caricature dad in thick black ink. She'd made him super-grotesque, with that scrawny neck and those meerkat eyes.

'Hey, isn't that your bike?' Susie the waitress asked from behind her counter.

I looked up in time to see two kids aged about ten hop on to the St Jude's bike, which I'd left propped against a lamp post. The one with the shaven head straddled the cross bar and began to pedal while the other with dark hair flopping down over his forehead perched on the saddle and stuck his legs straight out. As they wobbled out of sight I saw that they were followed by a brown-and-white dog.

Yeah, that was my bike. I thanked Susie, shoved Lily's diary into my pocket and was up out of my chair and on the pavement in five seconds flat.

Notice the dog.

The thieving little bastards didn't get far along the pavement – only to the Bridge Inn – before riding tandem on a one-person bike became too much for them and they both fell off. The dog barked, the kids hooted as they picked themselves up then kicked my bike while it was down.

I sprinted towards them. The dog, who was between me and my transport home, heard me and turned to bare its teeth.

'Go get her, Bolt!' the kid with the jailbird haircut cried, stamping hard on the front wheel.

'Kill, boy, kill!' the other one croaked.

For a second it looked like the dog would. It snarled like only a broad-chested, bow-legged Staffie can. So I stopped in my tracks.

Partly because of the dog, but also partly because Jayden had just stepped out of the alleyway down the side of the pub.

He didn't say anything, just shoved the kids to one side and picked the bike up from the ground.

Stubble Head swore like an underage trooper while Floppy Hair slunk off without a word.

'Look at that!' I protested, pointing to the bike's buckled front wheel. 'It's wrecked. How do I get back home?'

Now Jayden did speak, not to answer my question but to swear back at the kid and thrust the mangled bike towards him. 'Take this into JD's – get it fixed.'

'Who's going to pay for it?' the kid retaliated.

'You are.'

'Who's going to make me?'

Would you have dared to stand up to Jayden this way? No – me neither. Anyway, Lily's ex was fired up enough to take the kid by the scruff of the neck, haul him off his feet and throw him and the bike in the direction of the car-repair place down the street.

While this was going on, Bolt the dog kept up a chorus of low growls.

'Sit,' Jayden snarled, and Bolt at least had the sense to do as he was told.

'So – same question,' I said as kid and bike got on their way. 'How do I get back to school?'

'Bus.' Squeezing one-syllable answers out of Jayden was like getting blood from the proverbial stone.

I was still mad, so I pointed after the retreating kid. 'Who is that, anyway?'

'Brad.'

'You know him?'

'I should do – he's my kid brother.' Jayden launched off in the opposite direction with Bolt close behind. Stick man and stick dog.

Running after him, I took a huge risk. 'You heard what happened to Lily?'

He halted, nodded then walked on with shoulders hunched, wearing a deep scowl.

'The funeral's Wednesday.'

He shook his head.

'Yeah, it is. I talked to Lily's brother, Adam.'

'It's not happening, not any more,' he insisted.

I overtook him and stood in his way. 'Why, what do you know that we don't?'

'No body, no funeral.'

'But there is – obviously there is!' I couldn't bring myself to say the word 'body'.

Jayden's hooded eyes were almost closed under that overhanging brow. 'Talk to Alex.'

'Alex who?' I looked frantically up and down the street, in time to see young Brad and the bike disappearing into JD Repairs.

'Driffield. You know him.'

'What's he got to do with anything?' I asked the question realizing that I wouldn't get an answer.

Bolt kept pace with Jayden as he turned off the high street down Meredith Lane – a road leading to a small housing estate built in the 1950s for council workers. The back end of a Staffie isn't attractive – thin, pointy tail curving up to reveal tight white anus and squat haunches. Is that too graphic for you? Anyway, they walk like bodybuilders on steroids.

Silence from Jayden and never a backwards glance.

What the –? What, dear Reader, was that all about? Jayden's kid brother destroys my bike. Jayden appears out of nowhere and reins him in. He tells me there isn't going to be a funeral. Hold the eulogy.

Driffield? Alyssa the Memory Girl gets to work. JD – John Driffield is the name of the guy who runs the car-repair garage. His name is in small letters under the main sign. Alex must be his son.

'Jayden!' I cried as man and dog turned into the garden of a house with an overflowing wheelie bin at the gate.

The door banged and then silence. And now I was on a

mission – straight back down the high street to JD Repairs where I saw my broken bike propped up inside the wide entrance. A bald man in overalls stood chest-deep in a service pit under an ancient Volvo. Radio 2 played loudly. There was a small office at the back of the workshop.

'Hi!' I called above Take That circa 1995.

The guy in overalls pointed me towards the office, where I found Brad sulking with Alex Driffield.

Brad's vocabulary of anatomically-based swear words was impressive for a ten-year-old. I won't sully the page.

'Eff off,' Alex told him as he swiped at the kid's head with the back of his hand. 'Sorry about that – the kid was out of order,' he told me.

Brad effed off and I shrugged, coming straight to the point. 'Jayden says you know something about Lily's funeral.'

Alex logged info into a computer as he talked. 'Yeah, it got held up.'

'How? Why?'

'No body, no funeral.'

'That's what Jayden told me. But how come?'

'From what I heard, the police aren't ready to release it.' This was right up Alex's street. What with his fascination for TV crime series, he relished being in possession of confidential police information.

'Who said?'

'A kid in school – Micky Cooke. His dad works at the morgue in Ainslee.' Slowly Alex revealed the precious, scavenged facts, savouring the moment.

My heart hammered at my ribs. 'And?'

'The pathologist handed over his report. He found something they weren't expecting.'

'For God's sake, Alex!'

'Chill. I don't expect it'll be anything too – y'know – gory.'

I bit my lip and steadied myself against the desk.

'Maybe nothing at all. They're not sure yet.'

Still I waited. The DJ segued from Take That into One Direction's latest number one.

'Micky's dad says it's just enough to make the cops think twice. Yes, Lily did drown, yes, she was pregnant and, no, there was no sign of a struggle . . .'

'But?'

'Like I said, they're holding on to the body for the pathologist to put in a second report.' Know-it-all Alex wouldn't let go of his big moment.

'Alex, for God's sake, this is real – not some poxy TV series!'

'You're right – sorry.'

'No, you're not. You're getting some kind of weird thrill.' I was really angry and didn't care if he knew it.

He shrugged. 'So now what?'

'So now you find out from Micky Cooke exactly what the pathologist found.'

'Just like that?' Alex made it clear he was done with me by turning his back and bringing up the messages inbox on his iPhone.

'Yes, just like that!' I yelled. 'You can't go around spreading rumours without any proof.'

'Watch me,' he muttered.

chapter five

Paige wasn't around – she was probably still at study group – when I got back to school, so I sat alone in our room, staring out of the window at the darkening scene.

Nothing had changed. There was a smooth lawn and a lake and beyond that an oak wood stripped of its leaves. Rooks rose from their untidy nests and circled in the dying light.

But everything shifted in the lengthening shadows – from sedate to sinister, sane to crazy, suicide to possible murder.

This could be a suspicious death! I said to myself as I put my finger on what had felt so wrong from the very start. Maybe Lily didn't kill herself.

I had nothing concrete to go on – only a funeral delay and a request for a second, in-depth pathologist's report – but the thought insinuated its way into my brain and I started to shake. *Murder, not suicide. Unlawful killing.*

But what about the email containing the desperate last thoughts of a gifted but unstable girl with an unwanted pregnancy and a boyfriend who'd dumped her the minute she'd told him about the baby?

Nothing too gory. I thought if I repeated Alex's phrase often enough it might make my racing heart slow down. *Nothing too – y'know – gory!*

But the lake and the woods still made me shudder. I almost saw Lily out there, or her pale ghost, standing at the water's edge, staring up at my window, begging for help.

I turned away but then it felt as if she was in the room, sitting cross-legged on her bed, breathing, beseeching.

'Lily, you have to help me. I don't know what to do!' I said.

Five minutes later Mercury knocked and came in (aka Zara, messenger to the gods). 'Hey, Alyssa. You look awful.'

'Thanks.'

'I'm just saying – I don't know, I thought maybe you needed someone to talk to.'

'No thanks.' Unlawful killing. Some terrible mystery about to be revealed. The new notion kept me in its iron grip.

'So anyway,' Zara said, 'Sam wants to see you.'

'When?'

'Now.'

'What about?'

Actually, the name Mercury doesn't suit Zara. She's too luscious for that – a goddess in her own right, although as a scientific genius she would reject the old, classical myths as stories invented by primitive peoples to explain away natural disasters. If she has a god, it would be Professor Stephen Hawking and her bible would be his *Brief History of Time*.

'D'Arblay didn't say.' She backed off from offering sympathy and reverted to that distant, don't-bother-me way she can adopt, except when she's seducing Luke or Tom or either of the two Jacks, in which case she's fully engaged in the task and doesn't have time for small talk. She looked at me a while longer then and her face softened again. 'Sorry, Alyssa. He just asked me to pass on the message. It's probably to do with Lily. Isn't everything?'

Ouch! 'Don't you care that she's dead?' I asked.

'Yes, I care, but spare me the shit.'

'What shit?'

'The shit that is about to hit the fan.' Zara led me to the window and pointed down the front drive to the main gates where cars were parked and a growing knot of people were milling around in the gloom. 'Journos. Cameras, reporters.'

I groaned.

'Vultures,' Zara said.

'Come in, Alyssa.' Saint Sam's voice was calm and quiet as I knocked on his door. 'Take a seat.'

I entered and sat, doing my best to ignore dapper, smart-arse D'Arblay who stood in the doorway that connected the principal's study with his own.

'First and most importantly, I wanted a private chat to ask how you're coping with the stress of Lily's death.'

'I'm OK.'

Head tilted to one side, Sam studied my face. 'We do have a counselling service,' he reminded me.

'I don't need it, thanks.'

'No. I can see that you're a strong personality. Besides we know that you're no stranger to tragedy – losing your parents at a young age and so on. You've already had to cope with a lot in your life.'

'I'm OK,' I insisted. Which of those two short words didn't he understand?

'Would you like us to inform your aunt? You could go home, perhaps skip the last few weeks of term then come back refreshed in the New Year.'

I looked down and studied my fingernails.

'Alyssa?'

'What about my eulogy?' It was a leading question, I know. I was digging to see if Saint Sam knew about the postponement.

'Someone else could do that for you,' he said without hesitating.

In the doorway D'Arblay nodded and smiled like the Churchill dog. O-o-oh yes!

'Alyssa?' Sam prompted again.

'No. I want to do it. Anyway, the funeral won't be Wednesday – it'll be later.'

I glanced up in time to see Sam react – maybe with annoyance, definitely not with surprise. But within a nanosecond he'd glossed over whatever emotion he was experiencing and he was back to his saintly, holier-than-thou self. 'What makes you say that?'

'It's true. Everyone in the village knows that the police won't release Lily's body.' I admit I took poetic licence here – Alex and Jayden weren't exactly 'everyone'.

'Ah.' The principal sighed and paused while his sidekick took two steps into the room. 'We were rather hoping that wouldn't get out. But Chartsey is a small place where everyone learns everyone else's business sooner rather than later.'

'Mr Earle won't be happy,' D'Arblay warned. 'And I must say I agree with him – the family deserves maximum privacy at such a time.'

Still sighing, Sam placed his hands on his desk and made his fingers into a steeple. 'It's important that we at St Jude's keep a united front,' he went on. 'Whatever we hear on the grapevine we keep to ourselves.'

I'd never had a gagging order before so at first I didn't understand what was going on.

'Meaning, Alyssa, you don't repeat to anyone, either to other students here or to outsiders, what you have just told me.'

'But it's true, so what's the point?'

D'Arblay was the one who laid it on the line, stepping forward with his hands clasped behind his back – one, two, three steps with mincing military precision. 'The point is the world's press is knocking on our door, but we still have to respect Robert Earle's request for privacy.'

Yeah, I'd been gagged. I got it now.

'Meanwhile we'll make a phone call and inform your aunt that you're under severe emotional strain,' Sam insisted.

'There's no need,' I began again.

'It's our duty.' He tapped his fingertips together. 'Oh, and before I forget, there was one other thing I needed to mention, also, I'm afraid, connected with this sequence of unfortunate events.'

I waited, knowing it wouldn't be good.

'As you recall, Adam and his mother have gathered up Lily's personal possessions from your room.'

I nodded but gave nothing away. Two can play at that game.

'There was one important thing missing,' Sam went on. 'An item that they particularly want to keep out of the wrong hands.'

'What?'

'Lily's diary. You wouldn't happen to have seen it, would you, Alyssa?'

'No,' I said, looking the principal directly in the eye. 'As a matter of fact, I didn't even know she kept one.'

I should probably have left out that last sentence. Methinks the lady doth protest too much. But I wasn't a practised liar so I overdid it, which meant that neither Saint Sam nor D'Arblay believed me. But what could they do, except corner Paige and ask her the same thing? Paige is more expert than I am in being economical with the truth, so I wasn't worried on that score.

In any case, I headed for the library where Saturday study groups meet, eager to update her and Jack.

I say 'library', but not in the old-fashioned sense. St Jude's still has one of those in the old building – the book-lined, traditional type with creaking shelves of leather-bound volumes, preserved for posterity. But the one students actually use is housed in the new technology building next to the sports centre. It's designed by a famous

Spanish architect, domed and clad with steel scales that make it look like a giant fish. *Nihil sed . . .* Inside there are a hundred Apple Macs, but hardly a printed book in sight.

'The question is – what do we learn about the First World War from Owen and Sassoon?' Bryony was winding up for the afternoon in one of the big, bright, open-plan study bays. 'Jack, is there any one image or phrase that stands out for you?'

She meant Jack Hooper, not my Jack. I realized this as I glanced around the group and saw that mine was missing.

' "I am the enemy you killed, my friend," ' was his earnest answer. 'Men wore different uniforms and fought on opposite sides, but under the uniform they were flesh and blood – no difference. They only killed the so-called enemy because that's what some dumb general ordered them to do.' Jack was on a roll and didn't stop when he saw me edge towards Paige. 'And the stupidest thing is they started the whole mess all over again twenty years later, only this time the Germans had Hitler and the Allies dropped the atom bomb.'

'Good. Then that's what you should construct your essay around, Jack – the insanity of war. Build up your whole argument from that starting point.' Logging off and packing up her well-thumbed volume of war poems, Bryony saw me hovering in the background. 'Hey, Alyssa.'

'Hey.'

'Are you looking for someone?'

'Yes – Jack Cavendish.'

'He left early for a lesson with his tennis coach.' As her

group of students dispersed and I failed to grab Paige's attention, Bryony stayed behind to share a smile and a joke. 'So much more important than dusty old war poets, eh?'

'Jack must think so. He's good enough to play at senior level for his county.'

'I don't doubt it.' Bryony Phillips is someone you want to stay and talk with, even when she's not saying what you want to hear and when you have something else important to do. Small and compact, with a wild shock of dark hair streaked with a flash of premature grey, she knows how to grab your attention both in and out of the classroom. 'Guy is always singing Jack's praises, but it leaves me cold. I'm not into competitive sports, I'm afraid.'

We strolled the length of the huge open space. 'Me neither.'

'But Jack has other talents?' She raised an arched, inquisitive eyebrow and her lips twitched into a smile.

'Some.' ('Sm'. I was swallowing my vowels again. This was a serious, recurring case of jack-itis.)

'Sorry, Alyssa – I overstepped the mark.'

'It's OK'. ('S K'.)

'No, it's not my business.' Stopping me in the glass entrance lobby, Bryony put a hand on my arm. 'Joking aside, how are you doing?'

'OK some of the time. Other times I can't believe this is real.'

'I know,' she sighed. 'We all miss Lily desperately. She leaves a big hole in everyone's lives – teachers and students alike.'

'The police won't release the body,' I blurted out without intending to.

Bryony took away her hand and sucked in a sharp breath.

'Ask Dr Webb.' There – I'd broken my gagging order. Not deliberately, but somehow with Bryony you wanted to tell it exactly how it was.

'What are they thinking – that Lily's death was suspicious?'

'Yes. Maybe. I don't know.'

Hurriedly I left the building ahead of Bryony, leaving her to digest the new information as I crossed the car park and dashed to the sports centre to find Jack.

A stranger had got into the sports centre, a spy in the camp.

'My name's Emily Archer. I'm with the UK Tennis Association,' she told Guy Simons who stood with beefy arms crossed. 'I scout for talent.'

'My arse,' Guy replied.

'No, really . . .' She was tiny and blonde; he was a gigantic thug. It was Tiananmen Square all over again, unarmed protestor versus tank.

'I'm trained to sniff out a talent scout at fifty paces,' he snorted, still blocking her way and now forcing her into a tottering retreat back the way she'd come. 'And my gut feeling is you don't know one end of a tennis racket from another.'

'Fine!' she snapped, backing into me and almost falling flat.

Journo, I thought. I would've let her fall and so would Guy, but Jack was more of a gentleman.

'You OK?' he checked with her, stepping out of the changing room, hair slicked back after his shower, and saving her just in time.

'Jesus Christ, I'm only trying to do my job!' she exclaimed at Guy as she righted herself and stormed off.

'Coffee?' I asked Jack, nodding my head towards the mezzanine cafe overlooking the indoor courts.

'You look upset,' Jack began. It was the first real chance I'd had to talk with him since he'd come and rescued me from the side of the lake, not counting the meeting in the Squinting Cat because Paige had been there and we'd only allowed ourselves that brief kiss. Dig deeper and you'd find that I was longing for him to put his arms round me and hold me close, for him to never let me go.

'Are you OK?'

'Yep.' I kept the hugging urge at bay and stirred chocolate powder into my cappuccino without looking up. Below us, on court number 3, Paige had challenged Luke to an impromptu game of singles.

'You're thinking about Lily, aren't you?'

I nodded and stirred.

'There's no problem between us, is there? You're not going to stop talking to me again?'

'Not unless you tell me you're flying out to Australia to another tennis academy,' I joked feebly.

'No chance.'

I was already kicking myself for my pathetic attempt at humour, when what I should have been saying was, 'How could there be a problem? You're the hottest guy around, plus the kindest and most sensitive. I really like you and want to spend more time with you.' Instead, I came up with the lame. 'That's OK, then.'

'And I'm definitely not going to drag you into any more shit with D'Arblay about late passes,' he promised.

'Water under the bridge,' I sighed.

'Tell me if I got this wrong, but I'm definitely picking up a bad vibe here. Are you sure we're OK?' Our coffees lay undrunk on the table. 'We're mates?'

'Mates.' A brief kiss and a hidden desire for more.

'More than mates?'

I took a deep breath then nodded and managed to smile. 'Anyway, I definitely promise I won't stop talking to you.' I reached for his hand across the coffee shop table. He has a broad palm and long fingers, which he wrapped tightly round mine.

'Game!' Paige cried as she served her second ace. Luke scurried to pick up stray balls.

'He hates to lose,' Jack muttered. 'Paige and Luke – are they on or off at the moment?'

'On, I think. At least, they went into the Bottoms together, to Tom's house.'

'When?'

'A couple of nights back.'

'If she thrashes him at tennis, they'll be off again.'

'Yeah, you're right. Hey, you want to know something

weird?' For some reason I hadn't jumped straight into the withholding the body mystery with Jack, but I knew I had to eventually.

'Do I?' he asked wryly. 'No, probably not. But you're going to tell me anyway.'

'OK, so I'll start from the beginning. I ran into Jayden.'

Immediately Jack was on edge. 'Where?'

'In the Squinting Cat – no actually in the street outside the Bridge Inn, about five minutes after you and Paige left.' And I told Jack about the bike episode and how I finally ended up talking to Alex Driffield. I spun it out for as long as possible.

'Hang on – you're saying Jayden was the good guy in this situation?' Jack reacted with disbelief.

'I wouldn't go that far. Let's say I didn't expect him to act the way he did – making his kid brother sort out the damage to my bike, stopping the dog from sinking his teeth into me.'

'That is weird,' Jack agreed. 'After what he did to Lily you'd think he'd lie low.'

'After what we *think* he did to Lily,' I reminded him, and ran the most probable scenario inside my head:

Lily: I'm pregnant.

Jayden: You're joking me.

Lily: I'm deadly serious.

Jayden: (after a long pause) So whose is it?

Lily (dissolving into meltdown) I can't believe you just said that!

Jayden: (turning away with Bolt the dog in tow) Anyway you told me you were on the pill.

Lily: Not me. I was never on the pill. You must be thinking about some other girl.

Jayden: Yeah, I sleep around, same as you (laughs). Same as every kid at St Jude's. See ya!

(She cries as stick man and stick dog walk out of her life.)

'You know what – now I'm not so sure,' I told Jack as Luke drew level on the court below – one game all. 'But that wasn't the end of it. I didn't get to the important bit yet.'

'The Alex bit?'

'He told me about some new forensic evidence. Micky Cooke picked it up from his dad, who works at the hospital morgue in Ainslee. It turns out Saint Sam and D'Arblay already knew this, but they're trying desperately to keep it out of the media spotlight. Fat chance though.'

Jack put his other hand round mine and my whole body trembled. 'Alyssa, slow down. I'm still not sure what this is about. What did they find?'

'I have no clue. Something's wrong – that's all.'

Cue the reappearance of Emily Archer, the lowlife journo, most probably wired up to an invisible recorder for all I knew. Don't expect an explanation of how she snuck back past Guy the gorilla – I just don't know.

'I think I can clear this up for you,' she told Jack smoothly, sitting down between us. She was in her late twenties, dinky and glossy in a black leather bomber jacket, jeans and knee-high boots, with obvious ambitions to read the Six O'Clock News. I made up that last bit because I'm a bitch and when Jack's around I feel threatened by any attractive older woman. 'Your girlfriend seems shaken up by the latest revelation – it's understandable.'

Jack pulled back from the table and looked at me to see what I wanted to do.

My mouth was dry, my heart thumping. 'Go ahead, explain,' I told Emily.

'The second pathology report on Lily Earle's death came through to the coroner earlier today and it seems it might blow the old suicide theory right out of the water, excuse the pun.'

Jack frowned at her, but said nothing.

'Yeah – sorry, I have bad taste. Anyway, they noticed something that may not have been accidental.'

'Not accidental?' Jack echoed the words in a low whisper.

'But they're not absolutely sure?' I croaked, my heart thudding down into my boots. So far the journalist's account wasn't definite, but it added to the questions arising from what Alex had already told me. What she said next added another layer of doubt – a major reason to shudder and grasp Jack's hand.

Emily Archer shrugged. 'The police haven't released any details yet, except that this is something that probably occurred after Lily died – *post mortem*,' she explained to Jack. 'They won't say any more until they've had time to study the pathologist's follow-up report.'

Letting go of my hand and rocking himself forward so that his elbows rested on the table, Jack raised his hands to his face, covered his eyes and rubbed his forehead.

'I know – too awful,' I sighed.

'Which begs the question – what is this?' Emily asked. 'I mean, what kind of warped psychopath would interfere with a corpse?'

chapter six

I'd already been sleeping badly, but now it became ten times worse. I lay in my narrow bed, tossing and turning with eyes wide open all through Saturday night, waiting for it to be light again. In the bed across the room I heard Paige sigh and turn over to press a button on her bedside alarm. The small light to show the time came on then went off again.

'What time is it?' I murmured.

'Six fifteen. Sorry, I didn't mean to wake you.'

'You didn't. What you told me earlier about the pathologist's follow-up report is what's keeping me awake.'

'Sorry.'

'Don't be. I'd have found out anyway.' There was a long, uncomfortable silence which Paige eventually broke.

Alyssa, there's something else.'

'What?'

'I've been thinking about Lily's email.' Her disembodied voice floated through the darkness and sounded different – quieter and less confident than usual. 'I don't want you to think I'm obsessing, but I'm trying to run through her entire message in my head, wondering why she would write the email if it turns out not to be suicide after all. I've got through the *Hey, Jack, I hope you're cool*

92

bit at the start, then Lily wanting to say goodbye to him because she knew he'd miss her. But what comes after that?'

'She says she's sober,' I recalled. 'Then she tells Jack she's pregnant – two tests and they both came up positive.'

'Right. Then she says the only person around here that she told was the baby's father.'

'Who she doesn't name,' I said pointedly. 'And anyway he didn't want to know. "Why should he?" Lily asked.'

'Because he's the baby's father, for Christ's sake, and it's a real live potential human being we're talking about!' Paige's voice rose in anger.

I sat up in bed and turned on my lamp, reciting the rest of Lily's note from memory. '"And I'm telling you now, giving you the reason why I'm going – it's because I don't want to go on living the out-of-control way I've been living these last few weeks that I'm out of here and won't be back (too shitty and painful and head-fuckingly awful, and anyway what kind of mother would I be?)."'

'It's OK, stop there,' Paige begged. 'Thanks, Alyssa.'

'So tell me – exactly why are we torturing ourselves by remembering this?'

Swinging her legs out from under the duvet, she paced from her bed to the window and back again. 'First off, to remind ourselves that she definitely didn't say it was Jayden.'

'Yeah, I got that. It bothered me too at first. But then I thought that was typical Lily – even then she was thinking about how he'd cope if everyone pointed the finger at him after she'd gone. She really loved him – she says so in her diary.'

'And, second, I wanted you to run through the message with me so I could be sure that Lily doesn't actually say that the plan was to kill herself.' Paige wasn't really listening to me. 'I mean, double check that with me – she doesn't come out in the open and say that that was her plan?'

I frowned and concentrated. 'No. She talked about saying goodbye – I suppose that could mean more than the obvious suicide thing.'

'"I don't want to go on living the out-of-control way I've been living these last few weeks",' Paige repeated, speaking faster and louder. 'That's not the same as wanting to die either. It might mean she was running away, aiming to find a new life where no one knew who she was.'

'"Too shitty and painful",' I quoted. 'But maybe you're right. 'You could read it another way – not that she planned to kill herself but that she was going away to get an abortion because she didn't think she could handle being a mother, and after that she would just disappear and start over.'

'I am right!' Paige said, sitting beside me in her cosy Joules pyjamas, dark hair tangled into bed-head curls. 'The way Alyssa wrote the email made it look like she was planning to kill herself because for some reason that's what she would want the school and her family to believe.'

'Yeah, because if people thought she was missing, presumed dead, the police wouldn't put so much manpower into finding her. She'd be on a missing-persons list – no big deal.'

'But she sent the email to Jack because he was the one who knew her best and she hoped that sooner or later somebody – him, you, me – would read between the lines and see that this wasn't a suicide note.'

'We were idiots,' Paige groaned. 'Why didn't we think of it earlier?'

'Lily was secretly telling us she would be on the run from the tyrant and the school.'

'And shit-face Jayden,' added Paige.

'No,' I argued, staring sadly at Lily's empty bed. 'We were wrong about Jayden too – *I* was wrong.'

I slid my hand inside my pillowcase and pulled out Lily's diary, flicking through the dog-eared pages then reading out loud.

Monday, July 4th. Met J after school. LOVE HIM!!!

I flicked again, through to September to the point where the circle with the dot hieroglyph first appeared. There was a question mark and a smiley face. 'This comes at the point where Lily and Jayden had the Upper Chartsey house all to themselves,' I reminded Paige. 'I still think the circle is code for when she got pregnant – it's a diagram of a human egg. But, look, she's using a different colour pen from the main written entry and there's a question mark as well.'

'Meaning she added the symbols later on and she wasn't sure if this was the correct date but she wants it to be. She'd be happy if she was right – look at the smiley face.'

'How come she wasn't sure?' I wondered.

'Oh, come on, Alyssa.' Paige's scepticism was back, full volume. 'Lily was probably still checking her cycle, finding out which was the most likely date. Maybe she didn't even know exactly how far on she was.'

I ignored Paige and followed my own train of thought. 'Or she wasn't sure because actually she'd slept with someone else around the same time. She's saying in code that she'd be happy if Jayden was the father, but she's not sure.'

This sent Paige off on one of her rants. 'Alyssa, Lily was not, I'll say it again – was *not* a slapper.'

I agreed. 'I'm not even saying she slept with this other guy because she *wanted* to,' I said slowly.

Paige snatched the diary away, slammed it shut and stood up.

We didn't come out into the open with the ugly scene that my words had conjured up. In fact, Paige went completely silent on me, grabbed her towel and stormed down the corridor to the shower room.

At 7.00 a.m., still sitting on my bed thinking, I received a text from Aunt Olivia.

Dearest A, Dr W phoned – thinks you should come home. Will send train ticket. Keep chin up. Love, Olivia.

Thanx. Am dealing with it, I texted back. Would rather stay here.

'Wakey, wakey.' Shirley Welford, our head of maths, came down the girls' corridor knocking loudly on doors, brisk and old school. 'Dr Webb has called a special assembly. All students to attend.'

We assembled, in uniform and all present and correct, at 9.30 in the new library and waited for Saint Sam to show up. The teachers gathered on a small platform at the far end of the room while students stood in huddles right down the brightly lit main body of the building. I stood with Paige and Jack as cold rain blew hard against the floor-to-ceiling windows, making everyone feel grateful to be indoors.

'What's he going to tell us that we don't already know?' Zara complained to Luke and Harry. She obviously hadn't had time to apply the lippie and mascara, or to fluff up her blonde hair, so she felt more like one of us – 'us' meaning specifically me and Paige.

'Search me,' Harry grumbled. 'But it had better be worth dragging me out of bed for.'

That was the general mood at that moment, I guess – scratchy and bad tempered, like you get when a train is delayed due to an accident on the line and you know you shouldn't criticize because someone was probably splatted out there and it's a total tragedy, but you're tired and it'll make you late home from wherever so you go ahead and have a good moan anyway.

'I should be writing an essay,' Zara went on. 'It's on quantum field theory in curved space–time. I have to finish it by tomorrow.'

'Fascinating,' Paige yawned.

Luke glanced towards the door for any sign that the principal was on his way. 'We'll probably get a lecture,' he predicted. By the way, he wasn't currently talking to Paige because, unwisely, she'd beaten him at tennis, six games to four.

'Here he comes!' Hooper warned from his position by the entrance. 'Oh no, it's only D'Arblay.'

I wasn't the only one who groaned at this.

'God, we could be here hours,' Zara said. 'We don't want him droning on as well.'

If he picked up on the hostile atmosphere, D'Arblay didn't show it as he skirted down the side of the crowd and stepped on to the platform. Soon afterwards Saint Sam came into the library and joined the bursar and a great hush fell.

Saint Sam waited before he spoke. He has perfect timing, I have to say. And he has a strong voice that carries well, an actor's voice, plus he's tall and he has presence – all good assets in the principal of a stupidly expensive private school or in someone about to play Hamlet or Macbeth.

'I wanted us to gather here for a special reason,' he began sombrely. 'And that is so that we can join together and remember Lily Earle during a minute's silence, each in our own way.'

He paused, slightly raised up on the platform, flanked by the staff, looking down on us with a sorrowful gaze.

'But before we pay our respects to Lily I wish to take this opportunity to remind you of some of the principles on which St Jude's was founded many years ago, and I hope this will bring you strength and comfort during this distressing time.'

'Here we go,' Harry grumbled.

'*Nihil sed optimus*,' Sam went on. 'Nothing but the best, and it's at times like this when the school motto comes into its own. Yes, we're sad and shocked that Lily is dead – that's only natural – but as a school we must work out the optimum way to cope with this disaster. We must look into ourselves and face it with truth and courage. We must stand together as a community.'

Ah, now I got it. Saint Sam was extending the gagging order.

'In other words,' he said, 'we have to behave with integrity. We do not run with false rumours or give way to pressure to sell our stories to the press. Instead we wait patiently and in a dignified way for the truth to emerge.'

Paige glanced at me and stuck her fingers down her throat. I grimaced at Jack then turned my attention to henchman D'Arblay who was nodding gravely and rocking occasionally on the balls of his feet, hands clasped behind his back.

Saint Sam looked down from on high. 'St Jude's has existed as a centre of excellence since its foundation in 1938 and I hardly need to remind you that each student here, from the school's inception to the present day, has exceptional talent, exceptional intellect and an exceptional ability to rise above the difficulties that life throws in their path.' (*Flatter your audience a la Mark Antony in* Julius Caesar. '*Friends, Romans, countrymen . . .*')

'That's why we now expect the very highest standard of behaviour on all of your parts.'

He paused for a mass squaring of mulberry-sweatered shoulders as we all got ready to accept the burden of his expectations. I'll say this for the kids of St Jude's – they were eager beavers. There was not much cynicism (except perhaps from me, Jack, Paige and maybe Harry, Luke and Zara), no twenty-first century apathy to dull their bright-eyed and bushy-tailed response to Sam's speechifying.

'But, of course, as members of staff at this outstanding institution we're also acutely aware of our responsibilities to you and we will play our part in reducing the emotional impact that Lily's death may have had on you. (*Soften the rabble-rousing tone, show a more empathetic side.*) In other words, my door is always open, as are the doors of all the teachers and administrative staff. If you have concerns that threaten to overwhelm you, please come and address them to us directly – we promise to listen and if necessary the school will take steps to seek professional help.'

It worked. One or two kids lowered their heads to sniffle and hide their tears, many more nodded.

(*Get everyone on side. Job done.*)

'So now, if we're ready, we'll collect our thoughts and stand in silence.' Sam's voice was laden with solemnity that was one hundred per cent effective. Even I gave way to the pressure of the moment, looked at the floor and painfully remembered Lily.

*

There weren't many places on the school campus where Jack, Paige and I could talk without being overheard. The stable yard was one of them.

'So what do we think?' Jack asked, turning to me. 'What's the answer?'

'What's the question?' Paige got in like a shot. 'C'mon, you two – are we still talking about them refusing to hand over Lily's body?'

'You told her?' Jack checked, and I nodded.

'Jesus bloody Christ, this sucks!' Paige groaned.

Jack and I waited for Paige to finish mixing a bucket of feed for Mistral.

'To make things worse, if anything could do that,' I told Jack, 'Paige and I went through Lily's diary again and we think maybe Jayden isn't the father.'

Jack blinked then gritted his teeth – yet another unwelcome shock. 'How sure are you?'

Paige jumped in quickly again. 'Pretty sure. I know Lily doesn't come out and say so in the email, but once you've thought it through and studied the diary entries, it does begin to make sense.'

'So when did we start liking Jayden?' Jack wanted to know, quickly stepping clear of Mistral's stable door as Paige led her grey thoroughbred out on to the yard. Like me, he sees a horse and thinks, Whoa, that's a thousand pounds of solid muscle and bone heading my way. It has a brain the size of an orange and I wouldn't trust it to save my life!

'We don't,' Paige insisted.

'No, we don't,' I agreed. 'He ditched Lily when she needed him most.'

'He's still a shit face.' Standing back, Paige watched her pride and joy lower his ripped neck and start munching.

'But that doesn't mean he was the father or that he was involved in her death – if anyone was, and actually we still don't know if this new detail in the pathologist's report is important. It may not be . . .' If, if, if. *If* she slept with someone she didn't want to. *If* her death wasn't straightforward suicide after all. *If* some crazy psycho guy had damaged the corpse.

Speculation brought the conversation to a halt and gave me time to realize, OK, so maybe I wasn't as anti-horse as I'd thought. I mean, there was something beautiful about Mistral's sleek combination of power and grace, as long as you kept a safe distance.

'So enough already,' Paige decided after we'd all silently chased our theories down dark cul-de-sacs.

Jack folded his arms and leaned against the high stone wall, just below our re-entry point after Tom's party.

'Do you realize you're in view of the security camera?' I reminded him, thinking that we might want to keep this conversation off the record.

'So? We're not doing anything wrong – we're helping Paige.'

'Better fetch me his saddle and bridle from the tack room, then,' she told him briskly, and Jack went off to find them.

'You're going for a ride?' I asked lamely.

'Duh – yeah! I'm hacking out with Guy, actually. That's

his horse, Franklin, the chestnut gelding next door to Mistral. He'll be here in five minutes.'

'Is this what you need?' Jack asked, standing at the tack room door with a saddle in his arms.

'No. Mine's the one with the green numnah – on a high rack at the far end.'

He disappeared back inside.

'So?' I asked. 'So, what?'

'So why are you brushing Lily under the carpet and refusing to talk to us all of a sudden?'

I admit it – I wasn't expecting Paige's next reaction, like Vesuvius erupting. 'Bloody hell, Alyssa, don't you know this was shitty enough for me without you introducing me to your latest lame theory?'

'I'm sorry, I thought we agreed. I didn't –'

'Didn't *think*?' she yelled. 'Look, I've known Lily ever since she started in Year Nine in main school. And yeah she could be bloody annoying and crazy and sometimes she was hard to live with, but even so she was my best, my *very* best mate, and she was my favourite person of all time and now you're trying to tell me she didn't actually drown herself in the lake, that there was a psycho who wanted her dead, and also that same crazy person or somebody completely different got her pregnant!'

Her explosion brought Jack running out of the tack room, gesturing behind him as if trying to warn us about something. 'What happened? What did I miss?'

'I-it's me. It's my fault,' I stammered.

Paige subsided as suddenly as she'd erupted. 'No, it's

not. I was the one who started you off. And it's not a lame idea – that wasn't fair. We'll talk about it again later – OK?'

I nodded, noticing that Guy Simons had followed Jack out of the tack room and there was a chance that he'd heard everything that had just been said.

If he had, he didn't comment – just nodded at me and Jack as he carried a saddle into Franklin's stable and bolted the door behind him.

'Guy rode Franklin in the trials for the Beijing Olympics,' Paige told us, as if she'd never lost it with me. 'He just missed out on a place in the UK team.'

'I didn't know that,' I said. I ought to have been more impressed, but Paige's outburst had shaken me, and, anyway, I didn't like Guy.

He spoke over the stable door. 'Why should you?' he grinned. 'Beijing is ancient history.'

'But you're still a great rider.' Paige insisted on being nice. Maybe it was a cliquey, horsey-person bond that I just didn't get.

Still steering well clear of Mistral, Jack said he hoped Paige and Guy would enjoy their hack. 'Fancy a walk to the Bottoms, Alyssa?' he asked pointedly enough for even Guy Simons to pick up.

'Ah, young love!' he mocked as he led Franklin out of the stable.

Ignore him! 'Yes, but let me go change my shoes,' I replied. I had a list of things I wanted to talk about and every reason you can think of for wanting to be alone with Jack Cavendish.

*

Looking back at St Jude's from the edge of the oak wood, across lake and frosty lawn, you'd still never have thought that anything bad had happened there.

The low, two-storey building stood as it had for four hundred years, ornate chimney stacks rising into a leaden sky, stone steps leading to a grand entrance, oak doors securely closed.

'You're shivering,' Jack said, putting his arm round my shoulders.

'It's cold. Let's walk.' We turned away from the dark lake and entered the wood.

A blanket of autumn leaves covered the ground, frosty and crisp underfoot. Gnarled trunks twisted and divided into stout, bare branches that formed a tunnel over our heads.

'You want to talk about something else?' he asked. 'I mean, other than Lily.'

'Nothing else seems that important.'

'And you can't stop thinking about her anyway. Me neither.'

'I'm glad we're doing this, though.'

'Me too.'

I genuinely was. It took me right back to the feelings I'd had at Tom's party. The lyrics to 'You're the One for Me' rang out inside my head. 'Love is a window . . .'

We walked on, through to the other side of the wood where Jack broke away.

'The stream's frozen over. Come and look.'

He was right – there was a thin sheet of ice and two ducks slipping and sliding miserably across the surface. On the opposite bank someone had thrown away two crushed Coca-Cola cans and a crisp packet, half hidden under a thatch of weather-beaten grass. I crouched beside him and touched the ice with my fingertips.

Jack stood up first and glanced back the way we'd come. 'Which way now?'

'I like walking in the wood,' I decided. It felt secret and sheltered, safer somehow.

'It feels good,' he agreed.

'Totally.' I smiled, and kissed him long and slow – a major move for me.

'So we're definitely more than mates?' He picked up on our earlier conversation in the sports centre as we walked on.

'You already know the answer.' I clicked back into being shy again for no reason other than I was suddenly scared of showing my feelings – a lifetime's habit, you could say.

'I want to be sure.'

'Be sure,' I whispered, looking straight into his eyes.

Jack pulled me up and kissed me back – another long kiss. I closed my eyes and breathed him in, put my arms round his neck and held him close. I might not be able to say the right words, but at least my actions would show him how I felt.

Then we retraced our steps, following the tracks our feet had made on the frosty ground.

'Why did we let all that time go by?' he wondered.

'You left the country, remember.'

'But when I came back, you didn't . . .' He hesitated and scuffed the ground with the toe of his boot.

'It felt complicated,' I sighed, thinking of the time we'd wasted – almost a whole term.

'I think we were both scared,' was his response.

'I definitely was. The truth is I didn't believe you would . . . choose me.'

He kissed me again. 'And then Lily happened,' he said.

I nodded. 'Jack, can I ask you something?'

'About Lily?'

'No, about Jayden.'

'OK.' He dragged his feet, ready to go on the defensive.

'It's a question I asked you before. At Tom's party, what did you two talk about? Why did Jayden grab you and drag you off to the other side of the room?'

'He did?'

'Yeah, you know he did. You need me to remind you of the details?' The colour of the carpet, the pattern on the curtains, the angry, feral look on Jayden's face.

'No.'

'So what did he want?'

'Nothing. He was being an idiot.'

I waited at the edge of the wood, looking up into the branches, feeling snow flakes begin to land on my face.

Jack walked on a little way then waited for me. 'OK – he asked me if Lily and I had got back together, like he was accusing me. I told him no.'

'What else?'

'I don't know if he believed me. I said so what if we had? He'd been the one who'd dumped her, hadn't he? What right did he have to be asking me questions?'

The carpet in the Old Vicarage was tasteful beige through-out, the curtains were bottle green, suspended from a brass pole.

'Tom, there you are!' Lily cried as I tried to work out what was going on between Jayden and Jack. She slid her arm round Tom's waist and kissed him on the lips.

I watched Jayden's face as Lily came on to Tom. He looked savage.

'Hey, Jayden!' She'd had too much to drink; Tom was annoyed; she began to totter towards her ex, totally out of her head. She didn't even make it across the room.

'Why was Jayden accusing you of getting back together with Lily?' I asked Jack at the edge of the wood.

'You'd have to ask him,' he replied. Definitely end of conversation.

And, anyway, we could see Paige and Guy riding along the edge of a ploughed field, hurrying home before the snow got too bad. They trotted towards us, their horses breathing clouds of steam into the cold grey air, cutting across our path.

'OK,' I told Jack. 'Maybe I will.'

I had to wait until the next afternoon before I could follow this through.

'Are you mad?' Paige demanded when I told her my plan.

'No. Jayden knows something we don't know,' I insisted. Lessons had finished for the day and I was heading back to our room to get changed out of my uniform when she appeared at the top of the stairs and I explained my next move. 'I'm sure of it.'

'Jeez, Alyssa. Does Jack know what you're planning?'

'I mentioned it, but he doesn't think I'll go through with it.'

'Well, hell, *quelle surprise!*' She came down the steps towards me. 'Seriously, Alyssa, you know by now that Jayden is not the kind of guy you drop in on for afternoon tea.'

'So tell me what else we can do,' I challenged. I'd sat through Bryony's class on the ending of *Lear* (yes, it had taken us a whole term to reach this point. The thankless daughters were dead but so was Cordelia. 'Howl, howl, howl, howl! O, you are men of stones!'), all the time obsessing about what to do next about Lily.

'Here are the options,' Paige began.

I haven't said so before, but one of her non-horsey talents is logical argument. That's when she's not being scornful or stubborn or displaying other similar character flaws. In fact, I can see her as a barrister in Crown Court, wig and all.

'One, we track down Adam Earle.'

'Why would we do that?' Personally I didn't see any good reason for more contact with Lily's automaton sibling.

Paige quickly explained. 'You remember in Saint Sam's

office – why was Adam so interested in what Lily had said to us the day she packed her bag and left? Why so cagey? Why no grief?'

'Good point,' I decided.

Paige and I sat down on the cold steps, ticking off items on our fingers. 'Following on from that,' I said, 'why did Lily tell us she'd been summonsed home to see her dad? I know from what Anna said that Robert Earle was still in Chicago.'

'Deliberate decoy,' Paige observed. 'Part of her plan to drop out of sight and never be seen again.'

'And there are questions about Mamma Earle. I know that she's bound to be shattered by her daughter's death, but, still, why is she so passive? No, that's not the right word. Why is she so scared?'

'Really?' Paige frowned and considered the question. 'Scared of the tyrant, I guess. Anyway, let's think of stuff right under our noses. Is there someone here at St Jude's who secretly hated Lily enough to harm her?'

'No way!' was my immediate response.

Paige, though, wouldn't let it drop. 'Keep it on the list,' she insisted. 'Stick with the school. Saint Sam and D'Arblay – what's with the control freakery?'

' "Be dignified. Don't speak to the press," ' they'd insisted. I saw what she meant but I had no answer.

'They're getting worse. Soon we'll be wearing straightjackets and be locked in our rooms.'

'Or they'll get us sent home.' Which only made me think that sitting here itemizing our options might appear sensible but it was wasting time. 'I have to go now,' I told Paige.

She jumped up from the step. 'You're not still thinking of going to see Jayden? Yeah, you are. Don't deny it, you totally are!'

'I can't sit and do nothing.'

'At least wait until Jack has finished his coaching session,' she pleaded. 'I'd come myself and back you up but I just saw Georgie pull into the car park.'

It was good advice, which I chose to ignore. 'Go do your dressage. If you see Jack, mention that I'm heading for Chartsey,' I told Paige, pushing past her. 'Tell him not to worry – I'll be OK.'

chapter seven

I took another school bike and cycled into the Bottoms, quickly calling in at JD's for a progress report on repairs to the first one.

Alex was there with Micky Cooke, whose dad works in the morgue. The two of them saw me talking to Alex's dad and straight away decided to give me a hard time for the hell of it. I was surprised because to look at Micky you would have thought butter wouldn't melt – open face, big smile, loose-jointed and laid back.

Alex started it with, 'Look who it isn't – the *numero uno* super-sleuth.'

'Miss Marple on a bike,' Micky laughed. They cut me off on the pavement outside the workshop and stupidly I rose to the bait.

'What did I do?' I asked Alex.

'You don't have to do anything, you just are.'

I made another wrong choice and went proper Miss Marple on them. 'Get out of my way, please.'

'"Get out of my way, please"!' Micky mimicked in a prim voice.

'OK, Colonel Mustard, where did the murder take place and which weapon was used?' Alex acted like the Cluedo analogy was hilarious.

'Why are you being like this?' I asked as I tried to wheel my bike past them and Alex grabbed the handlebars with both hands. 'Alex, let go!'

' "Alex, let go!" '

I pushed harder.

Alex braced himself and pushed back. 'What are you doing here, Alyssa?'

'What's it to you?'

' "What's it to—" '

Wrenching the bike from Alex's grasp, I swung the front wheel towards Micky and ran it over his toes.

'Wow!' Alex's hilarity knew no bounds. He was cawing like a crow and flapping his arms, hopping from one foot to the other. 'Didn't you know – Micky's feet are his fortune? Southampton signed him up for their junior squad. What are you trying to do – wreck his career?'

At this point I threw the bike on to the ground. 'Forget it – I'll walk,' I said through gritted teeth.

'Seriously, Alyssa.' Alex and Micky kept pace as I cut up Meredith Lane. 'You've got that famous don't-mess-with-me look.'

'Which we like,' Micky said as he faked a serious limp.

'Which makes us think more Sarah Lund than Miss Marple.'

'Minus the ugly sweater,' Micky added.

God, they were pathetic.

'Sarah Lund sniffing out clues.'

'Tracking down the killer – in this case Lily's.'

'*If* there is a killer . . .'

'Letting nothing stand in her way,' Micky said as he stepped right in front of me. 'She never lets up in her hunt to bring the villain to justice.'

'She doesn't show her feelings.'

'Which we also like,' Micky said, this time with a definite leer.

'So?' I yelled angrily (proving them wrong on the last point at least). 'What are you two going to do about Lily? What's the rest of the world doing?'

'See!' Alex crowed. 'We knew it.'

'She's a girl on a mission,' Micky agreed. 'Who's the killer, Alyssa? Really – we want to know.'

'Does he live in the Bottoms?'

'Or Uppers? Is he at Ainslee Comp?'

'Is it Jayden?' Alex dropped the raucous laugh. He stared me in the eye. 'Come on, Alyssa – is it?'

I stared right back.

Eventually I lost the two idiots and went on foot along Meredith Lane out of the village and up the hill to Upper Chartsey. A light snow had started to fall so it was good that I'd left the bike behind. As I entered the village, the street lights came on and the whole scene started to look sparkly and white, beautiful as a Christmas card but freezing cold.

A car crawled up the hill behind me, its tyres skidding and sliding into the kerb, then a four-wheel drive, stopping to unload two passengers outside the Smith's Arms. A guy on a motorbike rode slowly down the hill and turned into the pub car park.

I stopped outside the pub. What did I do now? I thought of walking in out of the cold and asking the bar staff where Jayden lived then decided against it. Snobby girl from St Jude's goes into pub desperate to find boy from Ainslee Comp – it didn't give a good impression, and even at a time like this I cared about my reputation. So did I find his number in a directory instead? Not unless I knew his surname, which I realized I didn't. Did I knock on doors? There weren't that many houses to choose from – maybe twenty or thirty in the whole village.

I walked on past ex-workmen's cottages, prettified with names like Swallow's Nest and The Old Granary, tarted up with rustic porches and double glazing made to look like leaded windows that didn't fool anybody. I began to lose heart and wonder how I would get home if it kept on snowing.

Then a kid shot out of a door and slammed it behind him. He skidded down the path and on to the snowy pavement. If I hadn't got out of his way, he would have mowed me down.

'Brad!' I spoke one word before he saw me, scooped a handful of snow off the top of the garden wall, compacted it into an icy ball and launched it right in my face. I ducked – it missed. He ran, slid and vanished round a corner.

Which left me with the obvious choice of knocking on the door Brad had just slammed.

I rehearsed it a few times before I plucked up the courage to walk up the path.

Knock knock.

'Hi, Jayden, I've come to talk about Lily again.'

Door slams in my face.

Knock knock.

'I just want to ask you one question.'

Door slams again.

Knock knock.

'Were you the baby's father?'

I knocked and a girl came to the door. This wasn't scripted.

'Yes?' Not a friendly 'yes' either – more a suspicious one and delivered out of the side of the mouth by a blonde-with-dark-roots girl about my age wearing heavy black mascara, half a dozen studs in each ear and a nose ring.

'Erm, does Jayden live here?' I asked. I was hatless, shivering and caked in snow.

'No.'

'Are you sure? Only, I saw Brad . . .'

'Still no.'

'So do you know where I can find him?'

'If I did, would I tell you?'

And she wouldn't – not to save her life. This, by the way, was a girl you wouldn't argue with in case she had a knife slipped inside her boot, or she wore a hat with a razor-edge rim like Oddjob in the old Bond movie. I'm exaggerating again, but you get the idea.

'Thanks anyway.' I turned and walked down the path, right into stick dog Bolt.

Whoa!

Bolt growled at me as I came out of the gate. He barrelled past and scratched and whined at the front door.

Scary girl opened the door and let him in.

Snowflakes landed on my eyelashes. This was turning into a blizzard.

'Jeez,' Jayden said when he saw me shivering outside his house.

He took me to a back room at the Smith's Arms and got his barman mate to make me a hot chocolate.

'Why are we here?' I wanted to know. 'Wouldn't it have been easier just to invite me into the house?'

He ignored the questions, hunching forward with both elbows on the table. 'What are you doing here?'

'Looking for you, obviously.'

'Why? And don't say to talk about Lily.'

'Yes, actually.'

'OK, so I'm out of here,' he said, but didn't move.

'Here' was a tiny, unheated room with four round tables, a dozen heavy wooden stools and a few tacky hunting pictures on the walls. I think it was where they served pub food to ramblers and furtive couples from Ainslee engaged in extra-marital affairs.

'Of course it's about Lily,' I told him. 'Who else? And listen, Jayden, you don't scare me.'

'Yes, I do.'

'OK, you do. And who was scary girl?'

'At the house?' he laughed. 'That was Ursula.'

'Ursula?'

'Her dad was Austrian. He's dead, the same as yours, but not in a plane crash.'

'How did you know that? Did Lily tell you?'

'Back to the same old topic,' he sighed, nibbling his thumbnail and spitting out the paring.

'She couldn't have. You'd dumped her before she knew me.'

Jayden's mouth twitched, but he let it pass. 'So what did you think of Ursula?'

'We didn't have much in common.' Besides dead parents.

'She's cool. She'll do anything I tell her.'

Wow, on my great-great-grandmother the suffragette's grave, I wasn't going to let that one go by. 'You like girls who do everything you tell them? Funny – I wouldn't have put Lily in that category. Is *that* why you dumped her? Or was it because she was pregnant?'

The who-dumped-who issue was what got to him, not the pregnancy. After I'd used the word 'dumped' twice in quick succession, he stood up and lurched across the room to wipe condensation from the window and stare out at the snow. Things were quickly coming to a head.

'You knew she was pregnant – right?'

'Sure I knew.'

I decided to push even harder. 'But you didn't want to keep the baby?'

Suddenly short of breath, Jayden slumped down on the bench beneath the window. He looked terrible and it took me by surprise.

'Sorry,' I murmured.

We waited an age without speaking. 'It wasn't mine to keep,' he said finally.

'Honestly?' I watched him like a hawk – every flickering muscle around his eyes.

'Yeah, really. Lily told me straight that I wasn't the father.'

Didn't I swear to Paige there was this whole new can of worms ready to be opened? Trying to keep a lid on my impatience, I let some more time pass.

'Sorry,' I said again, then a completely new idea hit me between the eyes. 'Did you think Jack Cavendish was the father? Is that what you wanted to drag out of him at Tom's party?'

Feral Boy had taken Jack away from me and cornered him. Jack had told me that Jayden wanted to know if he and Lily were back together. Jayden was putting two and two together – Lily back with her old boyfriend, making babies – and coming up with five.

'It wasn't Jack,' I told him now with condensation streaming down the windowpane and the hot chocolate going cold. 'Jack and Lily had moved on, they were mates – nothing else.'

'Yeah, right.'

'They were. Jack wasn't the baby's father.' I was a little bit shaky myself by this time and found a way out by shifting the focus. 'Listen, Jayden – are you sure Lily was telling you the truth? She wasn't just letting you off the hook?'

'Why would she do that?'

'Because she was Lily and she did crazy, self-destructive

119

things. Maybe she didn't want to trap you into a long-term relationship just because she was having your baby, so instead she lied to you and said it wasn't yours.'

He shook his head. 'I thought of that. I put pressure on her to let me take a paternity test once the baby was born. She agreed to that at least.'

'OK, I get it – you decided you definitely weren't the father so you ended it?'

He laughed, stopped, laughed again. 'Actually *Lily* ended it.'

I did a double take. Why had loved-up Lily done the very thing that would break her heart? 'Did she give a reason?'

'In a text. She said her family had told her to finish it, which might have been an excuse – I'll never know. Anyway, I'm clear in my own head that they did have total control over what she did. And the brother – he definitely didn't like the sound of me.'

'Adam?'

'Yeah, Adam.'

There was plenty here for me to work through. For a start, Jayden didn't seem like a guy to keep a lid on his temper or to follow a rich man's rules. And of course Lily was volatile too. I began to picture a new scenario for Lily's final hours – the email calling her home to face a family crisis (maybe Adam somehow finding out that she was still in contact with Jayden), followed by Lily panicking and finally deciding she needed out of her old life, packing her bag, writing the email to Jack and sneaking out through the grounds. She didn't get very far though before she ran smack bang into Jayden, hiding in the woods – full of jealous rage and frustration. Big argument. Vicious insults are flung in each other's faces. Jayden loses control . . .

'Don't even go there.' Jayden read my mind. Or his gaze was so intense that was how it felt.

'I'm not saying –'

'Yes, you are. You figure I was crazy-jealous.'

'No.' I could tell by his angry tone that this conversation was almost over.

'You're wrong – I didn't want Lily back. She'd kicked me into touch – I'd moved on.'

'You were already with Ursula?'

He nodded and I sighed. First Jack and now Jayden – everyone had moved on from poor Lily.

'End of story,' Jayden said. He got up, opened the door and let in an icy blast and a flurry of snow. He mumbled a last, throwaway line before leaving. 'You need to find out what was in the pathologist's report.'

'You sod off back where you came from!'

Alex had me backed up against a dirty brick wall. I could see Micky and Ursula grinning over his shoulder. All three had jumped me as I'd slid and slithered my way back to the Bottoms to collect my bike. They'd dragged me along the main street and flung me into Alex's dad's dingy, oil-stained workshop.

The smell of petrol and the pressure of Alex's hand round my throat made me gag. I was struggling to breathe.

'Stop stirring it.' Ursula the she-wolf leaped to her

121

boyfriend's defence. She pulled Alex back and came right into my face. 'The murderer – the guy who supposedly killed your slut mate wasn't from round here. It wasn't Jayden.'

You need to find out what was in the pathologist's report. It was true. Now that Alex wasn't trying to throttle me I began to think straight. 'I wasn't accusing him.'

'So why did you come here?' Ursula grabbed my arm and manhandled me towards the door. 'Look outside – it's not what you'd call visiting weather.'

Actually the snow was easing and the yellow council trucks were already out, spewing grit across the roads.

'Yeah, whatever it was, why couldn't it wait?' Micky asked.

Of the three, he seemed the least likely to snarl and bite. I turned to him. 'Listen – if you found out there was a chance your best mate had been murdered, would you hang around and wait for better weather?'

He sucked air between his teeth. Alex grunted. Ursula shoved me out on to the pavement, where I skidded and sprawled forward on to my knees.

'We don't want any of your lot snooping around.' This was Alex trying to be reasonable. 'St Jude's means trouble – always, end of!'

It was Micky who helped me to my feet and pointed me in the right direction. 'Leave the bike here. Call a taxi,' he suggested.

I nodded and set off along the street into the glare of the gritting lorry's headlights. As it trundled by, I felt a sharp spatter of salt and gravel against my legs. I turned my head to see if the others were following me, found that I was alone outside St Michael's church and took out my phone to order a cab.

I made the call and slipped the phone back into my pocket, prepared to wait. Then I saw a red car crawl into a driveway, heard the engine cut and a door slam. After that a motorbike edged out of Meredith Lane on to Main Street – a single headlight, the low purr of a powerful engine, rider crouched low over the handlebars.

There was a slow-motion moment when the rider turned his handlebars and trained his headlight on me – enough time to wonder why he'd done that and to hear the purr turn to a roar as he accelerated towards me, to see that a visor completely covered his face.

He was ten metres away and accelerating, five metres and ploughing through deep snow on to the pavement.

'Move, Alyssa!' Tom yelled from across the street.

I flung myself backwards under the lychgate, staggered into the churchyard, stumbled and fell against the nearest gravestone. Sacred to the memory of Alfred Ernest Hathaway, 1837–1891. The motorcyclist braked and swerved. He clipped the gatepost, skidded away.

Tom ran across from the Old Vicarage and helped me up. 'Are you OK?'

Apart from the fact that I was covered in snow and shaking like a leaf. Apart from the fact that a guy on a motorbike had just tried to kill me.

*

A log fire burned in Tom's living room. The bottle-green curtains were drawn and early Christmas cards stood on the mantelpiece.

'Am I crazy, or was that deliberate?' I asked. One minute I was calling for a taxi, the next I was face down on Alfred Ernest Hathaway's grave.

'Difficult to tell.' Tom wouldn't commit. 'All I know is I saw you caught in the headlight, not moving out of the way.'

'He didn't stop,' I pointed out. The total opposite – he'd clipped the gatepost then swung back across the pavement on to the gritted road. You could see the arc of the tyre prints.

'So he was over the limit.'

'Maybe.' I remembered that a motorcyclist had parked outside the Smith's Arms. Could it have been the same one?

'He was over the limit and he didn't want to get done for drunk driving.'

'Nice guy!' The warmth of the flames was thawing me out. 'You didn't get his number by any chance?'

Tom shook his head. 'It was over in a split second.'

'I know. I just get the feeling . . .'

'That he *wanted* to run you down?'

I nodded. 'But when you come out with it like that, I do begin to sound a little crazy, don't I?'

Then again, when your roommate is dead, your world view does darken and you begin to see everything through a sinister glass.

*

Tom cancelled the taxi and made me wait for someone from the school to pick me up. 'You shouldn't be alone,' he said as he called St Jude's.

'We may be some time,' D'Arblay warned. 'The snow's bad and traffic is backed up all the way into Ainslee. Is Alyssa happy to wait where she is?'

Tom told him yes and made me take off my wet boots. He put them by the fire to dry.

'Where are your parents?' I asked.

'At work. Not back until late.' He sat down beside me, picked up the remote and flicked on the TV, running through channels with his feet up on the coffee table, as if nothing had happened.

'Thanks,' I told him.

'For what?'

'You saved my life.' And that's not a sentence I expect to say very often.

An episode of *The Wire* came up. 'That's OK. Let's say you owe me.'

'I do?'

'No – I'm kidding.'

'Not funny.' I could say whatever I liked to Tom, and vice versa, and it would stay low key. He was just one of those easy people. And I guess I liked him, basically, because he'd taken care of Lily at his party.

'Don't give her any more of anything. I don't know what she's had, but she definitely can't take any more of whatever it is.'

We were forty-five minutes into *The Wire*, during an ad break, when the doorbell rang and Tom answered it. I could

125

see and hear him through the open lounge door.

'Come in,' he told Paige and Jack, my Jack. 'She's in the TV room.'

Paige rushed in first, carrying cold air with her. 'Jesus Christ, Alyssa! Didn't I warn you not to see Jayden?'

'It wasn't anything to do with Jayden.' I sprang to Feral Boy's defence as Jack came into the room. 'This was some random guy on a motorbike.'

Jack pushed past Paige and took hold of me. He held me close before he started to fire questions at me. Was I sure I was OK? Was I in shock and did I need to see a doctor? Did I call the police? Did anyone get the guy's number?

When he'd run out of steam and I'd answered the best I could, given that he was half squeezing me to death, he relaxed his hold.

'D'Arblay drove us,' Paige told me. 'He's waiting in the hallway.'

I took a deep breath and turned to Tom. 'Thanks again.'

'No problem.' Still normal, still easy, even though Jack had made it plain that he should step aside now because he, Jack, was taking over from here.

'You ready?' he asked, one arm round my shoulders.

'Bye,' I told Tom as I shoved my feet into my steaming boots, put my jacket on and tucked my hair inside my collar.

'Bye,' he said, going back to *The Wire*.

Out in the hallway, the bursar stood expressionless. 'The traffic is easing,' he reported. 'We should be home in fifteen minutes.'

In danger of dying one minute, receiving a traffic report the next. That's how weird life is.

D'Arblay opened the door to lead the way to the car. There was an old-fashioned wooden coat stand by the door, loaded with jackets and scarves, with a shelf underneath for boots and bags. Tom's family wasn't the tidiest – there were slippers and sandals from last summer, sports bags, a shopping basket and Lily's overnight bag. Or what looked exactly like Lily's bag, unzipped with a pair of jeans spilling out and a glimpse of silver sequins.

It took a while for me to register.

'Come along,' D'Arblay insisted.

Paige went ahead. Jack waited for me. 'What's wrong?' he asked.

I pointed to the bag. His eyebrows shot up and he spread his palms in a gesture of confusion. Then we stepped outside.

'I spoke with Dr Webb,' D'Arblay informed us on the way back to St Jude's. 'He intends to make strenuous efforts to identify the motorcyclist.'

'Yeah, like we have the registration number!' Paige scoffed from the front seat. 'We know the colour, the make, the model – everything.'

Jack sat holding my hand in the back of the car. 'Do you remember anything, Alyssa?'

For once in my life I was forced to admit that my freakishly accurate memory had deserted me. 'It was dark, the headlight shone in my eyes.' Then I was face down on top of a grave. I tried to link it with the bike I'd seen outside the pub in Upper Chartsey, but even supposing it was the same one I didn't have any more details, except maybe it was a neon green colour. 'No, sorry.'

D'Arblay drove at twenty along narrow, snow-covered lanes. 'We'll contact the police, of course. And Dr Webb has informed your aunt.'

I was looking at the back of his head, noticing how his ears stuck out and working out how much his leather gloves had cost, trying not to take in what he was telling me.

'She agrees with us.'

'How do you mean – she agrees with you?' Paige asked.

D'Arblay steered the car past the huddle of journalists and then through the carved stone pillars at the entrance to St Jude's. 'Alyssa's aunt wants Alyssa at home for the rest of the term. It's clear to everyone after the trauma of recent events that she needs complete rest and recuperation.'

'You can't decide that,' Paige argued. 'What if she doesn't want to go?'

'That's irrelevant,' D'Arblay said. The grounds of St Jude's had never looked more beautiful under their pure white covering of snow. The house itself looked like a painting by a Dutch master. 'Tomorrow afternoon at the latest Alyssa leaves for Richmond.'

chapter eight

Aunt Olivia doesn't do afternoon tea. At that time of day she's usually on a train or a plane looking at spreadsheets, sending emails. But this Tuesday she sat with me in the Art Deco surrounding of Bentley's, an up-market tea shop in Ainslee – light oak panelling, faux-medieval tapestries on the walls, antique Clarice Cliff teapots set on a high shelf.

She was wearing Jaeger from head to toe – lilac silk scarf, grey cashmere sweater, tailored black trousers, plus her usual businesslike expression as she poured her Earl Grey into a bone china cup. 'OK, Alyssa, I need to know what's really going on. Why do they want to send you home?'

'Don't worry, I'm not being suspended.' It wouldn't have been the first time it had happened so I felt I had to reassure her.

'And you like the school?' She gave me a sharp, inquisitive look.

'I do.' My answer didn't have to be thought out. I do. I like St Jude's. I like Bryony Phillips and the French teacher, Justine Renoir. I like the library and the science labs and the freedom the staff give you to follow your own interests. I especially like Paige, Zara and Jack.

'You want to stay?'

'For sure.' For the first time ever I was starting to feel that this was where I might one day be comfortable with who I was.

'So what's this all about? I know it's to do with the poor girl who drowned, but tell me more.' I saw Aunt Olivia glance at her watch as she sipped her tea – no surprise there.

'I was Lily's roommate so they think I must be suffering from stress.'

'Understandable under the circumstances.'

'Yes, but what they don't realize is that I'll be under even more stress if they send me home. I need to be here, Aunt Olivia.'

'Why? What good can you do?'

'I can keep an eye on Paige for a start. She's Lily's other roommate. It's hit her hard.'

'And?'

'I want to be on the spot while the police investigate. They might want to ask me some questions about the last time I saw Lily.'

My aunt's expression changed from detached curiosity to something approaching concern. 'The police are investigating Lily's death?'

'Yes. Didn't you know? You saw the reporters at the gate. It's been in the news.'

'I don't pay any attention to news reports. I assumed that the poor girl had committed suicide.'

'So did everyone – at first.' Fiddling with my teaspoon, I hesitated over how much to tell her before deciding to leave out the bit about the request for a second pathologist's report because that was unusual and anything out of the ordinary would freak her out more than she probably already was. 'If you were me and you'd found out that something suspicious could be going on, wouldn't you want to know more?'

'I don't like mysteries, certainly.'

I'd relied on the family sniffer-dog gene, inherited from my Bletchley Park great-aunt and I had Aunt Olivia hooked. 'So that's why I want to be here.'

My aunt nodded her elegantly coiffed head. 'That's all very well as far as it goes, Alyssa. But this D'Arblay man – he seemed insistent.'

'I know they want me off the scene, especially since yesterday.'

'Ah yes, yesterday. Tell me.'

'It was snowing. The roads were bad.'

'You had a near miss with a motorcycle.'

'It skidded on to the pavement.' Which was the truth, but probably not the whole truth because I needed Aunt Olivia to skim over this incident too. 'Honestly, the school's got this wrong. I'm perfectly OK – see!'

She studied me then told me with a sigh that I was exactly like my mother. 'Helena was always convinced she was right too.'

I was sitting calmly across the table and my aunt has almost zero imagination so she takes things at face value – if I look OK, as far as she's concerned I am OK.

'So I shouldn't worry too much about you?' she double-checked.

'It's the school – they're overreacting.'

'And I don't suppose I'm obliged to take their advice,' she said cautiously. 'After all, they can't force you to leave early.'

I may have looked calm and composed, but my heart was setting up a new world record for most beats per minute. I *had* to stick around to find out why Tom had Lily's overnight bag at his house for a start, and for a hundred other reasons.

'Alyssa dear, I don't mind admitting that I don't know what to do for the best.' My decisive aunt was suddenly dithering. 'I came here with the firm intention to follow Dr Webb's advice and take you home. Even though I'd explained to him I frequently worked in Geneva and that you might have to spend a considerable amount of time alone in the Richmond house, he was still of the opinion that it would be best to remove you from the school.'

I shook my head. 'No, Aunt Olivia. I have to stay here – it's important.'

She nodded and thought some more. 'Then I have to trust your instinct,' she decided.

The words fell from her lips like shiny gemstones. I'd got the reprieve I'd been working for. Be still, my beating heart.

'I'll drive you back to St Jude's and insist on an interview with the principal. I'll tell him in person that I wish you to continue until the end of term.'

'So that's that.' I sat with Paige in our room, enjoying one small victory. 'They can't get rid of me, even if they want to.'

'But *why* would they want to?' Paige wondered. 'Why not me as well? I was as close to Lily as you were.'

'Closer.'

'But they're not putting the same pressure on me.'

'Maybe it's something to do with not trusting me. I'm still an outsider.'

'And brainy with it.'

'Not compared with some others around here.'

'Alyssa, you're bloody clever. And you've got this memory thing going on, which none of the rest of us have. It's like they're scared of you remembering some little detail that might get the school into trouble.'

'With who?'

'With the Earle family, or the journos – I don't know.'

We heard footsteps stop outside our door so the guessing game had to stop.

Knock, knock, followed by a hissed request. 'Alyssa – Paige – can I come in?'

It was Jack's voice so I was the one who shot to the door. 'What are you doing? You're not supposed to be here!'

At St Jude's we have one long corridor for the girls, one for the boys – visits only allowed between 10 a.m. and 6 p.m. It was now 8.30 p.m. Punishment for breaking the rule – immediate suspension.

'I know. Paige, you have to stand guard.'

She huffed and puffed and effed but eventually she went to sit on the top step at the end of the corridor.

'So can I come in?' he asked. He stepped into the room without waiting for a reply and before I knew it, his arms were round my waist and he was pulling me towards him and kissing me.

I went weak at the knees, my heart raced – you know the usual clichés. Again, before I knew it, I was kissing him back until more footsteps dragged us back to earth.

'Jack, is this a purely social visit, or is it important?' Paige burst through the door and caught us eating each other's faces. 'I'm out here freezing my tits off.'

'Sorry.' Blushing, he stepped away from me. 'Get back out there, Paige. Call me if anyone comes.'

She closed the door and stomped off.

'What if someone does come?' I asked. 'Will we have a *St Trinian's* moment of you climbing out of the window and down the drainpipe?'

Jack grinned. (You know what I'm going to say – Oh, that grin! I had to kiss him again and again.) 'So, anyway, I dropped in on Tom at the Old Vicarage.'

'When?' I gasped.

'While you were busy with your aunt. How did that go, by the way?'

'Excellent. She's cool with me staying.'

'Great.' Another pause for more kissing before we got back to business. 'So Tom and I arranged a date for the next five-a-side match.'

'No, really? Did you sneak another look at that bag?'

'Maybe.' Jack looped his arms round my waist.

I leaned my weight back against them and looked straight at him. 'And?'

'I found this.' Suddenly unclasping his hands and letting

me stagger back against the window ledge, he put his hand in his pocket and pulled out a red smart phone.

'Lily's?' Yes – Lily's secret phone that she was rummaging for after her September meeting with Adam and Saint Sam, when she was crying and chucking stuff across the room, wailing that 'they' wouldn't let her speak to 'him', before she took a knife to her latest masterpiece. 'Did you ask Tom how come he had the bag?'

'No. I decided I didn't want him to know that we knew.'

'You *stole* it?' It was a rerun of Paige with Lily's diary. With Paige it didn't surprise me, but with Jack it did. He must have planned the whole thing, invented the five-a-side excuse to get inside the vicarage then somehow distracted Tom's attention while he went through the contents of the bag, found the phone and slipped it into his pocket. And he'd kept his nerve and walked away with what could be a vital piece of new evidence.

'Yeah, if you like. But right now it doesn't tell us anything.'

'Didn't you look at her voicemail and messages?'

'I couldn't. It's out of battery.'

'Right – of course. We need the charger, but Adam and Anna probably cleared it out with the rest of Lily's stuff.' Still, there was a small chance that they'd left it behind so I started to search in the top drawer of Lily's old bedside cabinet.

'Anything?' Jack asked.

A single silver stud earring shaped like a star, a handful of fluff, three pink paperclips. I shut the drawer and looked in the cupboard where I found a hair drier without a plug. Then I peered underneath and fished out the very thing we were looking for. Standing up straight, I dangled the charger from my forefinger.

Jack's phone started to vibrate. He checked it. 'Warning call from Paige. Someone's coming.'

'Jack, quick – you've got to get out of here!' I dashed to the window and opened it.

'Who do you think I am – Spiderman?'

Footsteps headed down the corridor. 'Get out!'

'It's bloody freezing.' It turned out he was a reluctant superhero. Still, he did throw Lily's phone for me to catch, then made a risky exit into the cold night.

I still had the phone and its charger in my hand when the door flew open and Paige made her second entrance, crouching low with an imaginary gun in her hand. 'Everyone, freeze!' she said in an American gangster accent.

Jack had gone to a lot of trouble over Lily's secret phone. Paige and I charged it up then checked her messages, which were all from Jayden and dated early September:

Lily, I need to see you.
Lily – meet me – Smith's Arms, back room.
Lily, answer your phone

And so on. Then we checked her missed calls – all from Jayden again. And her voicemail:

I need to talk to you. Why won't you answer?
Call me. Let me help you.
We need to talk. This is driving me crazy.

Lily hadn't answered any of them – neither messages nor calls. They came to an abrupt stop in the third week in September.

'All those heroics for nothing,' Paige told Jack when we saw him at breakfast next morning. 'There wasn't a single message from Lily to Jayden. She totally cut him dead.'

'Yeah, but we did learn something new from the whole bag situation,' he argued. 'About Tom and Lily and the fact that she didn't pack her bag, run out of here and throw herself straight in the lake.'

'Doh – we already knew that she didn't throw *herself* in!' When Paige runs down a blind alley, she gets irritable. Today she took it out on her boiled egg, which she quickly and cleanly decapitated.

I pushed my own plate to one side. 'You're missing Jack's point. He's saying that Lily and Tom met up – we don't know where.'

'Or why,' Jack added.

'But they must have done because Tom now has Lily's bag with the belongings she packed for her supposed trip home, which means she gave it to him for some reason.'

'Or he took it,' Jack said. 'From Lily or from someone else.'

'And he hasn't brought it back to the school or taken

137

it to the police.' This led to the one thing I really couldn't explain. 'Or said a word to anyone about being involved in Lily's disappearance.'

I ran into D'Arblay in the corridor as I went into my French class.

'Alyssa.' He acknowledged me with a stiff little nod then went ahead of me into the classroom to speak with Justine Renoir.

Inside the room, Hooper smiled and moved his bag to make room for me on the chair next to his.

I was glad of the smile. Hooper isn't someone you notice in a crowd – he's self-effacing and it takes a while to get to know him. Still, there was something about him that I instinctively warmed to.

'*Ça va?*' he asked.

'Hi, Hooper. Yeah, I'm good thanks.' I'd only just got settled when D'Arblay left and Justine called my name.

Justine is unbelievably chic and uses Chanel Coco Mademoiselle. She has a sexy gap between her two top front teeth and plump, cushioned lips. Anyway, she told me that D'Arblay had asked permission for me to leave the class early and go to Dr Webb's study – all in French, of course. In ten minutes, she said. *Dix minutes.*

'What does Saint Sam want?' Hooper asked, keeping to the spirit of the lesson. *Qu'est-ce qu'il veut, Saint Samuel?*

'He's probably changed his mind about sending me home,' I groaned.

'*En français*,' he whispered as Justine began the lesson. Ten minutes later he murmured *bonne chance* when I got up to go.

I decided there and then that I love Hooper – his deadpan expression, his way of trying to keep dark situations light.

To get to Dr Webb's office I had to pass through the main entrance hall and I glanced out at fresh activity at the far end of the drive. I guess we'd got used to a dozen or so reporters, photographers and a couple of satellite vans hanging around, even in this weather, and no one had tried to sneak in since Emily Archer's undercover entry into the sports centre, so I'd pretty much stopped noticing them. Today was different though.

'Whoa!' Harry remarked as he noticed the scrum at the gates. He happened to be exiting the bursar's office as I headed for my appointment with Saint Sam. A limo had just driven into the grounds. 'Guess who!'

'Who?'

'Anna Earle. According to D'Arblay's secretary, she's due any time.'

And Anna it was – still in black, still pale and fragile as the car pulled up at the main door and she stepped out. She recognized me and gave me the ghost of a smile before Saint Sam opened his door and invited us both into his office.

The principal offered Anna a seat and left me standing by the door. He waited for her to begin.

'I'm so sorry to take up more of your time, Dr Webb.'

'Not at all. We're happy to help in whatever way we can.'

The word 'help' had a grating effect – too impersonal, too polite for the occasion of losing your daughter in potentially violent circumstances. Anna Earle's eyes closed briefly and she sighed.

Saint Sam quickly tried to up his game. 'Of course, we're very disappointed that the request for a new pathologist's report is holding up the funeral arrangements. We can only imagine how terrible it must be for the family.'

Let me out! In fact, what am I doing here in the first place?

'It's the waiting,' Anna said. The voice was as ghostly as the smile. 'The not knowing.'

'We understand.'

She shook her head. 'I realize – I have to accept – that Lily has gone and I'll never get her back, but there are so many unanswered questions.'

Dr Webb did the steeple thing with his hands, tapping his fingertips together. I guess at this point he'd run out of platitudes and was trying to think of something meaningful to say.

'I only want to know what happened.' Anna's voice quavered and quivered to a halt. 'I have to do something. I can't sit at home.'

I totally get that. Paige and I – we feel the same way.

'No. Honestly, Mrs Earle, I do understand. Many of us at St Jude's wish we could do more.'

I sure do. Wanting to do something is the reason I

chased after Jayden and almost got myself mown down in the process.

'What exactly are the police doing? Have they involved the school?'

'Of course. I gave them a statement yesterday, as did Guy Simons, our head of physical education, who was the last teacher to see Lily on the day she disappeared, as indeed did our bursar, Terence D'Arblay, who gave his permission for Lily to leave school and travel to London.'

'What about you, Alyssa?' Turning with sudden eagerness, Anna drew me into the conversation. 'Have you spoken to the police?'

'Not yet,' Dr Webb answered for me. 'Inspector Cole understands the need to tread carefully as far as Lily's fellow students are concerned. He plans to interview Alyssa and Paige at a later date. Meanwhile, there are many other demands on police time.'

You're being much too bland again, Saint Sam. And how come you're answering for me?

'I see.' Anna left a long pause before she spoke again. 'You'll let me speak to Alyssa? I can take her out of school?'

Ah – that's what I'm doing here!

'We'll do anything that can be of comfort to Lily's family,' he assured her. 'We've taken Alyssa out of lessons especially to be here, though whether or not she can provide any answers . . .'

Anna Earle stood up with more determination than I would have expected. 'That's beside the point, Dr Webb. Alyssa was one of Lily's closest friends.'

'I understand,' he said again as he stood and made his way across the room to open the door for us. 'Take all the time you need, but with one proviso – that you don't leave Alyssa to find her own way home. You'll send her back to school with your driver?'

'Oh my good God!' Anna sank back on to the white leather seat as her driver coasted down wintry back lanes. The press feeding frenzy at the school gate was over – faces and lenses pressed against the car windows, reporters yelling heartless questions. 'How are you feeling, Anna?' 'Where's your husband?' 'Have they decided that Lily was murdered?'

I sat beside her in silence, seeing myself in the driver's overhead mirror as Anna leaned forward and closed the privacy screen.

'That man!' she sighed. 'Did they cut out his heart before they made him principal of St Jude's?'

I was expecting her to shrivel at the onslaught of the piranha press, not launch this attack on the sainted Sam.

'Sorry,' she sighed. Her hand trembled as she flicked her hair back in a gesture that reminded me so much of Lily that it took my breath away. 'What else could I expect – Dr Webb has to keep things on a professional level, doesn't he?'

'It's the way he is,' I agreed.

'He can't get personally involved – I realize that. In any case, over the years I've learned to deal with men like Dr Webb.'

We cruised on along the lanes, the hedges and fields still laden with snow.

'Lily went to many different schools before she settled at St Jude's,' Anna explained. 'Each one had a principal who was no doubt good at his or her job, but who never showed a scrap of genuine emotion, even when they were excluding her.'

I said I knew what she meant.

She looked hard at me. 'There's something about you, Alyssa.'

I blushed then stared out of the window.

'No, I noticed it the moment I saw you.'

'What exactly?'

'I realized that you and Lily are similar – you don't follow the rules.'

'Only if they make sense to me.'

'Yes, I can definitely spot that in you. That's why I wanted to have this time with you. You know, Lily is a free spirit. Her father doesn't see it, but I do.'

I let Anna do the talking, but each time she spoke of Lily in the present tense it gave me a small shock, like static electricity.

'Robert tries to rein her in. I tell him you can't tame Lily's creative spirit, she has to be free. We've had this battle for as long as I can remember, ever since Lily began to show signs of what they termed bizarre behaviour and I saw as the beginnings of her creativity.'

'You could say that about a lot of kids,' I said, meaning myself. I remembered being afraid of turning the light off because I was sure that witches would burst through my bedroom wall when I was asleep.

'Lily had an imaginary friend called Peter with a magic pebble that allowed him to make wishes come true.' Anna smiled at the memory. 'It didn't matter to her that she had no real friends because we moved around the world so much when she was young. She always had Peter. But it worried Robert because as a newspaperman he deals in facts and doesn't pander to the world of the imagination – he's very old school. And then of course eventually the doctors were involved. They put Lily through test after test until they came up with a diagnosis.'

After the unexpected torrent of words, Anna lapsed into silence.

'How old was Lily when that happened?' I asked.

'Eight, nine, ten – it went on for years. First they said she was hyperactive, then she had attention deficit disorder, then borderline autism. And all the time I was desperate for them to leave her alone because they were all so negative and only seemed to make things worse. I pleaded with Robert.'

'Too much pressure on Lily,' I said quietly.

'On both of us.'

There were high, snow-laden hedges to either side of the road and a heavy grey sky overhead. I heard the swish of tyres, the purr of the powerful engine.

'I'll always regret that I wasn't strong enough to protect my daughter,' Anna sighed. 'I should have said no – no more tests, no more labels.'

'But you can't afford to think that way.' Guilt nailed

her to a cross, adding to her grief.

'Thank you, Alyssa.' She gave me that smile with nothing behind it and when she took my hand her fingers were ice cold. 'Talking to you like this is the only thing that brings me closer to Lily. And, even though it's painful and you have every right to choose not to give me an answer, still I have to ask you . . .' She ground to a halt, swallowed hard then shook her head. 'I'm sorry.'

'You're asking me what really happened that day?'

Adam's email was branded on my brain – 'Family crisis. Come home.'

Bee-stung Lily had packed her bag, the one that was now lying among the sandals and dirty sportswear at the Old Vicarage.

'Did you get permission from Saint Samuel?' Paige asked.

'Yep.'

'What's the crisis? Did somebody die?' I wanted to know.

'Not yet.' Lily said.

'Did your family business go belly-up?'

'No.'

'Does your dad want to make you the youngest ever MD of the digital-media section of his multi-national news corporation?'

'Give me a break, Alyssa.' Lily stuffed her jeans and favourite top into the bag.

'Sorry, but we're only trying to find out what's wrong.'

She went on with her breakneck packing then stopped to text Adam.

The answer's still no.

I'd seen the message on Lily's phone. I saw it again, clear as day.

I relayed to Anna this final conversation with Lily. Verbatim.

'So at that point, having told me about the pregnancy some weeks earlier, she's now refusing to talk the thing through with us,' Anna whispered. 'That was because of the pressure Robert was putting on her to have an abortion.'

'An abortion?' I felt another small shock when I heard the word. 'Was that the plan?'

'Yes. It was one of the reasons I didn't want to involve Lily's father when she first told me about the pregnancy, but he has a way of extracting information. The minute he found out, he decided abortion was the best solution. Obviously.'

Personally I didn't see what was so obvious. 'Lily didn't agree?'

'No, that was why I was desperate for her to come home – to work it out face to face.'

And probably the reason why she never got on the London train. Instead she'd written the goodbye email to Jack, bought a different ticket and got shunted off down her own fatal siding.

'So I have something huge to tell you and you can pass this on too if you like. I'm pregnant, Jack. Big breath. Read again: I'm pregnant. This is not a lie – I did the test twice and both times it came up positive. Careless, huh? You'd have expected better of a smart St Jude's girl like me.'

God knows which off-the-wall, crazy train she'd actually planned to take.

There on the back seat of the limo I made the decision to tell Anna everything I'd found out so far about Lily and Jayden – how, from the evidence in her diary, she'd hoped he was the father, how happy she was that the baby might have been his and how she'd cut him out of her life when she'd discovered he wasn't. Exit stick boy and stick dog.

'She loved Jayden?' Anna asked in that faint, surprisingly young voice.

'Yes. And he loved her.'

She sat very still to let this sink in then gave a little gasp, almost as if she had to remind herself to breathe. 'And the real father – we're absolutely certain that he didn't want to play any part?'

I had to shake my head and make her cry at the desperate rejection Lily must have felt. The loneliness of it.

chapter nine

Anna stayed in Ainslee while her driver took me back to school so I had plenty of time to think about her and her relationship with Lily.

She definitely loved her, but she wasn't strong or fierce enough to stand up for her. She didn't say, 'This is my daughter and she's beautiful and precious in her own right. She doesn't have to be the same as everyone else.'

She wasn't there for Lily.

I looked out of the window at bare thorn trees and snow melting into black earth. The driver looked straight ahead and didn't say a word.

I recognized famous media baron Robert Earle the second I saw him standing in the main entrance to St Jude's.

He was skinny and stringy beneath his double-breasted, dark-blue coat, wizened and practically bald, with those staring, dark-circled eyes.

The driver had glided past the press scrum at the gates, but when he saw his boss he braked hard and stopped ten metres short of the entrance.

'Thanks for driving me,' I muttered, quickly sliding out of the passenger seat and hoping to slip away unnoticed.

But one of Earle's minions spotted me, cut off my retreat and led me towards the great man.

Robert Earle came slowly, deliberately, down the steps. 'And you are?' he asked without preliminaries.

'Alyssa Stephens.'

He looked down his nose, inclined his head towards his up-to-speed aide who informed him that I'd been Lily's roommate.

I obviously wasn't interesting or important so the media man brushed me to one side and went to speak to the driver, ordering him to step out of the car. 'Where's Anna?' he demanded.

She'd checked in to The Swan Hotel in Ainslee, the driver told him. His orders were to return there and wait.

'Since when do you take orders from Anna?' Robert Earle demanded. It was a short sentence, but long enough for me to be sure that the driver's answer had annoyed the hell out of his boss. There was a mini eruption as Earle fired off orders to minions number one, two and three – get on the phone to his wife and tell her not to leave the hotel, demand an explanation from the school principal – how come he hadn't informed him, Robert Earle, of Anna's whereabouts the moment she'd arrived at the school? Make sure the press pack didn't get wind of his wife's latest movements.

'And you,' he told the innocent driver, holding out his hand for the car keys. 'You're fired.'

Whoa!

The man didn't see any point in arguing. He just shook

his head and stepped away, fading into the shadowy world of the unemployed.

Earle motioned for me to come forward again. 'You – Alyssa – what did Anna want?'

'Just to talk.' It was a free country, whatever Robert Earle thought. I wasn't going to dish up information on a plate.

He narrowed the bulging meerkat eyes. 'What about?'

'Your daughter.'

'Jesus wept, hasn't Anna talked enough without having to dump on total strangers?'

This was beyond brutal. I stayed silent while the aides rushed about Earle's business and Dr Webb appeared in the doorway.

'Whatever Anna said, you keep it to yourself,' Earle said in his narrow, nasal voice. Taking a phone from aide number one, he spoke to his wife. 'Don't move. Don't go outside. Wait till I send someone to fetch you.' End of conversation. He thrust the phone back into his minion's hand.

Anna was married to the guy. They had two kids together. No way would I have let him speak to me this way.

Saint Sam came down the steps, aware of the long-distance lenses trained on us all. He was keen to lead everyone inside the building but Robert Earle's anger, once roused, was wide ranging and random in its targets – first the driver, then Anna, now the school principal.

'I warned you about security,' he muttered. 'That includes not letting my wife roam the bloody Cotswold countryside with one of your students.'

'I'm very sorry,' Saint Sam replied, fear flickering behind

the smooth expression. 'Mrs Earle came to my office. It was impossible to refuse.'

'You should have called me – I'd have refused for you.' Earle gestured towards the journalists. 'Look at them – baying for my blood. They'll make a big deal of this – Anna coming here alone, secretly taking one of your girls for a country spin. They'll have pictures.'

'Come inside,' Saint Sam suggested helplessly.

Earle ignored him. 'This girl – Alyssa – they'll be after her like rats down a drain. They won't let up until they've got their story.'

'All our students have been warned about the need for discretion.'

Bland and weak again, Saint Sam. At times like this you need to be firmer.

'Bullshit,' Earle grunted. He turned and herded me up the steps. 'What exactly did my wife say to you?'

'Not much.'

'Let's pretend I didn't hear that and I'll ask you again – what did Anna tell you?'

I managed to look him in the eye. 'That she misses Lily. That talking to one of her school friends is the best hope she has of hanging on to her memory.' Let's see how you react to that.

There wasn't a flicker of anything in the dark eyes except fury. 'I expect she gave you the old sob story, how I failed to do my best for my daughter every step of the way.'

'Come to my office,' Saint Sam urged, getting desperate.

Robert Earle shrugged him aside. 'Yeah well, I don't need

that particular headache right now. You forget all the guff my wife gave you, OK?'

I stared back at him, trying to imagine him as my father. Lily had been right – 'tyrant' just about covered it and I decided that my no-daddy status was better than her monster-daddy one.

'You can rely on Alyssa,' Saint Sam tried to say.

By now we were inside, out of sight of the journos, and just when you thought Robert Earle might see sense and calm down, he fired off again, worse than before.

'"Rely"? Yeah – right. Just like I relied on you, Dr Webb, and look how that turned out.'

People were walking past, going about their business – Justine Renoir and Jack Hooper, Guy Simons, Harry Embsay. Everyone noticed what was happening between Saint Sam and Robert Earle.

'I hope you're not suggesting that we in any way failed in our duty towards Lily,' the principal said, struggling to keep his calm.

'You hit that nail right on the head,' Earle ranted. 'That's exactly what you did – failed in your duty. I told you right at the start that my daughter only came to St Jude's under strict conditions. Condition number one – your school nurse had to make a daily check to make sure she took her medication. Number two – you would alert us to any health issues – any mood swings or irrational behaviour – the moment they arose. Neither of which conditions you fulfilled. Number three –'

'I'll stop you right there, Mr Earle.' Really, Saint Sam

152

couldn't let it go any further. 'I assure you that we were perfectly aware of Lily's medical condition before she arrived. The school provided excellent care, even when her behaviour was at its most challenging.'

'And if you're "perfectly aware" of Lily's bipolar disorder, you'll also be "perfectly aware" of the deal we did to get her in here,' Earle reminded him at full volume. A freight train wouldn't have stopped this rant. 'You give my daughter a place and I fund your school to the tune of two million pounds.'

Dr Webb took a step back, as if he'd been punched in the stomach. 'It wasn't quite like that.'

'It was exactly like that. Remember, I was frank with you – I said, "Lily's a problem. She's been thrown out of every mainstream school we've put her in." You didn't miss a beat. You told me, "Here at St Jude's we believe in every child's right to express their individuality." I said, "Good on you, Dr Webb. You manage to keep my extremely individual daughter here for five whole years and I'll pump money into your Foundation – half when she arrives, half when she leaves." Needless to say, you bit my hand right off.'

At this point I just wanted to shut my ears. I know they run a business here, but this sounded just too cynical to bear. It didn't stop there, though.

'The problem is you didn't keep to your side of the deal.' Robert Earle lowered his voice at last, seeming aware for the first time that he needed to tone things down.

His aides looked at their watches and their phones. One

153

went to check out alternative exit routes.

Saint Sam hadn't recovered from the earlier body blow. He looked confused.

'Which means I don't deliver the second million,' Earle said, ready to be ushered out of a side door. 'Tell that to the next meeting of your board of governors, Dr Webb.'

Early next morning, Paige, the two Jacks and I gathered round an oak table in the old library. Zara already happened to be there, so she joined us too.

The old library was where they put the current editions of the daily papers – in among the dying technology of paper and print. The rows of decaying, leather-bound volumes made a musty backdrop to our conversation.

'Front page in the *Daily Express*.' Hooper read out the headline: *Grieving Anna Gets No Answers*. He showed us the clear, in-focus picture of me and Anna getting into her limo – not blurred or fuzzy – so we were easy to identify.

'Page four in the *Mirror*,' Zara said. 'They go for the family-in-crisis angle, with pictures of Anna and Robert arriving separately, Anna looking sad, Robert ready to commit mass murder, plus a paragraph about lack of police progress.'

'There's nothing in this one.' Paige leafed through another tabloid without success.

'That's because Robert Earle owns it,' Zara pointed out. She seemed knowledgeable about the redtops, maybe because she followed the Hollywood A-listers in their gossip columns.

'Ah.' Paige made a typical comment about not shitting

in your own back yard then turned to the *Independent*.

Meanwhile I was busy with the *Mail*'s headline – *School for Scandal* where the main picture was of the school building in all its ancient glory, with images of Anna and Robert Earle inset into the top right corner.

'Let me see that.' Jack finished with the *Mirror* and came to peer over my shoulder. 'Hey, look who wrote it.'

Emily Archer, young journalist of the year. It turned out Emily had tracked down Robert Earle's sacked driver in a pub in Gloucester and he'd given her the low down on the Earle family's reaction to Lily's death, saying that his ex-boss blamed St Jude's for his daughter's death and was accusing them of covering up certain facts about the discovery of the body – their lack of action when she first disappeared, their reluctance to involve the police.

'According to local opinion, the school has not always been free from scandal. Other unexplained deaths have occurred, dating as far back as St Jude's foundation in 1938.'

'Shit – D'Arblay and Saint Sam keep that one quiet,' Paige commented as Jack read aloud.

'You wouldn't exactly advertise it in the prospectus,' Hooper said.

It turned out Emily Archer had been thorough in detailing events. Then she wrote about ancient stone pillars and oak doors hiding unsolved mysteries, moved on to the tragic loss of a troubled young life and finished with *Police investigations continue. However, yesterday's apparently unscheduled visit by members of the grieving family fixes attention firmly on the building where tragic Lily Earle spent her last days and where her body was pulled from the lake.*

'What about the other unexplained deaths?' Hooper was the first to speak after we'd put the newspapers back in the stand and walked from the library into the main school building. 'Is that journos raking up any dirt they can find?'

'Yeah, it's ancient history,' Zara decided.

I agreed on that point. 'We need to concentrate on Lily.'

Neither of the Jacks said anything as we headed for our first lesson of the day.

School routine held me together through Thursday and into Friday morning. The subject of Lily came up regularly on the BBC News channel and again in the newspapers, and there was no way any of us could ignore the satellite TV vans or the paparazzi at the gate. Still, no journalists, not even Emily Archer, had managed to corner me, despite what Robert Earle had predicted, and I was in the new technology centre when Dr Welford invited Jack to spend his afternoon doing extra maths to get him ready for the Oxbridge entrance exams. Extra maths sounds like torture to most of us, but my Jack acted as if he'd been offered a second helping of sticky-toffee pudding.

He said yes please, he'd like a session on the Newton-Raphson method of solving equations, as long as they could fit it around his tennis-coaching session.

'Not that you need the extra tuition,' Shirley Welford told him with a smile. 'It's more that I enjoy the challenge of teaching you.'

She was happy, Jack was happy – it was win-win.

'When do you next get some free time?' I asked him as we went for lunch, resisting the urge to grab him and kiss him that I felt every time we were together. 'We still need to get hold of Tom and ask him about Lily's bag.'

'Yeah, well, just don't try that one by yourself.' Jack reminded me that my last solo excursion to the Bottoms hadn't worked out well. 'I mean it, Alyssa.'

'I hear you.'

'Seriously.' In fact, it was Jack who did the grabbing and kissing, right there in full view of the lunch queue. 'You know I couldn't stand it if anything bad happened to you.'

'OK. How about we both go tomorrow morning?'

He agreed that this would have to do and I made Jack a promise that I would stay in the school grounds, even though I had a free afternoon. 'What if the journos manage to grab me – what do I say?'

He made a zipping gesture across his mouth. Say nothing.

OK again. 'And if the police want to talk to me and Paige before we see Tom? Do I tell them about the bag?'

'Yeah, definitely mention it,' Jack decided. 'Let them put some pressure on him as well as us – it can't do any harm.'

We kissed again, lips brushing – a reassuring, we're-a-couple kiss – then parted.

But the journalists were penned inside a taped-off area outside the gate and Inspector Cole, the man in charge of the investigation, didn't come anywhere near St Jude's. Instead, he spent the afternoon in front of TV cameras, making an appeal for anyone with information about Lily's movements on the day she'd drowned to come forward. I watched him on my iPad.

'Alyssa – the bag!' Paige insisted. We were in our room and she was getting ready for a session in the indoor arena with Mistral, but she broke off to watch the broadcast. 'That's definitely information.'

'I know.'

'So go forward.'

'I will. Tomorrow, after Jack and I have talked to Tom.' Maybe this doesn't sound like my best decision and it probably wasn't, but, remember, I trusted Tom and wanted to give him a chance to explain. That's the only clear reason I can give for not going to the police straight away.

Paige said, 'Please yourself,' and went to do dressage while I spent an hour preoccupied with OCD things like rearranging the objects on top of my bedside cabinet three times and checking my phone for new messages every five minutes. I tried not to remember Lily sitting cross-legged on her now-empty bed, but failed. I saw her face, her dark hair piled on top of her head, heard her voice teasing me. God, I missed her.

'Jack?' she said. 'Jack Cavendish asked you to Tom's party?'

'He did.'

'You're sure it wasn't Jack Hooper?'

I remembered the debris of paint tubes squeezed out of shape, chocolate wrappers, her broken Kindle. I remembered it in so much detail that I had to get out of the room before Lily's ghost drove me crazy.

'I found out it was Sir Edward Bond's own daughter who died in 1938,' Hooper told me when I ran into him on my way to the sports centre to watch my Jack play tennis. He always slouched around the place looking disengaged – a fly on the wall, constantly observing with his bug eyes – so to have him volunteer this information without being asked was unusual. 'She was a student here, part of the first year's intake.'

I changed course and walked with him into the quad. 'How do you know this?'

'Easy – anyone can do it. I went online and checked the newspaper archives.'

'This stuff about the history of St Jude's – you think it could be relevant?'

'Maybe, maybe not. I'm just following my nose, doing a spot of research. That's what I do.'

'OK, so what else?'

'The daughter's name was Eleanor. Do you want to know how she died?'

'She drowned in the lake.' Call it a flash of inspiration or sixth sense. Anyway, I was right.

Hooper nodded. 'After that, Sir Edward was a broken man. He resigned as St Jude's chairman of the board, retired from all his business interests and turned into a recluse.'

'What about Eleanor's mother?'

'She's not mentioned.'

We'd reached the doorway up to the boys' dormitory and stood in the archway to finish our conversation. 'Do they explain how Eleanor ended up in the lake?'

'Misadventure – that was the verdict. In other words, it was a tragic accident. One other thing – St Jude's was damaged by German bombs during the war. Three more kids and a teacher were killed.'

'But we're miles from anywhere,' I pointed out. 'The nearest big city is Bristol, so how come German pilots were dropping bombs on poor little us?'

Hooper shrugged. 'Another case of misadventure probably. Anyway, St Jude was the patron saint of lost causes – which doesn't exactly inspire confidence.'

'He could have been the patron saint of martyrs – that would probably be worse.'

'Yeah, but not much,' was his parting comment as he climbed the stone stairs to his room.

When I retraced my steps and reached the sports centre, I found I'd got my timings wrong. Jack's extra maths came before his tennis coaching, not after, so I found Luke and Zara shooting basketballs into a hoop in an otherwise deserted space. Up on the mezzanine level, D'Arblay was deep in conversation with Guy Simons. When I say 'deep in conversation', I mean that D'Arblay was doing the talking and Guy was scowling – until I appeared and then they quickly broke apart.

What's that about? I wondered briefly.

With another hour to kill, I grabbed a coffee to go and

went for a wander in the grounds, drawn towards the woods at the far side of the lake where I could stay out of sight. It was one of those cold, grey December days when you need Christmas lights and town glitter and sparkle to lift your spirits – not bare, black trees and freezing fog creeping down from the hills.

I walked for ten minutes while I finished my coffee, slid the crushed, empty cup into my pocket then turned for home.

The next bit reminds me of a scene from *Jane Eyre* – the part where lonely, plain governess Jane is walking along a path towards Thornfield and a big grey dog dashes by, like a wolf in a fairytale forest. The dog scares her half to death. Then we get her first sight of Mr Rochester on horseback. He gallops up and rescues her, sets her back on her feet. Major frisson moment – love at first sight for our heroine. 'Reader – I married him' eventually.

Love wasn't in the air where I was, but the atmosphere was exactly the same – cold and bleak – when I heard a horse coming up fast along the bridleway and I was almost too late to step out of Harry Embsay's way.

I swore at him in an un-Jane-like way. He laughed and galloped on towards the main house.

First a guy on a motorbike tries to run me down, now Harry on horseback. This was not funny.

'Where is he?' I asked Paige as I strode into the stable yard after an angry dash past the lake, hard on Harry's heels. I was out of breath, hot and sweaty under my padded jacket and big scarf.

'Where's who?' She was heaving Mistral's saddle off his back and carrying it into the tack room while her horse stood patiently tethered outside his stable.

'Harry Embsay. He almost knocked me down, for Christ's sake!'

'He went out on Guy's horse.'

'I already know that!'

'He's not back yet.' Paige disappeared into the tack room while I checked the empty stable where Guy kept Franklin.

'See!' she said as she re-emerged.

'It was stupid,' I complained. 'Harry's a total idiot.'

'Tell me about it.' Paige got busy with brushes and combs, speaking more softly to her horse than she ever did to mere humans. 'You did pretty well with your transitions today, didn't you, boy?'

'Did you hear what I said, Paige? Harry practically mowed me down. He could've killed me!'

'Yeah, but it wasn't on purpose.'

'I don't know – maybe it was.' Harry must have seen me up ahead with my red hair and bright green scarf in all that greyness, yet he hadn't made any effort to avoid me – the exact opposite, in fact.

Paige stopped brushing. 'You don't think you're being a teeny bit par-a-noid?' she mouthed quietly. She winked and suddenly my tension melted away.

I grinned. Mistral stamped his hoof.

'Chill, my friend,' Paige said as she got back to her grooming.

162

Then without warning the tack-room door flew open. A figure in a grey hoodie, the bottom half of his face hidden by a black scarf burst out, a blade in his left hand. With his empty right hand he took hold of a tall green wheelie bin containing feed and thrust it straight at Mistral.

The bin smashed into the side of the horse. Mistral squealed and reared. The hoodie guy raised the knife to strike the horse, but the rope tethering Mistral to the wall strained, frayed and then snapped. He broke free and reared on to his hind legs.

The attacker slashed again at the horse's neck. He missed and, as Mistral crashed down to earth, hoodie-guy covered his head with his arms and cowered under the flailing hoofs. Then he scrambled out of reach.

Mistral reared again and before we knew it the hooded figure was scaling the wall, scrambling over the top, disappearing across the fields.

I remember the noise – the horse squealing, the thud of the bin smacking against him, Paige yelling, hoofs crashing down on to the cobbles. I'd moved out of the way, but not Paige. Fearless, she ignored the hoodie attacker and tried to grab the end of the rope, got in much too close to all that terrified bone, hoof and muscle.

She reached up as Mistral reared yet again, caught the rope and had her arms almost pulled from their sockets. I yelled at her to let go. She stumbled sideways, fell between her horse and the stable wall, was down on the ground as he landed on top of her.

Then there was silence. Mistral stood over a motionless

Paige, legs braced as if scared to move another muscle and hurt her more than he already had. She lay on her back. There was no blood.

The horse looked down. He quivered, flared his nostrils then let out a loud, broken sigh.

Paige didn't move. Her eyes were closed.

Guy Simons appeared. He'd heard the horse squeal and Paige cry out. He ran into the yard.

'Call an ambulance!' he yelled, dropping to his knees and putting his cheek close to Paige's mouth to see if she was breathing. 'Alyssa, call 999!'

chapter ten

'Why didn't I do something?'

Jack had heard me say this over and over. 'What? What could you have done?' was the question he put to me each time.

I would shake my head. 'I don't know – just something.'

He held my hand, didn't push me for a more logical answer as we waited in the old library.

The ambulance hadn't reached the stable yard until twenty endless minutes after I'd made the call. There'd been rush hour traffic, a thickening fog – the roads were chaotic.

'Don't move her!' I'd said to Guy, who was first-aid trained and had checked that Paige's airway was clear. He nodded then stepped back. There was no blood, like I said. She was unconscious, but maybe she would be OK.

I'd brought a horse rug from the tack room and gently laid it over her. Guy had cornered Mistral and led him into his stable.

Then other people had arrived – Zara and Hooper, Luke in sweatshirt and shorts. He'd knelt beside Paige and spoken her name, given me a quick, scared glance when she didn't answer.

'Don't move her,' I'd whispered automatically to anyone who went near. Then I told Zara and Hooper to chase after the person who'd caused this. 'A skinny kid in a grey hoodie. He climbed over the wall and ran away. But watch out – he has a knife!'

Zara was the first to react. Before I knew it she was hauling herself up and over the wall, yelling at Hooper to follow her.

Luke, Guy and I were the only ones left, waiting those endless minutes for help to arrive.

In the middle of our vigil Harry Embsay had ridden Franklin into the yard and immediately started yelling at people – blaming them. 'Somebody, do something,' he'd demanded as he vaulted from the saddle and seen how bad things were – Paige lying spread-eagled and white as a corpse, eyes closed, the minutes ticking by. 'Don't just stand there!'

I'd listened for every breath, watched for even the slightest movement and seen nothing.

Fifteen minutes passed then we'd heard a siren muffled by the fog, had another delay as the ambulance driver navigated through the press pack then discovered exactly where to come, blue lights still flashing.

Two paramedics – a man and a woman – had jumped out as Harry, Guy, Luke, and I stepped back to give them room.

After that I had the temporary memory collapse that comes over me when I'm in shock and everything becomes a blur. The paramedics had followed their procedures, testing vital signs and hooking Paige up to tubes and monitors before they immobilized her with back and neck braces then carried her on a stretcher into the ambulance. No one had spoken – I do remember that – not until the ambulance door was closed and the vehicle had backed out of the stable yard. We'd heard the fading siren, felt empty and numb in the silence that followed.

Then it had been D'Arblay who'd taken control. He'd issued the orders for Zara and Hooper to call off their search and return to school while the rest of us went back to the main building and waited in the old library for news. He said that no one should tweet or text about Paige's accident until her parents had been informed.

I did as I was told, was waiting with the others in the periodical section of the library, when my Jack finally caught up with events.

'Why didn't I do something?' was the first thing I whispered to him from a million miles away, from the vastness of a huge, hostile universe.

Something truly big and bad was happening – I already knew that – but it wasn't until the attack on Paige that I got really scared. Fear got into my bones and clutched at my heart, sent chills up and down my spine.

'Someone wants to get rid of us,' I admitted to Jack as Zara and Hooper reported back to D'Arblay and Saint Sam in the principal's office. Apparently they hadn't found any sign of the guy in the hoodie, and even the news hounds camped out at the gates had missed most of the latest drama, noting the arrival and exit of the ambulance, but then caught off guard when, half an hour later, two police cars had nee-nahed past them, sweeping through the gates and up the school drive.

'This kid – did he actually try to kill Paige?' Jack put into words what I was trying not to think.

'Whoa!' Harry muttered. 'That's crazy.'

But Harry hadn't been there, either when the guy on the motorbike rode straight at me or when the kid burst out of the tack room with the knife.

I re-ran the event in my mind and recalled some of the details – the hoodie kid gripping the Stanley knife in his left hand, the bottom half of his face covered by a black scarf. The wheelie bin slamming against Mistral's side as the kid raised the knife to slash at the horse's neck. 'No,' I told Jack. 'It was Mistral he was after. Paige just got in the way.'

Jack's logical brain took over. 'So these two – the biker and the hoodie kid – they're more likely to be scaring the shit out of you and Paige than trying to kill you.'

'You can't know that for sure,' Luke said, finding it hard to believe that his on-off girlfriend was in hospital. He'd dropped the uber-cool act and talked as if he was in a state of total shock.

I followed Jack's thinking and stepped in with an opinion. 'I'll say one thing – if they are trying to kill us, they're not very good at it.'

'We need to find out who "they" are.' This was Jack again, gripping my hand across the oak table, thinking furiously.

*

When D'Arblay had finished with Zara and Hooper, he came to the library and chose me and Jack to go to the hospital to wait outside the door to the ICU. 'Paige's parents are out of the country and it will take them some time to fly back,' he explained. 'If she regains consciousness, she may want Alyssa there to hold her hand.'

We found at the hospital that Paige hadn't regained consciousness – not yet – and it was almost midnight.

'She sustained the injuries approximately eight hours ago,' I heard one medic report to another as their soft shoes squeaked towards us down the polished corridor and they pushed through the wide doors into the unit. I saw four beds, all occupied by patients hooked up to tubes and monitors. It was impossible to tell which one was Paige.

'Three broken ribs, one punctured lung, broken collarbone . . . X-rays and brain scan . . . possible aneurysm . . . skull fractures, small splinters of bone lodged in the frontal cortex . . .' The words slipped out between the doors before they swung closed.

I gripped Jack's hand tighter. 'I should've pulled her clear,' I moaned. 'All I did was yell at her to get out of the way. She didn't listen.'

'She'll be OK,' he insisted. 'They know what they're doing.'

'Paige was trying to calm Mistral down. He reared up when the guy with the knife ran out of the tack room. She was in a corner, backed up against the wall. She didn't even put her hands up to protect herself.'

I paused to let my total recall kick in once again, as I knew it eventually would.

The tack room door flew open. A figure in a grey hoodie burst out, holding a Stanley knife. Grey hoodie and black scarf. A man, tall. Grey eyes with heavy lashes. A hoodie with an Adidas logo and three white stripes down the arms.

He took hold of the handle on a tall green wheelie bin and rammed it straight into Mistral's flank. He raised the knife. Mistral squealed and reared. The rope came loose.

'What was the guy doing in there in the first place?' Jack asked.

One of the medics came back out of the ICU and avoided eye contact as she hurried away.

'Hiding.' He must have been – otherwise Paige would have seen him when she carried Mistral's saddle in.

'And where did he go afterwards?'

'Up over the wall, across the fields.'

'You didn't recognize him?'

I shook my head. 'He had grey eyes with long, dark lashes. He was wearing an Adidas top.'

We waited until two in the morning, when Paige's mum and dad showed up and the hospital sent us home.

'Go and get some sleep,' a nurse advised. 'We'll keep in touch via the school.'

Jack and I used a taxi, sat in silence through the sleazy Friday night streets – guys reeling out of clubs and across the road, girls vomiting under the town's giant Christmas tree. We held hands along familiar country lanes until we reached St Jude's.

*

I didn't sleep. I stared at the ceiling remembering Paige's grey horse screaming, rearing up and plummeting down, the sound of hoofs thudding into bone and flesh, the silence afterwards.

I took my mind back to five minutes earlier.

'You don't think you're being a teeny bit par-a-noid?' Paige asked with a wink. 'Chill, my friend.'

Saturday morning brought no fresh news. Paige's parents were still at her bedside, the doctors were carrying out more tests. We were in limbo, with too much time on our hands.

'It's definitely linked,' I told Zara at breakfast, which none of us ate. 'My so-called accident with the motorbike and what happened to Paige.'

She shook her head and I didn't blame her. Who wants to believe a conspiracy theory when coincidence or cock-up falls within the same frame? 'We have to be logical about this,' she insisted. 'We can't let our imaginations run away with us.'

Jack, Zara and I walked out of the dining hall towards the new library. 'But what if I'm right? What if Lily's killer was after me and now he's targeting Paige?'

Zara shook her head angrily and veered off towards the library.

I ran after her. 'At least think about it.'

'No. I don't want to.'

Specifically, she didn't want to consider what might have been – Paige falling into a permanent vegetative state, me mangled under the front wheel of a powerful motorbike.

'It was a lime-green Toyota,' I told Jack quietly as we watched Zara go and my eidetic memory clicked in. 'Registration number KD58PDO.'

At least the attack on Paige meant that I finally got to meet Inspector Cole. He came hotfoot to the school that Saturday morning.

'Use the bursar's office,' Saint Sam suggested after the inspector and I had been introduced. 'Nobody will disturb you there.'

I sat on the edge of my hard seat, facing the inspector across Terence D'Arblay's wide desk. Behind him was a glass-fronted cabinet containing shelves of red ring-binders and curios such as conch shells, a bronze statuette of a horse, a carved silver box, military medals and old black-and-white photos dating back to the founding of the school.

'You're worried about your friend?' was Cole's first question.

'Yes. Has she come round yet?'

He shook his head. 'The doctors have decided to keep her in an induced coma until some of the swelling around her brain is reduced. That's normal procedure with an injury like this. It gives the patient a better chance of making a full recovery.'

'There wasn't any blood,' I told him, as if this made a difference. 'At least I couldn't see any.'

Mistral had trapped Paige against the wall, she'd lost her footing and gone down. A thousand-plus pounds of horseflesh had landed on her skull. But no blood.

'Tell me about Paige's attacker,' Inspector Cole invited.

'He was about five eleven, six foot, skinny.'

'How old?'

'Young – maybe eighteen, nineteen.'

'What colour was his hair?'

'He was wearing a hoodie so I couldn't see. And there was a black scarf covering his mouth and nose. He had grey eyes with dark eyelashes.'

'Good.' The inspector wasn't taking notes, but he looked as if he was taking in the details. He was an older guy – late forties maybe – a little out of shape, with a fleshy face and double chin. He wore his thinning grey hair short and had a bristly moustache that was darker than his hair. 'Anything else?'

'The hoodie was grey with a white Adidas logo. He was carrying a type of Stanley knife with a grey metal handle – in his left hand.'

'Very good. Trousers?'

'Tracksuit bottoms. They matched the top.'

'OK, so describe exactly what he did.'

This was no problem for someone with a brain like mine so I gave the inspector the action replay.

'Who did he plan to use the knife on – the horse or Paige?'

'The horse. He slashed at Mistral's neck, but he missed. Paige got in the way when she tried to stop him. Listen, inspector, you should look at the CCTV footage to see for yourself. They have a camera on the wall in the stable yard.'

He sucked his teeth. 'We would like to, but apparently it's out of action. Technical fault.'

'Oh.'

'They're fixing it as we speak.'

'Too late,' I said.

After this Inspector Cole took a short coffee break with Saint Sam. I'm sure they discussed Paige and probably me too, but I was also pretty certain at this point that no one except me and Jack was making firm links between yesterday's attack and the guy on the green Toyota, and how both things might be connected to Lily's death.

We resumed at eleven.

'Alyssa, the principal informs me you may have been involved in a hit-and-run incident in Lower Chartsey. When was this?'

'Last Monday.'

'You didn't report it?'

'There wasn't anything to report. The guy didn't hit me and he drove off.'

'But you think it could have been deliberate?'

I shrugged. 'There's no way I can be sure.'

'What were you doing in the village?'

'Talking to a friend.'

The inspector was good at his job and he winkled Jayden's name out of me. 'Did you see anyone else?'

More winkling then I gave him the names of Micky, Alex and Ursula and a little about the bullying that took place in the JD workshop.

Cole's moustache twitched as he wrinkled his nose, sniffed then reached for a pen. For the first time he scribbled a few things down. 'Clear something up for me, Alyssa – what was so important that you had to battle through a snowstorm to talk to these village kids?'

This hit a nerve with me and I rushed to answer. 'I wanted to find out about Jayden and Lily – how he'd reacted when he'd found out she was pregnant.'

'You thought he was the baby's father?' The moustache twitched again as if he was a furry-whiskered terrier picking up a fresh scent.

'No, I already knew he wasn't,' I replied. 'Or at least I'd figured it out.'

Inspector Cole nodded. 'You're a bright girl, but then you wouldn't be at St Jude's if you weren't.' The flattery suggested that he was bringing the interview to a close. 'Anything else you want to say?'

'I remembered the bike's registration number – the one that almost ran me down – it's KD58PDO.'

He wrote it eagerly on a sheet of St Jude's headed notepaper then looked up with pen poised. 'That's everything?'

'No – there is one other thing.'

'In connection with which incident – the motorbike or the horse?'

'Neither. This is in connection with Lily. On the day she disappeared, I saw her get the text from her brother and watched her pack her bag to catch the London train, only we know she never made it and now the bag's turned up at Tom Walsingham's house.' And I gave the inspector Tom's address – The Old Vicarage, Main Street, Lower Chartsey.

'Any idea how the bag got there?' Inspector Cole asked without showing any reaction. I'd have expected a twitch of the terrier moustache or raised eyebrows at the very least.

'No. I haven't worked that one out yet, but I will.'

He smiled as he shook my hand and said goodbye. 'Thanks, Alyssa. Be sure to let me know when you do.'

When the police move, they move fast. At midday on Saturday I received a text from Tom.

Cops came to my house! What the f . . . ! Am in woods by lake. Meet me.

I showed the text to Jack.

'I'll come with you,' he said, quick as a flash. It wasn't that he didn't trust me, it was that he wanted to protect me. Or at least that's what he said and what I preferred to think. OK, maybe there was a whiff of jealousy in there too.

Anyway, I was glad I wasn't alone as Jack and I headed out through freezing fog, skirting the lake and heading for the trees.

'Let's see if Tom can worm his way out of this one,' Jack muttered.

'He's got a hell of a lot of explaining to do, for sure.'

Jack held my hand and we walked on for a bit. When

I tripped over a tree root and stumbled, he was there to break my fall. 'It's OK,' he breathed as he held me close and pressed his lips against the top of my head.

We stood for a long time, blanketed in cold fog, warm in our embrace.

Then Tom appeared out of the mist and called my name. 'Alyssa, over here!'

Jack and I rushed to meet him, saw him suddenly duck out of sight behind a tree and were too late to stop ourselves from being spotted by a small posse of journalists who had broken free from the main gang at the school gates.

'Hey, Jack!' In spite of the fog swirling around, Emily Archer recognized him straight away and I recognized her. Action Girl in leather jacket and zippy boots, blonde hair upswept.

He frowned. We waited for Emily to arrive.

I jumped in with the first question. 'How did you get in?' The reporters would have needed to make a long loop across country, over the stream and then around the back of the woods to infiltrate the school grounds without being seen.

'What is this – Colditz?' she wanted to know, smiling exclusively at Jack, ignoring me for the moment.

Back off – he's way too young for you! Jealousy pounces and grabs you by the throat when you least expect it.

'Good to see you,' Emily told Jack as three fellow journos huddled behind her. 'We need a quote about what happened to Paige Kelly yesterday – the ambulance, the police cars. Something short to keep us in the loop.'

Jack shook his head and did his best to make it look as though we were here for some fresh air. 'We can't talk to you,' he said.

'Can't or won't? Oh, come on, this really isn't a prison camp,' she wheedled. 'You have freedom of speech the same as anyone else.'

Freedom of speech for you to misquote. My guard was up, as you can imagine.

'OK, forget yesterday. How much does the school keep you informed about the investigation into Lily's death or do they leave you completely in the dark?' One of the reporters lurking in the background rushed a question at us both.

No comment.

'What prompted the request for a second pathologist's report?'

'When are they going to hold Lily's funeral?'

No comment. No comment.

'Moving back to my original topic,' Emily said. 'What's the students' reaction to Paige's accident and do they know yet if she's likely to pull through? It *was* an accident, wasn't it?'

My stomach churned and I had to walk away fast, leaving Jack to Emily's tender mercies and heading back towards the lake so I didn't have to listen to any more of this. Only one of the reporters followed me – a small guy in a grey knitted hat and a red North Face jacket.

'You're the kid in the car with Anna Earle,' he said.

I walked faster. He ran to head me off just as I came out of the wood.

'Do you have special links with the Earles? How was

Anna?' he asked. 'Did you know they hospitalized her again the day after her visit here?'

'Again?' I echoed.

'Yeah, didn't you know? She was diagnosed with major depression back in 2003. Her only daughter dies and she goes into meltdown for a second time. Her husband sectioned her two days ago.'

I shook my head and tried deep breaths to deal with the panic battering at my rib cage.

'It's unofficial,' the guy in the red jacket said. 'Earle took out a super injunction for us not to report it – not in the public interest, blah blah.'

'Which hospital?'

'Private clinic, top secret.'

'Thanks,' I muttered, side-stepping him and breaking into a sprint across the lawn.

The reporter didn't follow me. Instead he went to join the rest of the pack in the woods. When I reached the safety of the quad, Tom had snuck ahead and was already waiting for me.

'Finally!' Tom said.

I'd smuggled him up to my room where we could talk in private. Lily's empty bed was in one corner, stripped of its sheet and duvet, Paige's opposite. Her bed looked as if she'd just stepped out of it and had gone to take a shower.

My heart was still pounding and I was looking out of the window to check we hadn't been followed. 'OK, Tom – what is it? What do you want?'

'The cops!' he said.

'Lily's bag!' I retorted.

'You told them.'

'Of course I told them. What did you expect?'

He paced up and down, tall, skinny and raw-boned. 'Without even telling me, sneaking behind my back.'

'What did you expect?' I repeated. 'Tom – that was *Lily's* bag!'

'I didn't know that, did I? Not until the cops came knocking.'

'How could you *not* know?'

'Because I didn't look. It was just there.' He let out a long breath, like a balloon deflating and suddenly there was no anger, no energy left. 'Jesus, Alyssa.'

'Wait,' I said, pacing from the window to the door. 'You're saying the bag had been in your hallway for weeks and you had no idea it belonged to Lily? Didn't anybody else notice it – your parents, for instance?'

Tom shook his head then changed his mind and nodded. 'My mum – actually. She took a look and asked me how come a girl's bag was left lying around. I said I had absolutely no clue. I was busy at the time – it went right over my head.'

'Tom, I don't know – do I believe you?' How scatty and haphazard could the Walsingham family be?

'It happens.' He needed to sit down, and chose the edge of Lily's bed. 'A lot of people sleep over at my place when my parents are away for the weekend. They're forever leaving stuff.'

'But this isn't just any old bag, this is Lily's bag.'

'How many times – I did not know that!'

'Did the police take it?' For fingerprints, DNA evidence and so on.

He nodded.

'You want to know what Jack and I did after we saw it in your house?'

'The night I saved your life,' he reminded me with a hollow laugh. 'Yeah, Alyssa, tell me why you didn't go straight to the cops.'

'We wanted to be sure. Jack came back to your place and snuck a look. He found Lily's phone.'

'*Then* you went to the cops!'

My turn to nod and feel the energy drain away. I sat on the chair beside my bed. 'Every single message on that phone was from Jayden,' I told him. '"Lily, please see me, please answer me, don't walk away." But she did.'

'How's Paige,' Tom asked suddenly, as if this could possibly be a more cheerful, less confusing topic.

'She's in a coma. She's probably got an aneurysm and definitely splinters of bone lodged in her brain.'

'Jesus.'

'I know. Listen, Tom, if you told the police what you just told me, you're probably in the clear.'

'Like you said yourself – will they believe me?'

'Yes, if it's the truth.'

'Well, thanks for that touching belief in the British judiciary system.'

'How does sarcasm help?'

'It doesn't.'

'It has to be true because, when you think about it, if you'd been involved in Lily's disappearance you wouldn't have been stupid enough to leave her bag lying around. The cops will work that out eventually.'

He took a sharp breath and sat upright, waited to hear what else I had to say.

'So how did it get there? Think hard – did anyone call at your place the day Lily vanished?'

'I have been thinking and, yeah, some kids came round after school.'

'Including Jayden?'

'Yes.'

'Micky, Alex?'

'Yeah. We were planning the usual end-of-term five-a-side tournament. Inter-school stuff – Ainslee versus St Jude's.'

'So who else? Anyone from here?'

'Luke was there,' he said. 'And Jack.'

'And?'

'Harry,' he decided. 'Any one of those could have dumped the evidence on me, couldn't they?'

chapter eleven

'What do you mean, you gave Emily Archer your number?' My voice rose a couple of octaves.

It was Sunday morning and Jack had received a text. He told me who it was from, on our way to visit Paige in hospital. 'She asked me for it and I gave it to her – yesterday, while you were talking to Tom.'

We were cycling through the Bottoms when Jack and I had this, our first major fight. Christmas lights winked in the daytime gloom around the windows of the Bridge Inn. A snow scene had been badly painted on the steamed-up window of the Squinting Cat as I put on my brakes and squealed to a halt outside St Michael's and All Angels church.

'Christ, Jack, you *gave* her your number!'

'Calm down, Alyssa. It's not a crime.'

'D'Arblay and Saint Sam will kill you if they find out.'

'Well, they won't unless *you* tell them.'

'So why?' I asked him, raising it by another whole octave.

'Because she asked me.'

'You already said that. Really, Jack – why?'

'Because it could be useful.'

'Who to? You or her?'

'Us,' he said sullenly. Jack in a bad mood is not something

you often see. He gets a mono-brow from frowning, he stops looking at you and develops a forward slouch.

'It's not useful to me,' I argued. 'Why the hell would I want to be in contact with any of those low-life ambulance chasers?'

'Chill, Alyssa,' he sighed. (*'Chill, my friend,' were Paige's last words to me before the attack. I hear them again, see her smile and wink.*) 'It's only my phone number. Don't you even want to know what the message says?'

'No, not remotely interested.' I steered my bike up on to the pavement and leaned it against the churchyard wall, peeled off my hat and scarf, and told myself to stop acting like a four year old.

'I thought we were on our way to the hospital,' he muttered, staying astride his bike. 'Can't we deal with this some other time?'

'What else did you give Emily, besides your number?' It was no good, I was still snarled up in nursery-school stuff.

Jack was so disappointed in me that he cycled ten metres down the road then stopped and threw a comment over his shoulder. 'Just trust me, Alyssa – OK?'

I wheeled my bike to join him. 'Not unless you explain to me why you wanted to keep in contact with Emily Archer.'

He spelled it out for me once more. 'She's a journalist – they find out useful stuff – it's their job.'

'Don't patronize me.'

'Don't *make* me patronize you. Are we going to see Paige or not?'

I swallowed hard then suddenly choked up. 'Sorry – I

don't know what we're doing or where we're going. I don't know anything.'

Jack observed my tears. He didn't rush to get off his bike and wrap his arms round me.

'I can't stand that woman,' I admitted.

He nodded and waited.

'I don't like her texting you behind my back.'

'It would only be behind your back if I didn't tell you about it, and I did.'

'True.' Slowly, reluctantly I came round from my preschool state and got my mind back in gear. 'OK, so what did she say?'

Jack blinked and looked relieved. 'She says the police checked the reg of the Toyota and identified the owner.'

I stared at him.

'It was registered with a guy in Balsall Heath, Birmingham. He reported it stolen ten days ago. The cops just found it abandoned in the Cineworld car park in Ainslee.'

Impressive investigative stuff. Emily Archer was good – even I had to admit.

Jack and I made it to the Queen Elizabeth Hospital ICU just as visiting hours began – not that the nurses were sticking to official hours in Paige's case because they'd let Mr and Mrs Kelly stay at her bedside twenty-four/seven.

'No change,' her mum reported wearily as they made way for me and Jack. 'We have to see that as a good thing, don't we?'

She meant that the medics weren't saying that Paige

had got worse, but Mr Kelly didn't seem to share his wife's optimism. In fact, he gave a small shake of his head as he led her away.

It was awful to see Paige still lying there. I'd seen her forty-eight hours earlier, hooked up to monitors and an oxygen supply, but at that time we were all still in shock, hardly able to take in what had happened. Today I really let the effect of her injuries sink in. Machines beeped and clicked while tubes connected to her body appeared from under a pale blue sheet in a spaghetti tangle, leading to saline drips and blood-transfusion equipment. Meanwhile the patient lay with eyes closed and stents inserted into her partly shaved head.

'You can talk to her,' a nurse told us when he came to check the monitors and make some adjustments.

'Can she hear us?' Jack asked in a whisper.

'Possibly. We don't know for sure. Anyway, why not give it a go?'

What do you say to someone you know well who doesn't look like the same person any more? You'll have realized by now that Paige is unstoppable, in your face and funny. She gallops across fields and charges over fences, heaves heavy tack and polishes bits and bridles. She isn't afraid of anything. But now, on this hospital bed, that 'she' just isn't there.

'Hey, Paige,' I said. 'It's me – Alyssa.'

A machine beeped; a jagged green line on a screen showed the erratic rhythm of her heart.

'Don't worry – you're doing great,' I murmured. 'They're

taking really good care of you.'

What did the various charts hanging from the end of her bed mean? Where did the tubes lead and what exactly did the tiny stents drilled through her skull do? For the first time I noticed massive bruising above Paige's left ear, extending up and back across the shaven area of her skull.

'You're strong,' I whispered as I stroked the back of her hand. 'You can do this.'

Another nurse came and smiled at us as she added the latest information to one of the charts – the reassuring, meaningless smile of a professional care-giver.

'Mistral is fine,' I told Paige, and for a moment I thought I saw a flicker of response – a tiny movement of her eyelids as though Paige had tried but failed to open her eyes. 'There's not a scratch on him. Guy and Harry are looking after him, giving him all his favourite treats.'

The nurse smiled again, then went on to the patient in the next bed.

'Everyone is missing you. They all said to say hi – Zara, Luke, Hooper. Especially Luke. They say to get well soon.'

Jack took a deep breath then got up from his chair and stood by the end of the bed.

'St Jude's isn't the same without you charging around everywhere telling us all what to do, making your sarky comments. Life's boring without you, Paige,' I murmured, and stroked her hand, then lapsed into silence until the first nurse came back.

'That's probably enough for now,' he told me gently.

So Jack and I said goodbye to Paige and tiptoed out, walking hand in hand down the corridor towards the lift.

Hospital parking is a nightmare. The Queen Elizabeth has an electronic barrier system that only lets a car in when another one leaves so there's always a massive queue out on to Longland Avenue, which is where Jack and I spotted D'Arblay and Harry in D'Arblay's white Range Rover as we set off on our bikes.

D'Arblay saw us and wound down his window to ask how Paige was.

'The same,' Jack told him.

'Well, we'll soon see for ourselves,' the bursar said, tapping his forefinger against the steering wheel.

Harry didn't say anything, sitting in the front passenger seat, speaking on his phone and nursing a bunch of Tesco lilies with the price ticket still on.

'They won't let you take those into the ICU,' Jack warned.

Harry frowned, checked his watch then stared straight ahead as the line of cars inched forward.

'So maybe they will – what do I know?' Jack muttered, deciding to cut across the car park and round the side of the hospital to avoid the busy main road. His route took us across the staff car park where we came across someone else we knew. I was still thinking it was weird that Harry of all people had brought Paige flowers when I heard Jack swear under his breath.

'What?' I had to brake suddenly and stop for an old red

Mondeo reversing out of a space without looking. Micky Cooke sat in the front passenger seat beside an older, look-alike driver, presumably his morgue-worker dad. Micky was speaking on the phone.

Jack swore again. He knew Micky had been in on the ambush in the JD workshop, along with scary-girl Ursula and Alex Driffield – reason number one that Jack wasn't happy. Reason number two was that Micky was on the list of people who could have dumped Lily's bag at Tom's house.

'Leave it,' I insisted as Micky came off the phone then spotted us. There was one other passenger sitting in the back seat, also talking on his phone, so we were outnumbered. Anyway we had no choice because Cooke senior seemed to be in a big hurry. The Mondeo spewed out a plume of black exhaust fumes as he revved and shot forward towards the exit.

Jack and I cycled out of town under fast-moving, grey clouds and a cold drizzle of rain. Neither of us felt like talking. I was glad to be using up some energy as we cycled against the wind.

In the silence I let my thoughts drift from the stupid fight I'd had with Jack about Emily Archer to the info she'd given him about the owner of the green Toyota, which took me back to my snowy close encounter outside the church.

I'd phoned for the taxi, the gritting lorry had trundled by. A red car had crawled in its wake. It had turned into a driveway just off Main Street – not just red, but specifically a red Mondeo.

'Jack, wait!' I called now, but he was twenty metres ahead of me and the roar of the wind drowned my voice.

A red Mondeo. I repeated that to myself in a couple of ways – emphasis on 'red', switch emphasis to 'Mondeo' – while realizing that I hadn't seen the driver when he'd got out of the car and slammed the door and, anyway, it might not be important. There must be thousands of the superseded rust buckets gasping their last, environmentally unfriendly breaths on Britain's roads, and in any case the driver hadn't been involved in what had happened next. No – what I had to focus on was the Toyota edging out of Meredith Lane, the rider dressed in black leathers, crouching low over the handlebars. In my mind's eye I was again able to see the registration plate clear as anything – KD58PDO, the black helmet with its inbuilt visor, a split-second glimpse of the eyes behind it when the rider mounted the pavement and was caught in the glare of a street lamp – ten metres away, five metres and accelerating. They were grey eyes, wide open and fringed with dark lashes.

'Jack!' I yelled above the wind.

'I love you.'

The words came out of the blue. Jack said them after we'd got back from the hospital in, of all places, the Boris-bike store outside the sports centre.

'Yes,' I said. Meaning, Yes, me too, vice versa, I love you.

Meaning a million whirling thoughts and feelings that were impossible to express.

It's never like they show it in the rom coms – *Four Weddings and a Funeral, Notting Hill, Love Actually*. But, anyway, the words were said and the feeling was mutual.

We jammed the front wheels of our bikes into their stands and faced each other, bedraggled and windswept, cold and scared.

'I do,' he whispered.

'I know. I don't know what to say.'

'Just kiss me.'

So I did and nothing mattered in that moment except that Jack and I had each other.

He was the first to pull back. 'This guy on the Toyota is the same as the one in the stable yard – you're sure?'

I nodded. 'I remembered the eyes.'

Jack shuddered then flung an arm round my shoulders. He didn't kiss me again, but instead walked me quickly into the sports centre. 'It scares the shit out of me.'

'I love you,' I repeated among the basketballs and weights, the gym mats and rowing machines.

It was seriously unromantic, one hundred per cent sincere.

Up in the mezzanine coffee bar, looking down on Jack and his coach, my heart soared.

He loves me. I love him.

We'd gone to Tom's party then fallen out over nothing. We'd been in lessons together, eaten meals, walked and cycled, fought and stumbled our way towards love.

He, Jack Cavendish, is in love with me, Alyssa Stephens.

I watched him play tennis with the balance, coordination and grace of a dancer. He pivoted and turned, ran and stretched, leaped and swung with total drive and focus. I loved him for that, and for being honest and for putting up with me when I acted like a spoilt brat and for understanding that it was because I'd lost Lily, and now Paige was lying in the ICU and we didn't in our heart of hearts believe she would make it.

'Hey, Alyssa.' Hooper broke into my thoughts. He sat down opposite me, with his back to the tennis courts – the one person I didn't expect to see anywhere near a ball or a racket.

I was pleased to see him, as always. 'Hey, Hooper. Did you sign up for weight training?'

'Yeah, funny. No, actually, I was looking for you because I've got something else to tell you.'

'Go ahead.'

'No. First of all, how's Paige?'

I shrugged. 'Nobody's saying anything. They're keeping her in a coma until the swelling in her brain goes down.'

'How did she look?'

I shook my head, unable to go into details about tubes, stents, bags and screens. 'It was like she wasn't there. Her mum and dad stay with her most of the time. We saw D'Arblay and Harry there too.'

'I heard D'Arblay press-ganged Harry into visiting.' Hooper pushed his glasses further up his nose then closed his eyes. He opened them again, forcing himself to change the subject and get on with the original reason for him being there. 'I did some digging and found out more about Eleanor Bond.'

'Anything interesting?' If I didn't sound fascinated it was because 1938 was a long time ago and I had a lot of current stuff on my mind.

'About her mother – you know she wasn't mentioned in the newspaper report and it turns out that was because she wasn't actually around at the time.'

'Why? Where was she?'

'Stuck in Vienna.'

It wasn't what I was expecting and Hooper now had my full attention. 'Go on.'

'The mother, Simone Bond, was Jewish. She'd flown to Austria on family business. The Bonds had an engineering factory in Birmingham and they'd been supplying engine parts to various European car manufacturers, including the VW Beetle factory in Berlin, but she got caught up in Hitler's takeover of Vienna in the spring of 1938.'

'Wrong place at the wrong time,' I commented. I knew about the rise of the Nazis in the 1930s, can even quote you an extract from *Mein Kampf* and Hitler's vision of the Aryan race – *Slim and slender, swift, tough – we must raise a new man!*

'The Nazis went into Vienna and rounded up every Jew they could find,' Hooper went on. 'Eleanor never made it back to England.'

'Never?' I repeated.

'No. Nobody in Austria was going anywhere at that time,

especially if they were Jewish. They think she got sent to a concentration camp on the German border and starved to death, so by the end of 1938 Edward Bond had lost his only daughter and his wife. No wonder he became a recluse.'

'And apart from it being really sad and a long time ago, what are you thinking, Jack?'

'I'm not sure. Something about this is getting to me – maybe it's just psycho man Hitler and his creation of the perfect Aryan race. Millions of people were persecuted and the guy who founded this school was directly caught up in that.'

'Really sad,' I repeated. 'But so what?'

'Anyway, I'm going to dig some more,' Hooper decided, getting up to quit the sports centre and return to his natural element – the new library with its banks of computer screens and access to infinite knowledge.

Soon after this I left my Jack with his tennis coach and went for a walk in the woods to clear my head, hoping that this time I wouldn't run into the young journalist of the year.

'Hey, Alyssa, are you skipping lunch?' Zara called from the entrance to the quad. She was with Luke and Harry, but took a detour to talk with me.

'What's the latest on Paige?'

'Ask Harry,' I told her. 'He visited the hospital after me and Jack .'

'Harry – how was Paige?' Zara called.

Harry shook his head.

'Come over here. Talk properly.'

194

My least favourite equestrian shuffled across, hands in pockets. Luke followed. 'They said Paige was too sick – they wouldn't let D'Arblay and me on to the ward. Family only.'

I groaned inwardly, but tried not to let either Luke or Zara know that this must mean Paige had deteriorated. 'She's a fighter,' I told him. 'We all know that.'

I was searching for more of the right phrases when I noticed for the first time that Harry's right eye was bruised and swollen and his bottom lip was cut. 'What happened to you?' I asked.

'Nothing. I walked into a door,' he mumbled.

'Yeah – a door called Jayden,' Zara mocked, making Harry swear and storm off ahead of her and Luke.

'Harry and Jayden had a fight?' I asked. 'When? Where? Why?'

Zara was obviously hungry and in need of lunch so she kept her answers brief. 'Last night. In town. Don't know.'

'But I saw Harry earlier today – at the hospital.' Then again, I'd only had a view of the left side of Harry's face as he sat in the passenger seat next to the bursar. 'He didn't say anything.'

'Well, you wouldn't advertise it if you came off worst in a fight with Jayden. And everyone does come off worst, including Harry even though Harry's twice Jayden's size. You should see the rest of him – his ribs, his knuckles, his knees – all bruised and busted to hell.'

Hand on my heart, I couldn't say I was sorry – not after Harry had galloped Franklin right at me and almost knocked me over – but I was puzzled. And the mystery of this scrap between Harry and Jayden was what stayed at the front of my mind as I split from Zara and Luke then walked on through the grounds, skirting the last patches of melting snow and hurrying towards the trees. So much so that I marched straight on and out the other side, over the stream and across fields into Chartsey Bottom with only one thing in mind – I had to find Jayden.

First I tried his house in Upper Chartsey.

'You're joking me,' Ursula snarled when she answered the door, before she slammed it in my face.

No luck there, then.

So I went down to the Bottoms and asked for Jayden at the JD workshop.

'Not here, love.' This was Alex's bald dad, speaking from the oil-stained service pit.

Then Alex came out of the office and confirmed it. 'I haven't seen Jayden all week,' he told me.

'Wasn't he in school?'

'Nope.'

'Did you know he and Harry Embsay had a fight?'

'Yep.'

'What about?'

Alex shrugged and offered me a piece of gum as he walked me out into the street. 'I'll tell him you were looking for him – if I see him.'

'Thanks.'

'For what?'

'For being nice all of a sudden.'

Alex blushed. 'I suppose you want a sorry from me after last time? Well, I am – I'm sorry.'

Noticing the two bikes from St Jude's propped against the wall, I asked him if they were fixed.

'Ready to go. Just waiting for someone from St Jude's to collect them.'

'I'll collect one now,' I decided. That way I could cover more ground in my search for Jayden. 'By the way, Alex . . .'

He stepped back in fake alarm. 'Whoa, when you say "by the way" I know it isn't. In fact, this is where I feel the knife go in, right between my ribs.'

'OK, yeah – it's important.'

'Aargh!' Alex staggered and pretended to fall. 'I knew it.'

'Listen to me. You didn't by any chance notice someone leaving a bag at Tom's house – the night Lily . . . the night you lot met to arrange the next five-a-side tournament?'

'Aargh, shit!' Clutching his stomach, Alex staggered out on to the pavement. 'Right in the guts.'

'Seriously – did you?'

'Seriously – no. And I do know the reason you're asking.'

'The police already came calling?'

'Zap! Kerpow!'

And Alex told me he'd had to give details of who else was at Tom's house that night, and now they were working their way down that list, taking fingerprints and DNA samples, matching them up with evidence on the bag.

'What's the problem? This should be right up your street, Alex – all the *Silent Witness* stuff.'

'Yep, except my dad went mental. He threatened to kick me out.'

'For something you *didn't* do? Or I presume you didn't do?'

'Yeah, but that's how he is – old-school strict. A knock on the door from the cops brings shame on the family, blah blah. Anyhow, from now on I've got to keep my nose snot-free and that means keeping my head down and staying in school even during my free periods, not hanging out with the wrong crowd, working with him in the workshop in my free time.'

'Sounds like you'll have lots of fun,' I sighed, ready to take a bike and carry on looking for Jayden.

'Yeah – thanks, Alyssa.'

'You're welcome – any time.' The sarcasm between us was heavy as lead.

Alex stuck his hands in his hoodie pockets (black Nike) and with a sudden change of tone from sarcastic to genuine said, 'Alyssa, if you really want to know where Jayden is right now, he's probably walking Bolt on Hereward Ridge.'

'Seriously?'

'Yeah, seriously. He does that most Sundays. Don't tell him I told you.'

chapter twelve

Cycling all the way up to the Ridge told me I wasn't nearly as fit as I thought I was and gave me plenty of time to wonder why Alex had had a change of heart.

When you think it through, it was definitely guilty conscience over the time he, Micky and Ursula had threatened me in defence of their buddy, Jayden. After all, bullying probably didn't come as naturally to him, or to Micky for that matter, as it did to scary Ursula.

Anyway, I panted up the last few hundred metres, keeping my head busy with theories about Alex so that I didn't leave room for darker thoughts. I saved those for the wee small hours, the nightmare moments when Lily's ghost came screeching through the bedroom walls like those witches of my childhood dreams. Lily staring at me, pleading for help.

Eventually I came to the brow of the hill where I got off the bike and stared back down into the valley. My breath rose like steam into the cold, grey air.

I stood in total silence, wondering in which direction stick boy might choose to walk stick dog. Way below, cars crawled along Ainslee Road like small, shiny beetles. Above my head, rooks rose from the bare trees. To my left, halfway down the hill, stood Upwood House, a Georgian mansion and National Trust property in its big, artificially levelled and landscaped garden. To my right was a stand of ash trees where the cawing parliament of rooks eventually settled. I looked in all directions then decided to follow a bridleway sign towards the ruins of a thirteenth-century Cistercian abbey nestled on the lower slopes of the next valley. I got on the bike again and started pedalling bumpily downhill.

Ten minutes later I was in the grounds of Ripley Abbey and wondering if Alex had made a fool of me.

'He's having a laugh,' I muttered as I gazed at deserted hillocks and hummocks, piles of ancient stones and the odd wall crumbling but still standing after seven centuries of winds and rain. The only part of the building left intact was a row of shadowy cloisters. I checked it out before wheeling the bike through a crumbling gothic arch towards a river that snaked through the valley bottom, all the time looking for signs of recent human activity – anything at all: a crumpled crisp packet, an empty can, footprints in the mud.

Caw! Caw! Even the rooks laughed at me from their giddy heights.

Then Bolt charged along the riverbank, teeth bared.

'Down!' I yelled, putting the bike between me and the Staffie and thrusting the frame into his snarling face.

But he only took orders from one master and that definitely wasn't me. He growled and snarled, crouched, leaped, barked then snarled and snapped some more. The bike didn't seem like it was a good enough defence so I looked for places to hide – behind a pile of stones, up a grassy hillock or some worn stone steps leading nowhere. Finally, still using the bike as a shield, I turned towards the river and saw Jayden standing calmly mid-river, perched on one of thirty or so stepping stones used by the old Cistercian monks.

'Call your dog off!' I yelled.

Jayden didn't move. He let the swift, strong, black current flow around him, watched me suffer.

'Stay down, Bolt!' I cried, driving the bike's front wheel straight at him. He ducked out of reach, teeth bared, spittle dribbling from his mouth.

'Jayden, for God's sake!'

Stick Boy moved at last, stepping from one worn, moss-covered stone to the next, balancing like a high-wire performer, arms stretched wide. The wind caught his unzipped jacket and made it billow like a sail.

Burly Bolt barrelled downhill to the water's edge, gave a throaty bark and trundled back. He repeated this three times as I tried and failed to escape. Jayden stopped two steps from dry land.

'Jayden!' The dog had me cornered against a heap of medieval stones. The look in his eyes said, 'Kill!'

Stick boy smiled and jumped clean over the final stepping stone, made a crunch landing on the gravel bank. 'Down, Bolt,' he said quietly.

Vicious Bolt stopped everything he'd been doing and lay quiet as a lamb. There must have been a switch inside his head, activated by the sound of his master's voice. But his brownish-amber eyes were still trained on me and my bike, ready for Jayden to flick the next switch.

'Alyssa,' Jayden began casually. *What are you doing here?* hung unspoken in the ancient air, whispering through the arches, along the dripping cloisters.

'That dog is seriously going to hurt someone,' I gasped.

He nodded.

'He's not going to attack me again, is he?'

'Not unless I tell him. Anyway, what do you want?'

As far as Jayden and I were concerned, we were done with the pleasantries long ago. 'Why did you and Harry fight?' I asked outright.

'Who says we did?' Shrugging and slouching up the bank, past the boulders towards the shadowy cloisters, Jayden expected me to follow. 'Stay, Bolt,' he muttered.

The dog watched me go, eyes darting after me. *Kill!*

'Someone gave him a black eye and a busted lip,' I insisted. 'It's on record that the someone was you.'

'He's lucky that's all he got.'

I was staring at Jayden's back, trailing along three steps behind. 'It wasn't. You damaged his ribs, knees, knuckles – you want me to go on?'

He turned and smiled. 'It turns out Harry isn't as tough as he looks.'

I sighed then – wait for it – here comes my most predictable question. 'It was about Lily again, wasn't it?'

'For Jesus's sake.'

'It was. With you, everything comes back to Lily. You

didn't move on.' In spite of being dumped by her, in spite of scary, multiple face-piercings Ursula.

Jayden stopped but didn't turn. He put his arm out and traced his forefinger up and down the nearest stone pillar, threw back his head and studied the uncanny civil-engineering achievements of the ancient, Cistercian monks.

'The cops finally got the pathologist's second report,' he said in a flat voice.

The news hit me like a physical blow to the chest. 'Not good news?'

'Brace yourself.'

'Jayden, for God's sake!'

'We're talking mutilation.' His eyes bored into me.

'Mutilation?'

'Deliberate. Not accidental.'

Silence enveloped us. I don't know how long it took for me to understand. In the end I just repeated what Jayden had said. 'Someone deliberately mutilated Lily's body?'

Jayden nodded. 'It turns out that one of Lily's teeth was missing.'

A tooth! This was so not what I'd expected. If I was thinking anything, it was that maybe there was a cut, a flesh wound, something similar.

'Back tooth – molar, bottom right, with the socket gaping open.'

'Don't – I don't want to hear any more!'

'Sorry, I thought you needed to know.'

'It's just too . . . nasty.'

'Perverted?'

'Yes.' I leaned against the pillar and tried to take a deep breath to steady myself.

Jayden's voice didn't alter – it was a monotone drained of emotion. 'So did Lily go to the dentist for a tooth extraction the week she died?'

'I don't know, Jayden – no, she didn't! She would have told us. It would have been a big drama.'

'Which means the pathologist is right – the tooth was taken out *after* she died,' he muttered.

The shock got to me and I felt sick. 'We have to find out who took it and why.'

'Right! If we knew that we'd have all the answers – is that what you mean? The guy in charge of the investigation . . .'

'Inspector Cole.'

'. . . maybe he already knows who took it?'

'I doubt it.' I said. 'But they're not sitting on their arses doing nothing. They're starting to collect forensic evidence – DNA, fingerprints – from the bag Lily packed the day she disappeared. You know they found it at Tom's house?'

Jayden didn't answer. Instead he grunted and stayed with his new favourite topic. 'The tooth – Harry didn't seem to have any answers either.'

'Good God, Jayden – you challenged Harry Embsay about Lily's missing tooth? That's the same as saying you think he killed her!'

'He swears he hasn't got it.' Still no emotion, no direct eye contact as Jayden ran his fingers over the rough, cold stone.

'Why? Why would he have Lily's tooth? You think he's

keeping it in a little jar somewhere – as a souvenir? In a drawer, on a shelf, hanging on a chain round his neck?'

Jayden didn't react. 'Me and Harry moved on to the tooth subject after we dealt with the who's-the-daddy topic.'

'Oh, Jesus!' I didn't know what to say or to think, except that it was possible that this time Jayden had totally lost it. OK, so I've said before that Harry Embsay isn't my type. Remember how he blamed everyone the second he saw Paige lying badly injured in the stable yard, how he was always throwing his weight around, even way back when Saint Sam addressed the whole sixth form in the new library?

'What's he going to tell us that we don't already know?' Zara asked.

'Search me,' Harry said, huffing and puffing. 'But it had better be worth dragging me out of bed for.'

Harry is big and sulky and doesn't stay out of your personal space enough for my liking. He's athletic without any grace and it's brute strength, not balance and finesse, that allows him to yank on the reins and control Franklin when he gallops him through the woods and almost knocks me down.

'He denied everything,' Jayden told me in a flat, slightly slurred voice, speaking without moving his lips as if he didn't really want to let go of the words.

'Of course he did!' I spluttered. 'Lily wouldn't . . .'

Jayden tilted his head to one side then turned to look at me from under hooded lids. He waited.

'She wouldn't . . .' I began again.

Another memory wormed itself out of the deep recesses of my brain. It reappeared verbatim – a conversation with Paige, in our room, sitting on our unmade beds.

Maybe the baby was a result of a one-night stand – this had been my theory.

Unshockable Paige had been shocked and defended her dead friend's honour. 'Lily didn't do one night stands,' she'd insisted.

Then maybe a holiday romance – a random waiter or beach bum?

'Lily didn't go on holiday this year.' *Paige wouldn't even listen to my idle speculation as we tried to work out who was the baby's father.*

'She didn't?' No luxury yacht, no penthouse suite overlooking the beach?

'No. She was in the UK, drifting, doing her own thing, staying away from her dad.'

'The tyrant.'

'Yeah,' *Paige said – the pre-accident Paige, the invincible Paige.* 'She came to see me ride in the Burghley Horse Trials. That was late August. Harry Embsay and Guy Simons were there too.'

I drew in a sharp breath then let it out, felt my head swim as I computed what this might mean. 'Harry – it could've been . . . Wait, Jayden – I'm not sure!'

He stared at me then started to walk jerkily towards the daylight at the far end of the cloisters. Stones dripped centuries of black slime; his footsteps echoed under the arches.

I ran after him and grabbed him by the arm. 'What exactly was Harry's answer?'

'He swore he hadn't screwed Lily,' Jayden said as he broke free. 'He shouldn't have talked about her that way, like she was nothing, just a piece of meat. That's the reason I hit him.'

And kicked and punched him, smashed his fists into his face, his feet into his ribs. I could definitely relate to why Jayden had done that.

'Come!' he told Bolt.

The gleaming-eyed dog was at his heels in an instant. They walked away from the ruins along the dead riverbank, stick man and stick dog.

I went back to school, found Jack in the sports centre and told him every detail of my conversation with Jayden.

Whenever I paused for breath, he repeated the same two small words – 'A tooth?'

'It's so weird,' I sighed. 'I mean – *why*?'

'Does a psychopath have to have a reason?' Jack wondered.

'No, you're right.' But the idea scared me. If there was no logic attached to the action, how could the police or Jack or me or anyone sane follow the clues? Holding Jack's hand across the table in the mezzanine coffee shop, I felt we were Hansel and Gretel scattering crumbs in the forest, using it as a trail to follow to get back home, only to find that birds had come along and eaten every last one.

Children lost in the forest – that was me and Jack.

*

Then, during a free double period next day, after I'd watched the morning headlines on TV – New Tragedy Strikes at Top Public School/Olympic Hopeful in Hospital Intensive Care – I pulled myself together and decided to slide Lily's diary from its hiding place under Paige's mattress and take it to the old library where I could find a quiet corner to reread it among the newspapers and magazines.

I handled the diary carefully, stroking its dog-eared pale blue cover before I opened it at random.

February 14th – Sent you-know-who a Valentine's card. ☺ Didn't get one back. Got one from Tom W and one from H. ☹ A not doing well so they changed her tablets. ☹☹

I read between the lines, worked out that she'd sent Jayden a Valentine's card and received one from Tom Walsingham (the only Tom W I'd heard of around here) and one from Harry maybe. She wasn't interested in either. 'A' was her mum, I guessed, taking anti-depressants that didn't suit her.

April 1st – P swears L is R-Patz lookalike – hah! I say J is more movie/rock-star material than L – think Joaquim Phoenix/Kurt Cobain. P played April Fool's joke on L – apple-pie bed, extremely juvenile. He was not amused. Met J in Ainslee – shh! ☺☺ 🧍

Interpretation – P is Paige and L is obviously Luke. Lily has hit on the stick man hieroglyph for Jayden, her secret, guilty passion.

On April 20th the stick dog made its debut, together with:

Walked with J and B on Hereward Ridge.

May 24th – Quiet time at J's house. Amazing.

Followed by the rectangle with four legs – definitely a bed to mark the first time Lily and Jayden had sex, I was convinced. And I noticed it appeared often through the rest of May and all of June, with snippets of information about J's life – his abusive father now living in a homeless hostel in Bristol, his love of football (Everton) and his dog. He found Bolt in an animal rescue centre and took him home without asking his mum. Bolt lived in the garden shed for three months until Jayden's mum relented and finally allowed him into the house.

July 2nd – Met J after school. LOVE HIM!!!

And just so there was no room for doubt –

July 4th – Met J after school – LOVE HIM!!!

Then the row of red hearts linked by the letters of Jayden's name and Am thinking of getting tattoo around ankle, etcetera.

The same entry had the reference to Lily's phone call with her mum, when the tyrant broke off their conversation – which made more sense now that I knew how sick Anna actually was. I envisaged how worried Lily must have been about her mum and how Robert Earle had done his usual thing of ranting and dishing out orders for what he might have thought were good reasons (to protect Lily, Anna or both), but which turned out to be lousy psychology because it ended up with Lily permanently hating him and Anna in a psychiatric hospital.

I flicked forward to September 5th – when the circle and dot drawing appeared for the first time – the date Lily wanted to be the day of conception, but with a question mark and written some time after the event in a different coloured ink. Then back to late August, where I read and reread each entry.

August 22nd – P's house. J texted me twelve times!!! ☺☺☺☺

August 23rd – P's house. Right now P hates L and loves Mistral. God, I despise horses – stupid, smelly crap machines!!! Only 5 texts from J today – MISS HIM!!! ☹ G and H arrived. The day just got ten times worse. ☹☹☹☹☹☹☹☹☹☹

August 24th – no entry. August 25th – no entry. How weird was that? I flicked back and forth through the diary and discovered that in the whole year she'd only missed one other day, right up until the day she disappeared. Yeah, that was definitely right – a gap on March 14th, which was marked The T's birthday – blank page – and now again for the two days when Guy Simons and Harry Embsay had stayed at Paige's house to watch her compete at Burghley. The two blank spaces told me absolutely nothing, or maybe everything, I needed to know.

A chime from the carriage clock on the mantelpiece of the gothic fireplace made me realize that I'd stayed in the old library longer than I'd planned, so I closed Lily's diary and slipped it into the front pocket of my bag, ready to sprint across the quad for my French conversation class with Justine. *'J'ai un problème, mademoiselle – un grand mystère. C'est Lily – le vingt-quatre d'août, the vingt-cinq d'août, elle n'a pas écrit son journal!'*

I was heading for the door when I came across D'Arblay speaking with Adam Earle in the European History section, a side annexe to the main building, where they obviously thought no one would interrupt them. I heard them just in time to backtrack and stay close without being seen.

'Yes, the new information in the pathologist's second report raises more questions than it answers,' D'Arblay was agreeing with what Adam had just said. 'I appreciate how difficult it must be for you and your parents.'

'Very frustrating,' Adam said. 'One part of me still says that this is a small, unexplained detail in an otherwise clear-cut case of suicide. But then of course I do understand that Inspector Cole has to investigate all possibilities.'

D'Arblay agreed again. 'The police have asked the hospital pathology department to double check their autopsy procedure, just in case there has been room for error.'

'An irregularity?' Adam surmised. 'Something procedural that might account for the missing tooth.'

'Exactly. In any case, Adam, please accept my deepest sympathy for the delay.'

'The family needs closure – my mother especially.'

'How *is* your mother?' D'Arblay made another cheesy attempt at deepest sympathy.

Adam didn't reply so I had to imagine a shrug or a shake of his head before he moved quickly on. 'The real reason I'm here, D'Arblay, is to offer you some reassurance over the question of funding for the school.'

'Ah yes.' The bursar was back in brisk business mode where he was totally at ease. 'That was an unfortunate incident. While we understand the personal pressure on your father at the present time, we still felt it wise to ask our lawyers to address the legal situation – in other words to study the original agreement between Robert Earle and the St Jude's Foundation. Of course the withdrawal of his generous donation would do great damage and we're hoping that in the cool light of day your father will reconsider.'

'That's why I'm here,' Adam assured him. 'To calm troubled waters.'

'Good, good,' D'Arblay murmured.

'I've looked into it myself and as a matter of fact there is no legally binding contract between my father and the school, but in spite of that I hope to persuade him that the obligation is a moral one.'

'Very good.' D'Arblay sounded less confident now that the media mogul's donation depended on his discovery of a sense of honour.

'Lily did well here at St Jude's,' Adam explained. 'I would say she even thrived.'

'Thank you, Adam.'

'She developed her artistic talents and she made good friends.'

'We all miss her.' (Cheesy again.)

It was so fake it made me want to puke all over the section of shelves containing books about the French Revolution. *We* do – *we* miss her! We feel it in our battered, bruised hearts. We don't just say the words!

'If only she could have kept her personal life on track,' Adam sighed, 'this terrible tragedy might never have happened.'

I pictured a nod, a sigh then back to business. 'So I can inform the principal that you'll work to secure the original agreement?'

'Tell him that I'll do my best.'

There was some handshaking and more murmuring before the two men emerged from the annexe and headed for the door. I stayed hidden until they'd left.

What now? I was already late for my French lesson – *'Je suis en retard. Je suis désolé, Mademoiselle Renoir'* – and I felt one of my sudden urges to talk to Adam Earle, the person behind the suit. I watched from a library window as he exchanged a final handshake with the bursar and walked slowly towards his car. Reckoning I still had time to intercept him, I left the library by a side door and sprinted towards the car park.

Adam was opening his car door as I slipped into the passenger seat.

'Alyssa!' he said in a way that suggested he expected trouble, but was ready to deal with it.

'Do you mind?' I said hurriedly, one eye on the journos at the gate. 'I thought we could talk.'

'Here?'

'No, while you're driving, if that's OK.'

He nodded and didn't say anything as I slid out of my seat and curled up on the floor. 'Why the cloak and dagger?' he asked once we were clear of the journalists and I was sitting normally again.

'I don't want to attract attention – it might not be good for my health.' I explained about the Toyota incident and the attack on Paige's horse.

Even Adam couldn't conceal his surprise. 'You say you're being threatened, intimidated – for what reason?'

'Maybe because they think we know too much.'

'"They"?'

'Whoever killed Lily.'

'*If* Lily was in fact murdered!' Adam's guard was up again as he drove along the familiar lane. 'I take it the police are following it up?'

'Yeah, they're trying to trace the guy who stole the Toyota and the kid with the Stanley knife, who it turns out is the same person.'

He reacted again – not in a big way, just by raising his eyebrows a notch. 'You're sure about that?'

'Yeah, I saw them both. His role is to scare us and he's definitely doing a good job.' *Too* good a job, with my roommate in intensive care. 'I don't think the plan involved actually hurting Paige – that was just the way it worked out.'

Adam stared at the narrow road ahead, evidently trying to block any normal, sympathetic response to the surprise news. His car tyres swished through deep puddles, throwing spray at the windscreen. 'This Toyota/knife guy – you're saying he's scared you might have a vital clue that could lead to my sister's killer?'

'I guess.'

'And do you?'

I paused for a long time, watching the windscreen wipers' metronome motion and wondering how far I could trust Lily's big bro. 'Paige and I were there the day Lily died, right up until she packed her bag and left,' I said in the end. 'Five days later we watched them pull her body from the lake. We've gone over and over it in our minds.'

'So if anyone can work out what happened it would be you and Paige?'

'But right now just me.' I thought again of Paige in the ICU, pictured the beeping, erratic graph of her heartbeat.

'You shouldn't be here,' Adam decided.

'In the car with you?'

'No – here at St Jude's. You should be at home while the police sort everything out.'

'That's exactly what Dr Webb said, and the bursar. They

both put pressure on me, but I refused to leave.'

Stopping at a T-junction, Adam turned left on to a long, straight Roman road running parallel to Hereward Ridge. 'I appreciate your loyalty and determination on Lily's behalf, Alyssa. But I agree with –'

'No,' I insisted. 'Lily would've done the same for me or Paige – *if.*'

'I hear you. If it had been one of you in the lake. But it wasn't. So where does that leave us with all this? Are the police anywhere near to finding an answer?'

'Not really.' This was me being realistic, watching the dreary, rhythmic to and fro of the wipers.

'So you're absolutely sure it has nothing to do with errors in the autopsy procedure?'

'How could it?'

Adam stared ahead along the straight, narrow road. 'You're saying it was murder, even though there were no other signs of violence?'

I seemed to be waiting forever for a non-automaton, behind-the-suit reaction. We were discussing the death of his sister, remember.

In the end it was like buses – you wait all day for one and two come along together.

'For Christ's sake!' Without warning Adam raised his fist and slammed it against the steering wheel. The car veered violently on to the wrong side of the road then swerved back again. He gripped the wheel until his knuckles turned white.

Where did that come from? And, by the way, thank God for seat belts.

He slammed on the brakes and punched on his hazard lights – the beginning of reaction number two. 'How long is it going to take to clear this mess up? How many more people have to suffer? First Lily, then you, Alyssa, now Paige.'

'And your mother,' I reminded him, which really broke down his robot defences.

Pulling up on the frozen verge of the Roman road, Adam slumped forward over the steering wheel. 'My family is falling apart. I don't think we can get through this!'

'I'm sorry,' I began.

But he shook his head and pulled himself upright. 'Anna is in hospital,' he told me more calmly.

'I know.' Even then I noticed all the small things – the fact that he called his mother by her first name and that he wore a ring on his wedding finger even though Lily had never mentioned a wife.

'She's convinced they'll never let her out, that she's in there for the rest of her life. She says she wants to die.'

'But it won't always be like this. They can treat her depression like they did before.'

This seemed to pull him back from the emotional brink. 'You knew about that too? Did Lily tell you?'

I shook my head. 'Lily didn't talk about Anna. It was in the press at the time it happened.'

'Yeah, that was ironic. The Earles own half the world's media, yet even pre Twitter we couldn't keep Anna's breakdown off the front pages.'

'I guess there are things that even you can't control.' I

didn't plan to be mean and after I'd said this I regretted it. After all, the guy was suffering enough.

Adam gave a hollow laugh. 'You know what Anna's done? She's only turned her back on the psychiatrists and gone religious on us. Yeah, right! She asked for them to let a rabbi visit the clinic and they said yes. Apparently she opened up and relived the events of the last few weeks with him – poor guy, it must have felt like being hit by an express train.'

'Your mother's Jewish?'

'Non-practising until this latest meltdown. I guess it's like a drowning man crying out for help . . .' When Adam realized what he'd just said, the simile proved too much and he broke down a second time. 'I'm sorry, but this latest thing with Anna – I wasn't expecting it. Honestly – not after how well she coped with the news of Lily being pregnant. Back in September she had the strength to stand up to my father. She said Lily should be allowed to keep the baby if that was what she wanted. All that mattered was that Lily should be happy.'

I remembered what Anna had told me – that Robert Earle was in favour of ending the pregnancy. 'He didn't agree?'

'You're kidding. He was still in Chicago but he went right ahead and fixed up for her to have an abortion. He wouldn't listen to Anna or Lily, just went ahead and made the arrangements.'

'And that's why he ordered Lily to come home – to have an abortion?'

'Yeah, and she obviously suspected what he'd planned.'

'That makes sense,' I agreed. 'But we think that she never really meant to get on the train. She just packed her bag and planned to disappear for good. That's what Paige and I worked out from the email she sent Jack.'

'So what happened? We know that she never even left the school grounds.'

'Sorry, I can't answer that.'

'Do you think she'd arranged one last meeting with the baby's father – the boy from the village? Is that what you're saying?'

Which is where I had to go over more of the ground I'd covered with Anna and explain to Adam that Jayden wasn't the daddy after all, that he'd really loved Lily and had wanted to be there for her regardless. Stick man wasn't the villain – it was someone else.

'And if it wasn't Jayden, who was it?' Adam asked with a touch of the familiar robotic detachment.

I didn't know this either, I confessed. Not yet. Not for sure.

'Give me a name.'

'I can't.'

You're reading this and thinking that the first name that comes to mind is 'Harry Embsay' and I admit I was tempted to share this theory with Adam, but Harry was still no more than guesswork and gut feeling so I had to keep him to myself for now.

'But we're supposing it was someone she knew?'

'I'm not even sure about that – sorry.' If only Lily's

diary had given me more to work on, instead of two blank pages. 'I was wondering, though – can they still do a DNA test?'

'To establish paternity? I guess so.'

'Well, I think they should if they haven't already – so they can make a match when we find the right person.'

Adam agreed that he would contact the coroner as soon as he got back to his office. He turned off his hazard lights then signalled and eased back on to the road before he had one more little, human blip.

'Poor Lily,' he murmured, short and sweet.

'Poor Lily,' I sighed, short and angry.

She was bipolar and sixteen, for God's sake, pregnant either by a guy she didn't love or by a total stranger, hurtling towards an abortion she didn't want. Things couldn't have got any worse.

Then they did. She came face to face with psycho killer. The end.

chapter thirteen

Christmas was looming. So was the end of term.

'I swear I'm going to miss you every day, every hour, every minute of the holiday,' Jack told me in the stable yard where we'd shared our first kiss all those weeks – a lifetime – ago. 'I don't want to go home.'

'Not even if your dad lets you drive the Maserati around your country estate?' This was me, trying to lighten the atmosphere. Boys' toys – vroom-vroom.

'No, Alyssa – you're supposed to say, "I'll miss you too, Jack." We're meant to kiss and swear eternal love.'

That's one in the cornucopia of good things about Jack (maths genius who knows everything there is to know about conic sections, he of the amazing quads, hottest boy on earth) – he can do lightness yet still come through with the genuine emotion. I kissed him in between the bits and bridles of the spotless tack room where the kid in the hoodie had hidden. For a few precious moments I lost myself in that embrace.

'A kiss but no promises,' I warned.

'No eternal love?' He pouted then said, 'You're right – nothing is forever.'

After that he grinned, went into the tack room and got on with tipping feed into a bucket and adding water, giving it a stir. He and I had agreed to help Guy Simons look after Mistral while Paige was in hospital – the very least we could do.

Outside in the floodlit yard, cold rain came down. There were puddles everywhere and the sky was leaden. Bored horses stared out over their stable doors, knowing that no rider would show up until the weather brightened. I smiled back at Jack then carried the bucket across the yard into Mistral's stable.

Smiled then sighed. It was hard and perhaps not even right for me and Jack to stay cheerful and in love after what had happened to Paige. You realize how much my world view has shifted since the heady few days leading up to Tom's party? Look back and you can see how that was paradise and this is pure and simple hell.

'I wonder how Paige is,' he murmured, reminding me that we hadn't had an update recently. 'What do you say we go and visit once we're done here?'

'Yeah, good – if they'll let us in.' I opened Mistral's door and put his feed down in his usual corner, stepping back quickly before he shoved me to one side in his eagerness. When I came out and re-bolted the door, I looked up at the security camera that had failed to capture the evidence of the attack on Mistral – one glance was enough to throw me back in time and trigger total recall.

'Where is he?' I asked Paige, rushing into the stable yard as soon as I'd recovered from almost being knocked down by Harry and Franklin.

'Where's who?' She carried Mistral's saddle into the tack

room, leaving him tethered to the wall. She went in and didn't spot the kid in the hoodie hiding in there. She came out again as if everything was normal.

'Harry Embsay. He almost ran me down, for Christ's sake!'

Pause and think further back. Out on the edge of the woods Harry had laughed at me and galloped on. This meant he should've arrived back at the stables before me. So where was he?

'Not back yet,' Paige had replied.

Why not? Had he deliberately stayed away because he'd known what was about to happen?

I remembered Paige brushing Mistral and speaking sweetly to him, telling me that Harry was an idiot, but that he hadn't tried to mow me down on purpose.

'Yeah, but it wasn't deliberate.'

'I don't know – maybe it was.'

Yes, definitely it was on purpose now that I reran it. If at first you don't succeed in scaring Alyssa off the scent of Lily's killer by employing a hit man to stage a motorbike accident, then try, try, try again with a thousand pounds of horseflesh to turn Paige into a quivering wreck, to get us both hauled out of school early.

But Paige had stopped brushing and sighed.

'Just a teeny bit par-a-noid?' she suggested, and she winked to ease the tension. 'Chill, my friend.'

Then hoodie boy burst out, carrying the knife in his left hand. He looked at me then at the angle of the security camera fixed high on the wall. He detoured to stay out of shot, meaning he at least thought it was working and he already knew enough

about the security of the place to avoid being caught on camera.
Then he grabbed the wheelie bin and shoved it straight at Paige's
horse, raised the knife to slash at his neck.

Up went Mistral, hoofs flailing. Hoodie boy backed off. He
moved fast, yelled at me to stay out of his way as he panicked
and fled directly under the lens, creating the perfect photo op.

Come on, come on! I told myself. Recall every last detail.

As Mistral squealed and came crashing down to the ground,
the kid scaled the wall. He sat astride it and leaned out to sever
the cable with his knife. He slashed it clean through. Then he
swung both legs over the wall and jumped down. Gone.

'Harry Embsay was definitely in on it,' I told Jack as
the rain spilt over the gutters on to the cobbles below. 'He
stayed away to give the kid with the hoodie time to do what
he had to do. And, cross my heart, I swear I'm not paranoid.'

There was nowhere at St Jude's more out of Hooper's
comfort zone than the stable yard on a cold and rainy
winter's day, not even the sports centre. Yet here he was,
splashing through puddles without a jacket and looking
like a drowned rat, as Jack and I got ready to leave.

'What are you doing here?' I asked, in a hurry to get to
the hospital to see Paige.

'Wait – it's important,' he insisted.

'What?' I asked, feeling the hairs at the back of my neck
rise. How important did it have to be for Hooper to drag
himself out here?

'Before I start, I'm not making any of this up – OK?'

'OK, we believe you,' Jack said quickly. 'Just tell us.'

'I went back and did some more research on Eleanor Bond.'

'Not this again, please!' I was already shaking my head before he reached the end of his sentence.

'Yes, this again.' Hooper dug in his heels.

'What about Eleanor Bond?' asked Jack.

'I started with the whole Bond family. The mother, Simone – she got caught up in the Nazi takeover of Vienna – remember I told you, Alyssa? That was for obvious reasons, because she was Jewish. So I started looking at Edward Bond, who, it turns out, wasn't Jewish, but he had pro-Jewish business interests in Birmingham and all through Europe.'

Jack realized there was a lot of history to get through and like me he was eager to get out to see Paige. 'Where are we going with this?'

'Somewhere you're not going to like,' Hooper warned. 'Listen. All through the 1930s there were marches in the streets of the main British cities – London, Manchester, Birmingham – it's well documented. You've heard of Mosley's Blackshirts and those extreme fascist groups? Yeah, right. They organized the marches, targeting communists and Jewish groups and it turns out they included Edward Bond in this target group because of his wife and his businesses, and because he was known to be offering a place of safety to Jewish refugees. He went public about the evils of Nazism – even wrote articles about it for some national newspapers. That caused an argument about him setting up St Jude's in 1938 – nimby residents in Ainslee viewed Edward Bond as a troublemaker. They didn't want the school anywhere near.

They were right, in a way, because the Nazis tried to bomb St Jude's during the war.'

I was tuning in now, listening more carefully, paying attention to those tiny hairs standing up on the back of my neck.

'That was the atmosphere back then – people over here mostly didn't see fascism for what it was until after Hitler went into Austria then Czechoslovakia then finally Poland. They didn't diss his haircut or laugh at his moustache. He was building the VW Beetle – the people's car – and they thought he might actually be a good guy.'

Jack's attention was also fixed on the emerging story. 'Come on, Hooper – what are you saying?'

'OK, as we know – Edward Bond was an idealist. He went ahead and set up St Jude's Academy anyway. He ignored all the political stuff and founded it on the principle of *nihil sed optimus*, focusing on the talents of the individual student, fostering brilliance. Then his wife was swallowed up in a Nazi pogrom in Vienna, which happened without warning, and in the same year his daughter – a pupil at this school – was found drowned.'

'We already know this!' I exclaimed. 'So what's new?'

'OK, I moved on from Edward and Simone Bond to the daughter, but you have to take into account the political stuff I've just mentioned. Now, Eleanor – the first verdict was misadventure, but it turns out that wasn't accurate. I shouldn't have stopped investigating at the point where she died; I should have moved on into 1939 when someone – presumably Edward Bond – asked for Eleanor's body to be exhumed for a second autopsy and the coroner agreed.'

'Oh my God!' I sighed. Of all the shit life throws at you, exhuming your daughter's body is about as bad as it gets.

'I know. Bond must have had a good reason – a suspicion, maybe some proof that they'd got the wrong verdict first time round. It turns out he was right. They eventually did a second autopsy and found that the body had been mutilated . . .' Hooper paused then began again at top speed to clear up any doubt we might still have. 'Yeah, it was a missing tooth. I swear this is true, Alyssa. It turns out it was a kind of signature – a tooth missing from a corpse had happened at least four times before in the Midlands and south-west – all in the mid to late 1930s.'

'A signature?' Jack prompted. 'What does that mean?'

'It's where a serial killer leaves a kind of trademark to let the police know it's the work of one man.'

'Like Jack the Ripper?'

'Exactly – only in this case, less obvious and messy. But it must have been totally premeditated, which makes it even creepier. And here it wasn't one killer – it was a small group of right-wing fanatics, an offshoot of Mosley's Blackshirts and the British Union of Fascists, who wanted to persecute prominent pro-Jewish political activists like Edward Bond. They would pick on a family member, someone vulnerable.'

'Like Eleanor?' I said.

'And they would target that person and . . . and eliminate them.'

The word sent nasty shudders down my spine and I

forced my attention down a different channel. *We have to find out who took the tooth and why*, Jayden had told me.

'But that was then,' Jack protested. 'Not now. We've moved on – we're living in the twenty-first century!'

'And we still have problems in Israel and the Middle East, and our society still breeds fanatics.' Hooper drew breath and waited for me to respond. *Répond, Alyssa. Dis quelque chose.*

Find out who took the tooth and why. This is where the personal becomes political.

'Anna Earle is Jewish and Robert Earle's Comco is planning a neo-Nazi exposé,' I reminded the two Jacks quietly.

It was there, clear as day in Lily's diary – the headline that read *Comco Leads Campaign to Expose International Fascist Cells*. There, you see – more proof that my memory hangs on to every tiny detail.

The personal becomes political and maybe Lily's death isn't just Jayden any more, or Harry, or a random guy killing her in a fit of rage or jealousy or fear. No – Lily is a small part of something enormous, a victim of forces none of us could even begin to get our information-stuffed heads around.

'Hooper was born to do research,' I decided as Jack and I rode in a taxi through Ainslee's Christmas streets. 'He should write a historical novel set in Nazi Germany. Isherwood's *Cabaret* for the modern reader.'

'He probably already has,' Jack agreed.

'So who would know the history of St Jude's well enough to do a carbon copy of Eleanor Bond's killing?' I wondered. 'Besides the principal and the bursar,' I added. The school's rocky pre-war start had been officially laid to rest and no way would Saint Sam and D'Arblay want it resurrected.

'Yeah, they would know,' Jack agreed.

Christmas lights twinkled, carols drifted out of shop doorways and manic shoppers hurried along the wet streets.

'So why aren't Sam and D'Arblay making the connection between Eleanor and Lily?'

'Maybe they are,' Jack said.

The taxi dropped us at the hospital gates where a couple of die-hard smokers stood in the rain, taking last drags at their cigarettes before they stepped into the no-smoking grounds.

THIS BUILDING WAS OPENED ON 5TH MAY 1986 BY HER MAJESTY QUEEN ELIZABETH II said the brass plaque at the main entrance. A door glided open and Jack and I stepped inside. We crossed Reception and followed the arrows to the ICU – up one floor in the lift, left past Swallow Ward and Nightingale Ward, down a long, empty antiseptic corridor, before reaching the outer door to the ICU. I pressed the buzzer. For a long time nothing happened, then we heard a click and the invitation to speak.

'We're friends of Paige Kelly,' I said into the intercom.

There was another click and the locked door opened. We stepped inside. A nurse waited at the end of a short corridor. 'Come this way,' she said.

She led us into a small waiting area with out-of-date

magazines spread carelessly across a low pine table, six red chairs backed against the wall and a coffee machine in one corner. Amateur watercolours on the wall had been donated by grateful patients.

'When can we see Paige?' I asked the nurse.

'You're from her school – right?'

'I'm her roommate.'

'Well, the doctors are with her right now.'

There's a specific moment when extreme fear kicks in. It explodes like a bullet in your heart. This was that moment.

Doors opened and closed, medics rushed to save a life. I saw a nurse accompany Paige's weeping parents out of the ICU.

'Wait here,' our nurse told us.

They couldn't save her. Paige died at 9 p.m.

The hole in your heart gets bigger. You can't feel, you can't think.

At 9.30 our nurse took us down to the taxi rank. 'You're sure you're both OK?' she checked.

We nodded. Paige was dead, but we were OK. We took a taxi back to St Jude's in silence. Neither of us could utter a single word about how we felt.

That night I tried not to think about the tubes and stents, the fragments of bone, the unstoppable bleeding inside her brain. Instead I tried to picture Paige riding Mistral across country, windswept under blue skies, clearing those fences by a mile.

In the morning when I turned on my bedside light, I noticed that Paige's bed was still unmade.

I fixed it, carefully smoothing down sheets and plumping up pillows. Then I got dressed and went downstairs, looking for Jack. He was waiting for me in the quad.

'I was thinking, now that this has happened, maybe you should go home,' was the first thing he said. He looked like he hadn't slept either. 'Listen, Alyssa, what we . . . what *you*'ve been doing is too risky.'

He wanted to protect me because he loved me, he said. He wanted to wrap his arms round me and never let me go, but he was too scared for me to stay.

'I know it,' I told him gently.

But there was a gaping hole in my heart and no one, not even Jack, could persuade me to leave St Jude's until it was knitted together by answers and solutions.

We went to the dining hall where Bryony Phillips came to sit with us while others stayed away, as if we were contagious and they might catch our grief. I noticed that Zara was with Luke at a nearby table and I was glad he had someone to help him through the day.

'Any time either of you need to talk, you know where to find me,' Bryony confided. 'Forget the student-teacher relationship, I'm here for you both, any time, day or night.'

It helped a little.

When Bryony left, I joined Zara and Luke. Both had the blank expression that comes with the internal agony of grief. Zara didn't say anything – she just took my hand

and stared at me with her lovely, luminous blue-grey eyes brimming with tears. It was Luke who wanted to talk.

'I thought she would make it,' he mumbled. 'I was sure she would.'

'Me too.' She was invincible, unstoppable Paige.

'Why didn't she?'

I shook my head, knowing now wasn't the time for medical details.

'She *should* have made it.'

'I know.'

We lapsed into silence then Shirley Welford delivered a message from the principal – both Jack and I were excused from lessons and did I feel strong enough to see Dr Webb in his office at 9.30?

Twelve hours after Paige's death, Saint Sam's face was ashen. He looked like a man under siege, standing by his stained-glass window, hands clasped behind his back, rocking on his heels and clearing his throat. Inspector Cole sat calmly in a chair by the principal's desk. I noticed that his suit jacket was crumpled and his shirt cuffs were grubby.

In its time the room had surely seen disaster and triumph and everything in between. Even before it became a school in 1938, it had absorbed four centuries of history, witnessed tragedy and acquired the patina of people breathing and loving, fighting and dying inside its oak-panelled walls. But this day was surely one of its worst.

'Did you tell the inspector about Eleanor Bond?' I didn't

hold back or wait to find out why I'd been summonsed – I just launched straight in.

Saint Sam almost staggered under the weight of the question. His smooth manner was nowhere to be seen.

'I'm talking about the first girl to die here,' I explained to Cole. 'It's weird how history repeats itself – Dr Webb should have discussed it with you.'

I wouldn't have expected Saint Sam to be dumb enough to deny all knowledge, but he was. 'I don't know what you mean, Alyssa. Please sit down and explain.' He pointed to an empty chair underneath a framed black-and-white photo of the first ever intake at St Jude's Academy – fewer than thirty co-ed kids with pudding-basin haircuts, wearing gym slips or grey serge trousers and all in red-and-green striped blazers.

I pointed to the carefully posed picture. 'Which one is Eleanor?'

Saint Sam apologized for me. 'I'm sorry, Inspector. Yesterday was extremely traumatic for Alyssa. I'm hoping that now she'll take my advice and leave school early to give herself some time at home with her aunt.'

Not that old tactic! 'Which one is she?' I repeated stubbornly.

Again he ignored me. 'Don't expect rationality,' he warned Cole. 'She really is very upset.'

Inspector Cole took time to study his fingernails before he spoke to me. 'What do you mean about history repeating itself?'

'Eleanor Bond – 1938. Lily Earle – 2012. Google it.'

'Why don't you just tell me?' Cole invited.

So I drew the parallels – two bodies in the lake: accidental death, suicide or murder? Two missing teeth, with four other identical mutilations back in the bad old, neo-Nazi 1930s. Two reactionary, right-wing, racist groups who collected molars and put them in a jar (OK, I made up the part about the jar).

'I'm afraid this is nonsense,' Saint Sam sighed. 'In any case, I'm sure what happened over seventy years ago is of no relevance to your current investigation.'

Cole tilted his head to one side and picked at the dead skin surrounding his fingernails. 'Maybe, maybe not. Go on, Alyssa.'

'Lily's mum is Jewish. It's possible the Earles give money to support an Israeli cause – I don't know for sure. But I do know that Comco is planning an exposé of neo-Nazi groups – which in my opinion is all the link you need.'

'We can definitely check that out,' the inspector agreed. 'But I'm wondering why a fascist group, if it exists, would target Lily specifically.'

'Quite,' Saint Sam said with a complacent air, but once more he'd misjudged the situation.

'Because they knew they could get at Robert Earle via his daughter, the same way the Blackshirt splinter group picked on Eleanor.'

'And why take the extreme measure of killing her and mutilating the body?' Cole wanted to know.

'Again, because Earle's threatened exposé is putting them under serious pressure. Plus, the killer is probably a lunatic, right-wing racist and he sees that no way will Robert Earle pull his journalists off the topic. And so it ran out of control,' was my gut-instinct answer. 'That's how Lily ended up dead.'

I thought Saint Sam was going to rock so far back on his heels that he would crash straight through the leaded window. He was so thrown that he didn't try to object when Inspector Cole asked for a few minutes alone with me.

'Somewhere private,' he emphasized.

Saint Sam suggested the old library and I led the way, aware of long-distance lenses trained on us from the gate and a new police presence in the shape of two patrol cars and four uniformed officers. Cole held the library door open for me as we went in.

'What will you do?' I wanted to know as we sat in the deep tweedy armchairs in the periodical section.

'About what?'

'About Dr Webb.'

'What would you like me to do?'

'Charge him with withholding important information. He must have known about Eleanor Bond – he knows the whole history of St Jude's. It's something he should have told you.'

'Difficult to prove,' Cole said. He watched me closely then morphed unexpectedly into a caring father figure. 'Anyway, right now I'm more concerned about you, Alyssa.'

'I'm fine,' I muttered. My heart was still in tatters over Paige, but at least my brain was beginning to work again.

'We're in a position to offer you protection if you would like – as a precaution.'

'No, I'm cool thanks.'

'Stop a moment. Take time to think before you reject it outright. I'm not saying your new theory necessarily holds water – yes, this is probably the work of a seriously deranged individual, but it still doesn't mean he or she has any connection with what went on during the 1930s. Either way you mustn't put yourself in any more danger – not after what happened to Paige.'

Bang – another bullet enters my tattered heart. I wince and shut my eyes.

'I made a connection between the kid who attacked Mistral and the kid on the stolen Toyota,' I confessed, eyes still closed. 'It turns out they're the same person.'

'Name?' Cole asked.

'I don't have that yet, but he has grey eyes and dark lashes, about five eleven, six feet tall. He's left-handed. I gave you all that before.'

'You'd be able to pick him out in an identity parade?'

'Definitely.'

Cole was fully focused and he spoke more seriously than before. 'St Jude's might not be the best environment for you, Alyssa. Why not take the principal's advice?'

It was like a chorus of monkeys jabbering the same words – *Go home! Go home!* – so I decided that lying was my best option. 'Maybe I will,' I murmured. 'But first I want to ask you about a couple of other things.'

'Go ahead,' Cole said, inspecting his nails again.

'About Dr Webb and Mr D'Arblay – they said there was no CCTV footage of the guy who attacked Paige's horse. Well, I think there was. In fact, I'm certain the camera was working fine right up until the point where he climbed the wall to escape. That was when he used his knife to cut through the cable. Can you check that out?'

'Again, difficult to prove that evidence has been concealed.'

'But you'll try?'

He nodded. 'What else, Alyssa?'

'Can you still do a DNA test on the baby to prove paternity?' I tried to stay detached, but couldn't stop myself from shuddering.

'We can. Adam Earle asked the coroner the same question – I'll check it out to see if it's been done yet. What else?'

'You know the first autopsy on Lily? Well, it said there were no signs of a struggle.'

'No bruising, no broken bones, no signs of strangulation,' Cole agreed. 'And she was still alive when she went into the lake because she inhaled water.'

'But she could have been unconscious?'

'Yes.'

'So what if the killer drugged her somehow? Say the drug was slipped into a drink . . .'

Cole nodded again. 'An overdose of tamoxifen or Rohypnol, some date rape drug – yes we got the pathologist to test for the obvious ones. He didn't find anything.'

'But you could do more tests?'

'We could and we will,' he agreed.

'It wouldn't necessarily have been in the school grounds. Lily could have arranged to meet up with her killer in the village or in town, or else she ran into him by accident. He drugged her then afterwards drove her back here to put her in the lake to make it look like suicide. There was a four-day gap, remember.'

'A wide window,' Cole agreed. He was finally done with his fingernails, so he stood up and rubbed his nose instead. 'Where's home for you?' he asked.

'Richmond.'

'So we can get in touch with you there if you do decide to leave early?'

'Yes,' I said.

It was another lie. In fact, I'd already fixed on what I was going to do next, and it did involve a train ticket to London, but not to stay with my aunt.

chapter fourteen

I didn't discuss my plan with anyone – not even Jack. Maybe not a great move after what had happened to Lily and Paige, but I wasn't thinking clearly and it was something that on the spur of the moment I decided to do alone.

Hi, Jack, I texted. Am taking train to London. Don't tell anyone and don't worry about me – A xxx.

I put the message into Drafts, ready to press Send when I was actually on the train so he couldn't follow me.

That was early Wednesday morning as I left my room and walked down the stone stairway, before Hooper cornered me in the quad.

'Are you ready for this?' he challenged, noticing the overnight bag I was carrying, but choosing to ignore it for now.

'I don't know – am I?' You rarely saw Hooper before ten in the morning so whatever he had to say must be something else important.

'Lion Films,' he said enigmatically. 'Have you heard of them?'

'No. Should I?'

'Lion Films is owned by Comco. I came across it in a

list of companies set up and run by the Earles. They have offices in London, New York, Chicago and Tel Aviv.'

'Making blockbuster movies and raking in mega-buck profits?'

'Actually no. Lion specializes in documentary programmes with a high political content – films about the situation in Afghanistan, Israel, Palestine . . .'

'We're talking propaganda movies?'

'Yeah – some of them with a pro-Israeli bias. Comco also prints free newspapers and *What's On* magazines throughout the Middle East. They also own a TV station broadcasting out of Tel Aviv, but available in Egypt, Palestine and Syria.'

'So Lion Films is the branch of Comco that's setting out to investigate the neo-Nazi groups?'

Hooper nodded. 'They include it in their list of current projects. The website says they've already looked at cells in America and the UK. The documentary's due for release in July next year.'

'You definitely did your homework,' I told him. 'Thanks, Hooper – it could be a big help.' Genuinely, because it gave me good information for my up-and-coming, secret talk.

'So what's with the bag?' he asked.

I hitched it higher on my shoulder. 'To make Saint Sam assume I'm heading for Richmond. I want him and D'Arblay to think I'm taking their advice.'

'But you're not?'

'No.'

'Why not?'

'I need some space.'

'On your own?'

'Yeah. I'm feeling claustrophobic hanging around here all the time.' I told Hooper that I'd spent another night alone in the room I'd shared with Lily and Paige, going round and round in circles like a hamster trapped inside its wheel.

'So you're not going to tell me where you're going? No – I can see that.' He looked unhappy. 'Alyssa – you won't do anything stupid?'

I gave him my best patronizing smile and patted his shoulder. 'Don't worry. If anything bad is going to happen to me, it'll happen here at St Jude's or in the Bottoms, not in the place where I'm going.'

Who did I think I was kidding?

Hooper watched me set off towards the lake, his imagination working overtime. After thirty seconds he ran after me. 'I really don't think you should be doing this without Jack – whatever it is.'

I walked steadily on, skirting the frozen reed bed and flat expanse of grey water. 'It's OK, Jack and I are not joined at the hip. Anyway, I'll send him a text.'

'You know that's the identical bag that Lily had.'

His observation skills caught me off guard and I broke my stride. 'I know. We bought them together – from the same shop on the same day.'

'That creeps me out, Alyssa. It's like an action replay – you and Lily both sneaking off like this. Honestly, I don't like it.'

We passed the lake and entered the woods. 'Hooper,

what do you want me to do? Lily and Paige are both dead and no one can work out why. I can't sit around and do nothing – it's driving me crazy!' I picked up pace and began to jog along the bridle path, past the spot where Harry and Franklin had given me my Jane Eyre moment. Pretty soon I'd be crossing the stream then coming out at the far side of the woods on to the back lane that led to the Bottoms. If I hurried, I could get from there to Ainslee in time for the 10.05 Paddington train.

With his long legs Hooper had no problem keeping up. 'What am I going to tell Jack?'

'Tell him not to worry – I'll be safe. Honestly, you have to stop following me. Go back and cover for me with Saint Sam, do some more research – whatever.'

I suppose I sounded snotty because Hooper suddenly stopped and let me run on. I'd obviously hurt his feelings.

'Sorry,' I called over my shoulder. And I was. But not sorry enough to change my plan or even to give Hooper the explanation he deserved.

I came out of the woods on to the lane, which was free of early-morning traffic except for a farmer trundling past on a muddy tractor and a woman swishing by in a white Porsche. I was slightly out of breath after jogging away from Hooper so I stopped a while on the grass verge to watch a kestrel hover over unseen prey on the far side of the high hedge. After a few seconds it swooped out of sight and I continued past the Old Mill – an expensive conversion – and on again to the first straggle of tarted-up ex-farm-workers' cottages leading into the Bottoms.

I hit the village proper just as Tom drove out of the Vicarage on to Main Street.

I didn't expect him to stop, but he did and wound down the window. 'Hey, Alyssa – look who just passed his test!'

'Cool, Tom. You're sure you're speaking to me again?'

I hadn't seen him since the day he'd savaged me for telling the police about Lily's bag, but by now he'd had time to calm down and was back to his old, considerate self. 'Yeah. Where are you going?'

'Ainslee train station.'

'I'm on my way to school, but I can drop you off.' He leaned over and opened the passenger door, hardly giving me time to fasten my seat belt before he set off. 'I heard the news about Paige,' he said without any more small talk. 'I'm sorry.'

I nodded.

'You don't want to talk about it?'

'No.'

'Fair enough.' As we passed the Bridge Inn and the turn off up Meredith Lane, Tom saw Jayden loping down the hill. 'Do you mind if I give him a lift too?'

I shrugged and we took on board another passenger.

'Hey, Alyssa – how's Harry?' Jayden barked as he slammed his door shut and Tom set off again.

I tensed up but made an effort to keep the conversation under control. 'The swelling's going down nicely, thank you, but he still can't see out of his left eye. Tom, did you hear what Jayden did to Harry Embsay? Can I tell him, Jayden, or will you?'

'He was asking for it,' Jayden grunted as he cracked his knuckles. Cooped up in the back of Tom's small car, he looked moodier than ever and totally out of his element. 'Never mind me telling Tom what I did to dick-head Harry, what have you been up to lately, Alyssa? Have you found out who killed Lily?'

Tom took a sharp intake of breath, gripped the wheel and stared straight ahead.

'Jayden thinks it was Harry,' I explained as Tom drove out of the Bottoms on the Ainslee road. 'Hence the fight.'

'Christ!' Tom said.

'I know. I told Jayden you can't go round accusing people.'

'Not "people"!' Jayden said. 'Just Embsay. And he's not a person – he's an animal.'

'And was it?' Tom asked me. 'Was it Embsay?'

'That's a maybe,' I said, nervous that Jayden's temper would snap if I said anything too definite. 'There's a chance he was involved.'

Our back-seat passenger snorted down his nose. 'Meaning Embsay said he didn't screw Lily but he did, meaning he said he didn't kill her but he did.'

'Christ,' Tom said again, this time *sotto voce*. He seemed relieved when we came into the outskirts of town and he took the route to the station, arriving just in time to see a load of Ainslee Comp kids step off a local train.

'Thanks for the lift,' I told him, getting out of the car as fast as I could, but having to step aside to avoid the tide of uniformed kids. I checked my watch and saw that I would easily make the Paddington train.

Tom nodded and said goodbye. Jayden scowled. I turned towards the ticket machine, bought my ticket and glanced across the railway lines to the opposite platform.

I saw Alex Driffield unwrap a chocolate bar and bite into it, talking with his mouth full to Micky Cooke and an older lad who I didn't know. There seemed to be an argument. The older lad stabbed his forefinger into Micky's chest then stood in his way when Micky tried to step off the platform on to the steps leading to the narrow metal bridge over the track. He pushed him back against the chocolate machine.

'The next train to arrive at platform two is the 10.05 to Paddington,' a voice announced over the intercom.

Across the tracks on platform 3 Alex joined in the argument. He chucked away his chocolate wrapper and let it fly in the wind. Then he dodged round the older lad and tried to grab Micky by the arm. Micky resisted and decided to stay with the older lad after all so Alex went on alone, taking the metal steps two at a time.

My supercharged memory cells kicked into action and I began to think I'd seen the older lad somewhere before. He was hidden by my train as it pulled into the station so I had to wait before I could board and peer through the window at platform 3. The older, mystery lad and Micky had disappeared behind a service trolley, then the lad reappeared without Micky, phone in left hand pressed to left ear.

Where had I seen that before?

Backtrack in time before the train leaves the station – really concentrate. Try to place the tall, finger-stabbing, left-handed lad with the phone.

It had been weird, that time in the hospital car park – Harry had brought Paige flowers. He sat beside D'Arblay waiting to visit while Jack and I were leaving.

Jack swore under his breath.

'What?' We were on our bikes. I didn't see the old red Mondeo reversing out of a space and I had to jam on my brakes.

Inside the car were Micky Cooke and presumably his morgue-worker dad. Jack and I were concentrating on Micky, watching him speak into his phone – right hand, right ear.

Jack swore again because it was Micky who had ambushed me along with Ursula and Alex, and because Micky was on the list of suspects who'd met at Tom's house the night Lily disappeared.

'Leave it,' I'd told Jack. There was another person in the back of the car, also talking on his phone.

Remember more – every tiny detail. Make it fast!

The Mondeo spewed out a plume of black exhaust smoke, the man in the back glanced out and met my gaze. He was left-handed and his eyes were grey with thick dark lashes.

Good! That's what I'd missed before. But now . . . good – very good!

Now I was back in the present, looking out of the train at the lad on the platform. The same eyes and lashes, the same hostile stare when he saw me watching him. He backed behind the service trolley and I lost him again.

Alex came off the bridge and ran past my carriage, heading for the ticket barrier. I leaned out of the door. 'Who was that?' I yelled.

He didn't stop to answer, just threw a name in my direction – 'Micky Cooke!'

'No, not Micky – the other one!'

'Chris – Micky's brother. He's a wanker.'

The words faded, doors slammed, the station manager blew a whistle and my train pulled out.

Chris Cooke – Micky's brother, alias the guy on the stolen Toyota, alias the man in the stable yard in the grey Adidas hoodie. Things rolled and glided into place like the chilled drawers containing corpses in a hospital morgue. They closed with a soft thud on the lives of the two people who had died.

Lately we'd been through what felt like an age of freezing rain and heavy skies, but today was sunny – forgive the weather report, but it was a decent distraction while staring out of the window. My train sped smoothly through the countryside, in and out of tunnels.

We were thirty minutes from Paddington and I'd turned off my phone. I hadn't sent the text to Jack.

Chris Cooke – Chris Cooke – Chris Cooke. The name clicked rhythmically through my head. Sunlight to shade, sunlight to shade.

It turned out that the figure at the centre of all the bad things that had happened since Lily's body was dragged from the lake was Micky's brother. I was stuck on this fact, not getting any further until I changed focus – the guy at the centre of all the bad things was the *son* of the man who worked at the morgue!

All workers at the hospital would need ID; they would know codes to get them into certain high-security areas, including the morgue. Maybe Chris's dad was careless with his badge or pass, maybe he jotted down security-code reminders at home in case his memory let him down – in which case it was plain sailing for Chris to pick up confidential information and access his dad's workplace.

I was thinking – yes, Chris Cooke could definitely find a way to get inside the hospital morgue and perform that mind-blowingly nasty mutilation on Lily's corpse.

Chris Cooke – Chris Cooke – Chris Cooke. The tempo slowed as the train approached the suburbs. I looked out of the window at graffiti sprayed on to concrete walls, at the backs of big terraced houses, row after endless row.

From Paddington I took the tube to Euston and came up the escalators on to the wide concourse leading out on to Euston Road. From there it was a twenty-minute, traffic-swamped walk to the Comco offices.

Yeah – Comco. This was the secret plan that had grown in my brain and was just about to bear fruit.

I passed office blocks belonging to banks and building societies, walked across paved plazas with Costas and Starbuckses, then a grassed area with contemporary sculptures then more shiny office blocks.

Outside the Comco tower were two cold, coatless women

and a man in shirtsleeves smoking and drinking coffee. Inside was a reception area with white leather sofas and acres of travertine on floors and walls. Two receptionists, a man and a woman, sat behind a vast glass-and-steel desk and viewed me with cool disdain.

'I'm here to see Adam Earle,' I told the one nearest to the revolving glass door.

'Do you have an appointment?' he asked.

'No, but he'll see me.'

'I don't think so.'

'Tell him it's Alyssa Stephens.'

The receptionist was unimpressed. 'I could tell him it was the prime minister and you'd still need an appointment to see Mr Earle.'

At this point I felt like banging my head on one of the travertine walls. 'Look, are you even going to try?'

'Not unless you make –'

'An appointment!' I snapped. Funnily enough, I hadn't predicted this problem, which shows you I didn't yet belong to the world of work.

A woman in a suit tip-tapped by in stilettos, a courier in a helmet handed a parcel over the desk.

'OK, I'll make an appointment,' I conceded. 'Can you put me through to Adam Earle's PA, please?'

The receptionist was busy looking at a screen and tapping at a keyboard. Behind him a lift door opened and, guess what, Robert and Adam Earle stepped out with their entourage. Within ten seconds they were through reception, out on the pavement and getting into a supersized silver car.

I don't know if the Earles even glanced in my direction and if they did they certainly didn't acknowledge me.

'Maybe write the PA an email?' the receptionist suggested with a big dollop of triumph.

It had been easy to look up the location of Comco, but I guessed Adam Earle didn't advertise his home address. I Googled him over a cup of coffee at the nearest Pret a Manger.

No – right. I was stuck unless I hung out here within sight of Comco's revolving door and waited for Adam to come back from whatever meeting he and his tyrant dad had gone to.

Three coffees later I was buzzing from a caffeine overdose and still waiting.

'Hello, Alyssa,' a voice said over my shoulder.

I jumped out of my skin.

As I steadied myself, Adam sat down on the stool next to mine. He was dressed in a dark blue suit and white shirt, but his pale blue tie was loosened and the top button open. 'I'm sorry about Paige,' he said.

'I'm sorry, you're sorry, everyone's sorry.'

'I saw you in reception. I invented an excuse and got back as quick as I could, hoping that you'd hang around. I knew it must be important.'

'Thanks.' Thanks that he'd made this special effort, and thanks that he'd come through as a genuine, caring human being and not the automaton that he'd first seemed.

'Has anything happened? Did you find out any more about the baby's father?'

'No. I heard you made them do the DNA test.'

'No result yet, but it won't be much use anyway until the police are able to pin down a suspect. They'll need to find a match.'

'There is something else,' I confessed against the clink of crockery and the hum of conversation. 'Just a few hours back, in Ainslee Westgate, I found out the name of the guy who rode his motorbike at me then attacked Paige's horse. He's called Chris Cooke – he lives in Chartsey and he would be able to get access to the Queen Elizabeth morgue.'

Adam had taken out his phone and was on the point of making a call to Inspector Cole before I stopped him.

'Yeah – I'm not finished yet. Chris Cooke is local, but I think there's something much bigger going on. That's what I want to talk to you about.'

'What do you mean – how could it be bigger?' Adam spoke slowly, as if what I'd said didn't come as a complete surprise. I saw him retreat temporarily behind his robot shield.

'Suppose he's a small cog in someone else's very big wheel,' I suggested.

'Which someone?'

'Not an individual, more an organized group.' I knew I had to come out and say what was on my mind, but it was proving tricky. I decided to find another way in. 'So how's Anna?' I asked.

'No change.'

'Is she still seeing her rabbi?'

251

'No, my father put a stop to that. He was convinced it was adding to her confusion.'

'Plus, I expect he doesn't want to draw attention to her religious beliefs,' I said pointedly.

The point must have been needle-sharp because Adam reacted as if he'd been stung or bitten – a silent *ouch!* and then an attempt to brush the insect off his neck.

'I guess you planned to mention her connection to Lion Films eventually' I went on. 'And the free newspapers, the TV station and especially the planned exposé of the international neo-Nazi groups?'

'What has this got to do with finding Lily's killer?' he protested. 'Isn't that what you're meant to be doing?'

'That's what I *am* doing. So tell me about Comco's ownership of Lion Films for starters. Who set that up – Anna or your father?'

'Anna,' Adam said reluctantly. 'She brought family money into the business when she married my dad – a lot. It makes her a major shareholder and she can make executive decisions. Besides which, her family has a long history of supporting Israeli-based arts organizations – dance groups, orchestras, theatres. It wasn't out of character for Anna to establish Lion Films. She named it after the biblical story of Daniel in the lion's den.'

'How long?' I asked.

'You mean, how long is the family history of funding the arts? It goes way back to the 1920s and 30s.'

'So have they ever been targets of fascist organizations before now?'

Adam nodded almost imperceptibly. 'Yes. Back then they owned a chain of cinemas, which were destroyed by arsonists organized by the IUF – the International Union of Fascists. That's partly why Anna was so determined to launch Lion Films and fund the exposé in the first place – as a tribute to her grandparents, who she thought were heroes.'

'And more recently?' I memorized the name – International Union of Fascists – then pushed harder. 'Have there been actual protests against Lion Films?'

This time the answer took even longer.

'Yes,' Adam sighed. 'Some big-name actors have refused to work for Lion and some premieres have been disrupted – one in LA, one in Chicago.'

'What was Anna's reaction?'

'Hmm.' Adam gave a small shake of his head. 'Anna may look as if a puff of wind would knock her over, but underneath she has a hidden stubborn streak. She said the protests wouldn't put her off making the big documentary.'

'And what about your dad?'

'Oh, well, he was in two minds. On the one hand, he didn't see any good reason to hang on to an offshoot of Comco that didn't produce much profit and was drawing the wrong kind of publicity. On the other hand, he always hates being put under pressure from extremists of any sort – it makes him bite right back. Look, Alyssa, this all seems miles away from what we should be focusing on.'

'Not really.' In fact, I had an increasingly heavy, depressing sense that history could, in fact, repeat itself. Mosley's Blackshirts and the boycotts and protests surrounding Lion Films might be separated by eight decades, but there were too many similarities to ignore. 'Anyway, who won the argument – Anna or your father?'

'It's ongoing,' he told me. 'Or it was until he had Anna sectioned and tucked safely away. Now, God knows.'

'And who led the recent protests?' I had to know who we were talking about and how they might have tentacles long enough to stretch into a Cotswold backwater like Chartsey Bottom.

Adam's brain was busy making the same connections as I'd made and his replies came more slowly then ever. 'We investigated and found out it was an obscure group called the CRP – Campaign for Racial Purity. They're associated with other right-wing nationalist parties but they're less organized and more secretive.'

'And more violent?' I added. CRP – Campaign for Racial Purity – here was another name to hand over to historical bloodhound Hooper.

'I can't say that for sure.' Adam did more head shaking and seemed lost in that maze of uncomfortable thoughts. 'What I do know is they kept up the pressure against Comco and my father.'

'And?' I prompted.

'They said if he didn't halt the investigation into the CRP, they would take action against members of his family.'

'Ouch!' I shook my head in disbelief. 'Why didn't this come out earlier?'

'Because Comco is an enormous, multinational organization and the world is full of crazy individuals. We get phone hackers, spies and nutcases contacting us every day of the week.'

'You didn't take the threat seriously?'

'Alyssa, you have to believe me – neither I nor my mother knew about it at the time it was happening. It's not something my father told us about until after Lily disappeared.'

This helped explain why Adam hadn't hit the panic button when Lily first disappeared, why he and Anna had waited almost a week to show up at St Jude's. 'She was meant to come home,' I reminded him.

'When she didn't make it, I wasn't surprised,' he explained. 'She was seriously off the rails by this time and I resented the fact that my father had left me to do the dirty work as far as Lily was concerned. He wasn't on hand to deal with family stuff – remember, he was still in Chicago.'

'And when he did find out about her disappearance, how did he react?'

'Dad says he still didn't link it up with the CRP. He just blamed Lily for refusing to obey the order to come home.'

'Unbelievable,' I said, shaking my head in total disgust. I'd taken as much as I could stomach for now of the dysfunctional, mega-rich and ruthless Robert Earle so I picked up my bag and walked away from Adam without saying goodbye.

Turn right out of Pret A Manger then left down the Euston Road, striding out at top speed. Take the tube to Paddington and a late-afternoon express train straight back to ye ancient Cotswold town of Ainslee.

chapter fifteen

All the way home I made a million high-speed neural connections, synapse to synapse, and by the time the express train pulled into my station I had a clear new map of events in my brain.

Tyrant Earle had ignored the CRP threat to harm his family. Dealing with it had been so far down his to-do list that he hadn't even informed Anna, who had pressed ahead with her plans for the CRP exposé, oblivious. And, what do you know, the bunch of political activists, or at least one lunatic member of the group, had eventually got mad enough with the head of Comco to carry out the threat. The kidnap had gone ahead.

Stay with me on this.

Lily had been going through her own personal Armageddon. She'd got pregnant by someone other than Jayden – she'd already flown to the smiley-face heights of hoping that he was the daddy and plunged like Icarus into a shark-infested sea of despair when she'd learned he wasn't.

Did she want to keep the baby anyway? We'll never know. Maybe her fleeing-from-St-Jude's-disguised-as-suicide plan included an abortion, or maybe she intended to go through with the pregnancy and put the baby up for adoption, or even keep it. In any case, into this gut-wrenching mix comes a bunch of racial purists and one or more of them kidnaps her before she gets the chance to decide.

What happens next? Does the CRP put more pressure on Robert Earle? Does he still refuse to play their game? Do they lose it with him and kill Lily? Or does something else go wrong? I hadn't figured out that part before the guard's announcement came over the intercom: 'This train will shortly be arriving at Ainslee Westgate. Please remember to take all your belongings with you.'

The forecourt was busy with tourists, tramps looking for a warm place to spend the night and couples saying goodbye.

I came through the ticket barrier and ran into Mr and Mrs Kelly. They stepped out of a taxi, their faces dazed and pale, not speaking to each other as they checked the departure board. When Paige's mum saw me, she gasped then made a desperate little rush towards me.

'Alyssa,' she said, then stopped.

Paige looked like her dad rather than her mum, I noticed. He was tall and had dark curly hair, going grey at the temples, dressed for the journey in a dark brown Barbour jacket and checked scarf. He'd put down their bags, but hung back as Paige's mum approached me.

'Mrs Kelly,' I murmured. There was no need to say sorry because they absolutely knew.

'You were there,' she said. 'You saw what happened.'

I nodded.

'Did she . . . was she . . . ?'

'She was protecting Mistral.'

'Did he . . . ?'

'No. The guy went for the horse. It was meant to scare her, but it got out of control.'

'Did she know what was happening? What I mean is – did she feel any pain?'

'No, I'm sure she didn't.' It had been over in a second – Mistral rearing, Paige overbalancing, Mistral crashing down.

Mrs Kelly took in my answer then frowned and bit her bottom lip.

You're wondering why I didn't go on and give her Chris Cooke's name right there and then – something concrete for Paige's parents to hang on to. But I held it back, intending to hand it over to Inspector Cole first. Telling Mr and Mrs Kelly the name would be like lobbing a hand grenade into an already devastated war zone.

'Joanna, we'll miss our train if we don't hurry,' Mr Kelly said, still keeping his distance and re-checking Departures.

She nodded. 'Thank you, Alyssa.'

I didn't smile or say goodbye, just watched Mr Kelly pick up their luggage and lead his wife through the barrier on to their train.

The world goes on. Three girls tippety-tapped across the metal footbridge dressed in office-party high heels, short skirts and shiny, strappy tops. A guy in paint-spattered work clothes and scuffed builders' boots almost bumped into me as I turned suddenly and headed for the taxi rank.

I felt sick for the Kellys' loss.

There were about fifteen people ahead of me in the taxi queue, which meant a cold, dark wait of maybe five or ten minutes. I spent them Googling for info about the local branch of the CRP movement and found they had a website with an email address and a date for their next public meeting, but no actual names of party members.

I'll get Hooper on to it, I thought, putting my phone back into the front pocket of my bag.

Now there were only five people ahead of me in the queue. I hitched the bag further up my shoulder and watched another taxi arrive. Two guys stepped out and instead of taking the normal route on to the forecourt, they vaulted over the railing and crashed into me, almost knocking me off my feet. The woman ahead of me began to protest on my behalf, but I was too busy trying to hang on to my bag to make any noise. One of the guys had dragged it down my arm but I'd managed to hold on to it. I tugged it back towards me but they tugged harder. The bag was wrested from me and the two muggers ran away. I gave chase back into the station, across the forecourt, under the Departures board and over the ticket barrier. A female station guard in a grey overcoat and a dark red pillbox hat yelled for us to stop. I scrambled over the barrier with the two muggers still in view. They ran up the footbridge steps out of sight.

A railway worker in a high-vis yellow jacket charged along the platform and joined the guard. They stopped to discuss the problem – as far as they were concerned, three passengers without tickets had jumped the barrier and were headed towards platform 3. I drew breath and watched the station guard take out a phone to speak to her supervisor. It gave me a bit of time so I ran up the steps and across the bridge, only to find when I got to the other side that the muggers had vanished.

Which way had they gone? To the left was a long, crowded platform, to the right a row of vending machines and an arrow pointing to the toilets.

'Did you see two guys with a bright blue bag?' I asked the nearest onlooker.

He hesitated then pointed towards the Gents. Oh great – my overnight bag was currently being disembowelled in the men's urinals! Toothbrush and toothpaste, clean knickers, a spare top, my iPhone. On top of which, station security would have swung into operation and I would soon be arrested for unticketed entry on to the platform. Could my day get any worse?

Yes, actually.

'You want me to go in and take a look for you?' the obliging onlooker queried. He was an ordinary guy of about fifty, carrying a laptop, on his way home from work.

I nodded and hurried with him towards the Gents but before he had time to push open the door, my two bag thieves burst back out on to the platform and thrust him against the coffee machine. They ran straight at me and knocked me to the ground. One hooked his arm round my neck and started dragging me towards the edge of the platform. Within seconds he had his hands round my throat and I was overhanging the track, staring down on to gravel and sleepers and steel rails, listening to the sound of an approaching train . . .

And what do you know, my unremarkable, office-worker Samaritan did what the thieves hadn't expected any of the witnesses to do – he piled into the rescue. So did the high-vis railwayman who had followed his manager's instructions and pounded over the footbridge after me. That made two against two with me kicking and clawing my way back from the edge.

I heard yells, saw the muggers punch their way out as more passengers closed in around us. Soon it was five against two, I was on all fours, crawling away from the track, raising myself up. Someone called 999 and yelled that the police were on their way.

The muggers were overwhelmed and they knew it. They both drew knives from inside their boots. They slashed them through the air and everyone backed off, like the reverse of iron filings to a magnet. One lunged at me, but I managed to dodge and run back towards the bridge.

Two more railway security guys sprinted along the platform as the train arrived. I heard the whine and grind of brakes, saw the two muggers make a split-second, high-risk decision to jump down from the platform and make their escape across the track. Their feet crunched over gravel as I lost sight of them again.

The train seemed to sigh and groan as it came to rest.

'Are you OK?' the nearest onlooker asked. 'Did you get your bag back?'

I heard the *wah-wah* blare of a police siren, saw orange

flashing lights arrive in the station precinct, but I knew they were too late.

'It wasn't my bag they were interested in,' I groaned.

I'd been thrown to the ground, had stared over the edge of the platform at the oncoming train, seen the look in my muggers' eyes as they tried to throw me under its gleaming wheels.

Again it meant I got my next talk with Inspector Cole sooner than planned so I plunged in with a name. 'Chris Cooke.'

'What about him?'

'He rode the Toyota, he attacked Paige's horse – I saw him in Ainslee Westgate.'

'Good.' Cole waited while his female sergeant made a note. We were in Interview Room 2, back at the main Ainslee police station where I'd been driven at high speed through evening streets still crowded with Christmas shoppers. 'We'll pay him a visit. Now, on to this evening's incident, Alyssa. Did you recognize either of the muggers?'

I sat on a hard chair across the table from the inspector and his sergeant. The walls of the room were rodent-brown; a fluorescent light flickered overhead. 'No, I've never seen them before.'

'Can you describe them?'

'One was over six feet tall – six-one or two. He was wearing a black jacket and jeans, a grey knitted hat.'

'How old?'

'Twenty, twenty-one. He had a small shell-shaped tattoo

under his left ear – it was a Maori design or something like that. The other one was two or three inches shorter. He wasn't wearing a jacket, just a grey sweatshirt, jeans and trainers. They'd been drinking.'

'How do you know that, Alyssa?'

'I could smell it on their breath.' When they'd been bending over me, trying to shove and kick me off the platform under the wheels of the train. 'Did they get away?'

Cole nodded. 'We'll check out these descriptions. If the one with the tattoo is local, it shouldn't be too hard to trace him. But I can see you haven't finished yet. What else do you want to say?'

'It wasn't random – they didn't just jump out of the taxi and mug the nearest person. They specifically targeted me.'

'How sure are you?'

'One hundred per cent.'

'OK, but how did they know where to find you?'

'They arrived in a taxi so maybe someone at the station saw me arrive.' I thought back over events of the last hour and a half and remembered that I'd stopped to talk with the Kellys long enough for that person to make a phone call to the two muggers.

'Has someone been following you?' the inspector wanted to know.

'Probably Chris Cooke again. He could have been hanging around Ainslee Westgate all day, ever since I caught the 10.05 to Paddington. But there's more than one person involved.' I shifted on my seat and risked a quick glance at the deadpan sergeant, conscious that at this point she might easily suspect paranoia. 'An organized group,' I said quietly.

'An organized group?' she repeated without changing her expression. 'Is this group linked to Chris Cooke and the incident with the stolen Toyota then the attack on Paige Kelly's horse? And, if so, please explain the connection.'

'CRP – Campaign for Racial Purity,' I told Hooper and Jack.

It was almost midnight by the time I'd been delivered back to St Jude's in an unmarked police vehicle, sweeping past the hardcore knot of journalists at the gate. My Jack had seen the car drop me off in the quad and rushed straight across from the boys' quarters, collecting Hooper on the way. Together they'd broken School Rule Number One and snuck up to my room without being seen.

'Once I'd told Inspector Cole exactly what Adam Earle had said to me earlier in the day, he promised to check the membership of the local CRP branch, but I reckon we can do it faster. For a start we can take another look at their official website.'

Hooper agreed to begin there and then, and got to work on his iPad. 'I'd never heard of the CRP until now,' he admitted.

'Are they even legal?' Jack wanted to know.

'Yeah, we're living in a country that protects freedom of speech,' Hooper reminded him. 'You can march up and down streets carrying dumb-ass placards, and as long as you don't actually *do* anything to incite racial hatred you're OK.'

'OK, Hooper, so thanks for that and thanks for today,' Jack sighed.

'Yeah, thanks,' I echoed. Jack had already told me that Hooper had made sure he knew I was heading off with my overnight bag. Jack had immediately cut lessons and his regular tennis coaching session to chase after me into Ainslee, but too late to stop me getting on the train. The two of them had spent the rest of the day chewing their fingernails.

'Thanks!' Jack dropped him another heavy hint.

Hooper looked up from his iPad. 'What? Oh yeah – right!' He stood up and blushed awkwardly. 'I'll go back to my room and see what else I can find about the CRP. See you both in the morning.'

I waited until he'd closed the door behind him and the indrawn-breath moment where Jack and I would fall into each other's arms and proclaim everlasting love, only that's not what happened.

'So how are we meant to get through this, Alyssa?' Jack began, standing up from my bed where we'd both been sitting.

His question took me completely by surprise and I went on the defensive. 'Why, what did I do?'

He strode towards the door then to the window. 'You're telling me you don't know? You only go off the map and give me the worst day of my life, not knowing where you were or what you were doing. I have to find out through Hooper, for Christ's sake!'

'I'm sorry. I thought you'd understand.'

'I don't, so explain.'

'I was upset about Paige and wasn't thinking clearly – I needed some space – I don't know!'

'OK, you need space. I get it. But there's needing space and there's going to London without telling me, seeing Adam Earle –'

'I meant to send you a text.'

'You switched your phone off! Were you out of your mind?'

'I'm sorry.' I knew that Jack was right to be angry – after all, look what I'd walked into at the train station. 'What do you want me to say?'

'That you won't do it again – you won't shut me out.' He came back and sat next to me, spoke without looking. 'Don't you see what this does to us?'

'What do you mean?' Really, I had no idea what Jack would say next – anything from *this is goodbye* to *I love you forever* and everything else in between. I only knew I was plunged into fresh misery.

'How complicated it makes things. Now I'm back to thinking you don't trust me, the way you didn't trust me at first over Lily.'

'But I do.'

He shook his head. 'Not enough. I don't think you trust *anyone* enough to tell them what you're feeling deep down. You never come out and tell me – I've always had to dig, right from the start.'

'That's not true, Jack. Look at what's been happening – first to Lily and now Paige. You're always the first person I turn to.'

'But there's still a barrier.'

'What are you saying? I don't know how else to act. It's the way I am.'

'*That's* what I'm saying, Alyssa – it's the way you are. You can't change it.'

We came to a dead end and I felt my stomach twist in the silence that followed.

'I'm sorry too,' Jack sighed. He watched me stand up and drift to the window. 'Maybe it's me – I can't find a way through.'

'No, it's me.' Alone at the age of three after my mum and dad died, never fitting in, always on my guard. I stopped talking and stared at my own sad, fragmented reflection in the ancient, leaded panes.

I was in Bryony's class next morning, not listening to her critique of T. S. Eliot's poem, 'The Waste Land' – *April is the cruellest month, breeding lilacs out of the dead land.*

Instead I was secretly reading through the members of the Ainslee CRP committee, which Hooper had handed to me before the class began.

'Wow, that was quick,' I'd remarked. 'I take it you had to do more than look at their website?'

He'd nodded. 'Let's just say a little light hacking was involved.'

'Christ, Hooper, I'm impressed.' But actually it had been no more than I'd expected of my rat-down-a-drainpipe friend.

'I printed the list in alphabetical order,' he'd said. 'Read it, but try not to react – OK?'

- Audley, Charles – 204 Bristol Road, Ainslee (Chairman)
- Carter, Marion – The Old Mill, Chartsey Bottom (Meetings Secretary)
- Cooke, Matthew – 32 Main Street, Chartsey Bottom
- Morrison, Evelyn – Westgate Hotel, City Road, Ainslee (Treasurer)
- Morrison, Michael – Westgate Hotel, City Road, Ainslee (Membership Secretary)
- Simons, Guy – St Jude's Academy, Ainslee Road, nr Chartsey
- Troughton, Catherine – 75 Helston Avenue, Ainslee

'Today we'll study the First Quartet,' Bryony said. '"The Burial of the Dead".'

'It's still not illegal.' It was lunchtime and Hooper was trying to calm me down as we walked round the lake under a sky that was blue for once. 'Guy can be a teacher here and join any political group he wants. There's no law to stop him.'

'But the CRP!' I argued. 'You're not telling me Saint Sam would be happy about it if he knew.'

'Maybe he does know. Or D'Arblay – one or the other, or both.'

'If they don't yet, they soon will.'

'Alyssa, don't . . .'

'No, don't worry – I'm not about to march into the principal's office. But if Cole does his job and gets hold of this same list, he'll be over here asking questions right away.'

We walked on a little way then my messy feelings spilt out of my aching heart and I told Hooper out of the blue, 'Jack and I argued.'

'When?'

'Last night, after you left.'

He paused, glanced at me then kept on walking. 'There's no point me asking if you're OK.'

'No.'

'Is there anything I can do?'

'No – thanks anyway.' There was nothing anyone could do now that Jack and I had said how we both felt about my trip to see Adam Earle.

'Talking of Cole . . .' Hooper was the first to spot the police Range Rover at the gates. 'I guess his computer guys already found the list.'

An hour later I stood across the desk from Saint Sam.

Inspector Cole had been and gone, and I was sitting in Justine's European literature class when the call came via Luke.

'Dr Webb's office – now,' he'd told me out in the corridor after he'd knocked on the door and Justine had given me permission to leave her class.

'What's wrong? Am I in trouble again?'

'He didn't say – sorry.' Luke still hadn't come out of the traumatized, post-Paige phase and he seemed detached from the events taking place around him.

'How did he look?'

'I didn't see him. D'Arblay gave me the message.'

'Thanks, Luke!'

'Hey, don't shoot the messenger,' he'd muttered as he walked away, and I'd realized, too late, that I'd been too harsh.

Now I stood in the principal's office feeling like a prisoner awaiting sentence.

'These are my conditions for allowing you to stay at St Jude's until the end of term,' Saint Sam began in funereal tones. 'First, you must stay inside school grounds at all times. If for any reason you need to go into the village, you must ask my permission. You will not under any circumstances go alone. There will always be a member of staff with you.'

So I was a prisoner and this was my sentence.

'Let me be clear – this is because we can't risk a repeat of yesterday's events at Ainslee Westgate. And, before you speak, you need to know that Inspector Cole has given me a clear picture of the danger he feels you may be in from members of this right-wing splinter group – the Campaign for Racial Purity. Again, Alyssa, let me finish.'

'No, Dr Webb, you have to listen.' I was fired up enough to find my voice at last. 'Did the inspector also tell you that Guy Simons is on the CRP committee?'

'Stop there.' He raised his pale, slim, scholarly hands as if to push me away. 'I don't wish to discuss members of staff with you.'

But I wasn't finished. 'And Matthew Cooke is on the list too. He's Micky and Chris Cooke's father, who works at the Queen Elizabeth morgue. Micky could have been the one who dumped Lily's bag at Tom Walsingham's house. Oh,

271

and by the way his older brother, Chris, is definitely the guy in the grey hoodie who attacked Paige's horse and stole the motorbike and tried to run me over! Inspector Cole knows all of this.'

'We've been informed, Alyssa.' This was D'Arblay speaking as he came through the door connecting Saint Sam's office with his own. 'Christopher Cooke was in fact the main reason behind Inspector Cole's latest visit.'

'Why? What did he say?'

The bursar stood at my side of the principal's desk, his right hand resting lightly on the polished surface. He drummed his forefinger – once, twice, three times. I noticed for the first time that he wore a gold ring on the third finger of his right hand. 'The inspector informed us that they take your allegations seriously.'

'Extremely seriously,' Saint Sam echoed. He looked and sounded weary, unlike D'Arblay who was as smooth and dapper as ever.

'So much so that early this morning they went to Cooke's house with a warrant for his arrest,' D'Arblay said. 'They've taken him to Ainslee police station for questioning.'

chapter sixteen

Suddenly I was obsessed with hands.

Saint Sam in his wisdom had decided to move me from the room I'd shared with Lily and Paige to a smaller single room overlooking the quad, and I was staring out of the window down on a waterlogged winter lawn and paved walkways.

Hands – Saint Sam's, which were pale and meticulously clean; D'Arblay's stubbier and manicured.

Not so much hands as rings, in fact. I was remembering the one I'd seen on the third finger of D'Arblay's right hand – two narrow, interlocked bands, one white gold, the other a deeper rose-gold colour – wondering where I'd seen one just like it before.

It wouldn't be long before I remembered – my memory just needed the right trigger. Meanwhile I would arrange and rearrange my hairbrush and shampoos on my new bedside cabinet. I would re-hang my clothes in my wardrobe, arranging them by colour. I would get my possessions in perfect order.

At lunchtime Jack knocked on my door. 'Are you coming to eat?'

My heart leaped to hear his voice and see his face, but I tried to act casual. 'Thanks, but I'm not really hungry.'

'Come anyway,' he insisted.

We decided not to have lunch. Instead we walked in the grounds for a while then went for coffee in the sports centre.

'This is better than the dining room,' I sighed as we sat in a quiet corner of the mezzanine overlooking the tennis courts.

Jack didn't say much, just waited for me to start communicating.

'Thanks for not giving up on me,' I said. A night and a morning had never felt so long. Every minute of it I'd dreaded that Jack would never speak to me again.

He nodded.

'I honestly didn't mean to block you out,' I went on.

'I know you didn't.'

'I'll try not to do it again.'

'Cool.'

'And I do trust you.'

He smiled, reached across the table and took my hand.

Hands – pale and scholarly, manicured and stubby, or long-fingered, lithe and square-nailed like Jack's. Hands wearing rings, hands with nicotine-stained fingers clutching me by the throat, forcing me towards the edge of a train platform.

'Oh shit!' I gasped, standing up then sitting again in two jerky stages.

I reran yesterday's attack.

Two guys – one over six feet tall in a knitted cap, with a shell-shaped tattoo on his neck. The shorter one snatched my

bag, they ran with it over the bridge and into the toilets. The
tattooed one burst out ahead of the short guy, his tattoo grabbing
my attention as he hooked his arm round my neck and dragged
me towards the edge of the platform. He was a drinker and a
smoker – I could smell both on his breath as he choked me and
forced me down. His hands were bony and strong. He wore a
ring – two bands of interlocked gold.

'Shit!' I said again.

'Hooper – it's me, Alyssa.'

I called him from the sports centre while Jack absorbed the implications of what I was saying.

'Hey, Alyssa.'

'Listen, is there any chance of you finding out any more about the CRP?'

'What kind of thing?'

'Like, do they get some kind of membership badge when they join?'

'Jeez, Alyssa, they're not the boy scouts!'

'I know. Maybe not a badge – more a special type of ring. Can you find that out for me?'

'I guess.' Hooper sounded curious, as I'd hoped he would. 'OK, yeah – I'll try. Where are you now, by the way?'

'With Jack in the sports centre.'

'Are you two . . . ?'

'Yeah, I think we're good again, thanks.' Maybe not as good as before – it was too early to tell. But at least Jack had knocked on my door and we were talking. He hadn't given up on me, thank God.

'Cool. Speak later.'

'It would make sense,' I told Jack as soon as I came off the phone.

He shook his head. 'You're saying D'Arblay belongs to the CRP as well as Guy Simons. I'm not sure, Alyssa.'

'Think it through. We already said that D'Arblay would be one of the few people who knew the history of St Jude's well enough to recognize the parallels between Lily's death and Eleanor Bond's in 1938. We asked why hadn't he made the connection – especially when the info about the missing tooth emerged – remember!'

'I guess.'

'And actually D'Arblay could be the one who told them there was no CCTV footage from the attack on Mistral, which would mean he's been hiding evidence. Plus, look at all the times he wanted me and Paige to leave before the end of term. You see what I'm saying – he didn't want us here asking questions and stirring things up.'

'So Guy and D'Arblay together – they would both be aware of the CRP threats against members of Robert Earle's family?'

'They'd have to be,' I told him. 'Then when the whole thing blew up and Lily was actually killed, they were desperate to cover up their involvement, especially when her death looked like robbing the school of Earle's million-pound donation.'

Jack gave a wry smile. 'You know I never liked the guy. He's always been a control freak, but I never thought he would be involved with an extremist group. And this theory only hangs together if D'Arblay does turn out to be a member of the CRP,' he reminded me.

'Yeah, that's why I plan to focus on Guy for now,' I decided. 'Because you remember what we read in Lily's diary – Guy was with Harry when they visited Paige's house for the Horse Trials. And on the day Lily disappeared we know that Guy Simons was the last person at St Jude's to see her alive.'

It should have been straightforward for me and Jack to track down our head of PE, to watch him closely and pick up any dodgy behaviour that might drag him into the centre of the CRP involvement in Lily's death. But life around here is never simple.

In fact, we'd checked out the sports centre and Guy's small office beside the weights room, drawn a blank and decided to head for the main school building when a food-delivery van drew up in the car park. The driver from Askwith's Fruit and Vegetables stepped out, quickly followed by our favourite Rottweiler journo, Emily Archer. She must have bribed the guy from Askwith's to smuggle her past the police cordon.

'Jesus, you never give up!' I groaned as she ignored Jack and made a beeline for me. 'Anyway, you're wasting your time – I still can't talk to you.'

She darted across my path. 'Don't walk away, Alyssa – not before you hear what I have to say. I'm here to share information, not ask questions.'

I stared at her with grudging respect. 'So share.'

'First of all, the police questioned Chris Cooke earlier today.'

'I already know that, thanks.'

'And they released him without charge. I thought you should be aware so you didn't risk bumping into him by accident.'

My heart did one of those stop-start lurches. 'When did that happen?'

'An hour ago. I gather from sources inside the station that he gave them an alibi for both the motorbike hit-and-run and the break-in to the stable yard. Inspector Cole will check the alibis, but meanwhile they decided they didn't have grounds to hold him.'

'Thanks,' I told Emily. 'But I'm not about to bump into Chris Cooke – I'm grounded. He can't get into St Jude's and I can't get out.'

'If I can get in, so can Chris Cooke,' she pointed out. 'Be warned.'

'OK, I'll keep it in mind.'

Emily Archer seemed satisfied on that score and moved on. 'Secondly, I've been doing some research into Lily Earle's family and came up with some interesting connections.'

'Why are you telling me this?' I interrupted, while Jack stood between me and gusts of icy wind blowing across the car park and the Askwith's man carried trays of apples, bananas, cabbages and tomatoes into the school kitchens.

Emily took the interruption patiently. 'It's not stuff that's in the public domain, but it may be something Lily talked about with you and Paige.'

'I doubt it. Lily didn't talk about her family.' And, anyway, I was anxious to follow up my own Guy and D'Arblay suspicions. 'Sorry, I have to go.'

Being a journalist means you override the normal, polite keep-away signals. These are the people trained to thrust microphones under the noses of fraudulent financiers or cowboy builders who've robbed old ladies of their life savings – that's their job. So no way was Emily going to respect my feeble 'sorry, I have to go'.

'You know that Robert Earle isn't exactly the most popular guy on Planet Media,' she ploughed on. 'I considered that might be worth looking into and it turns out I was right. He has a long list of enemies, including a dozen editors he's fired without warning, rival newspaper owners – oh, and of course Dave Peacock, the guy he sacked on the spot for driving Anna Earle to see you, Alyssa.'

'You contacted him again?'

'Yeah, and according to Dave it's surprising what gets said during drives from one business meeting to another. He got to hear personal phone calls and off-the-record conversations with Earle's business associates. There was one in particular earlier this summer that Dave overheard.'

'To do with Lily?'

'Indirectly. This was about a protest staged outside Comco's offices on the Euston Road. Apparently Robert Earle totally lost his rag over it, yelled down the phone to the organizer of the protest, swearing and saying it didn't change anything, he wouldn't give way to threats or buckle under pressure and so on.'

'Was that all?'

'No. Dave says he heard the protest guy talking on Robert Earle's speaker phone – in other words he got both sides of the conversation and he didn't like what he heard – in the end the guy was actually threatening members of Earle's family.'

I took a deep breath. 'Thanks for telling me – I appreciate it.'

'But it's not new to you?' Emily was smart in picking up on my reaction. 'Which means we've been digging the same kind of dirt, you and me. Maybe you should consider a career as a journalist.'

'No thanks – no offence.'

'None taken.' She grinned like a co-conspirator. 'But if you want me to follow up on this anti-Comco group, which was issuing threats against Earle's family, I reckon we should pool our resources.'

'In other words, I just tell you what I know?' I glanced at Jack and saw him nod. He meant I should trust his journalist friend, which was a pretty big challenge for me, as you know. But I rose to it as part of my growing-up process. No more green-eyed-god jealousy towards Emily Archer from now on. 'They're called the Campaign for Racial Purity,' I told her.

She raised her eyebrows and sighed. 'Whoa, why do I *not* like the sound of that?'

The Askwith's guy had just finished his delivery and called to see if she wanted a ride out of the grounds. She told him yes.

'Be careful with these CRP people,' I warned. 'They're lowlife. Don't let them know you're investigating them.'

Emily nodded. 'Likewise,' she told me.

My warning to her was in time, I hoped, but hers to me was way too late. The CRP already knew I was on to them and were going to extreme lengths to shut me up.

Guy wasn't in the main school, and Jack and I had moved on to the stable yard when we heard two raised voices coming from inside Franklin's stable. We recognized them straight away – Guy Simons and Harry Embsay.

It turned out that stables are an ideal place to eavesdrop – you just have to stand in one stable and listen in to the conversation in the stable next to it. The sound drifts across the partitions separating one stall from the next.

'I'm not going in there!' Jack hissed when I put my finger to my lips and pointed to Mistral's stall.

'Shh!'

'Small stable – giant horse!'

'Shh, Mistral won't hurt us.' I had to hope that I was right. 'Hey,' I murmured as Paige's horse rustled through his straw and stuck his head over the door. I stroked his neck and finally managed to slide the bolt silently, signalling for Jack to join me inside.

'Jeez!' he groaned as he backed into the furthest corner.

We were in with Mistral and safe so far, though he didn't seem all that happy to have visitors. His ears had gone flat against his head and he rolled his eyes suspiciously.

'I think that's horse speak for "Get the hell out of my stable!"' Jack mouthed.

'Shh!' I needed to listen to Harry and Guy.

'I told you – I just spoke to him!' By the time we were safely hidden, Harry was almost bellowing. 'Chris told the cops he was with me both times – I'm his alibi!'

'So you just say yes, you were with him.' Guy made an effort to stay calm. 'You back him up. What's the problem?'

'The problem is – I wasn't!'

'They don't know that. You say you and Chris were together. Where were you, as a matter of fact?'

'Which time – when he rode the bike at Alyssa or when he attacked Paige's horse?'

'Both.'

'Number one there was a blizzard and I was stuck here until it stopped.'

'OK, so you say Chris paid you a visit in your room and you were snowed in together.'

'Number two – everyone knows where I was – I was out riding your stupid horse!'

Guy thought before he went on. 'You were out riding and you ran into Chris on one of the bridleways just outside the Bottoms. You stopped to talk. That's good enough. But you need to get together to work out the details. Where is he now? How soon can you meet up?'

'He went back to work.'

'Whereabouts?'

'With Audley at Upwood House. They're there all this week – that's what he said.'

'OK, so get over there now – before it gets dark.'

'And you'll give me a lift?' Harry laughed. 'Yeah, thought so – like hell you will!'

'I'm not the one in deep shit,' Guy told him. 'You are. Just get over there now and do what you have to do to firm up Chris's alibi.'

Jack and I heard the bolt to Franklin's stable door slide back and one pair of footsteps walk across the yard. We ducked down, well out of sight. In the stable next door we heard Harry swear and pick up a plastic feed bucket then slam it against a wall. Franklin gave a scared whinny and Mistral threw back his head and squealed a reply. I had to agree with Jack – all of a sudden the stable did feel pretty cramped and from our perspective crouched down in the straw the grey horse was a quivering mountain of muscle.

'Let's get out of here!' Jack whispered.

But we had to wait until Harry had taken out his anger on the bucket. It landed on the stone floor then he kicked it out into the yard, ran after it and stamped on it, went back to bolt Franklin's door and finally strode off after Guy.

'At least now we definitely know what we're dealing with,' I said to Jack as we left Mistral's stable. 'Chris Cooke, Harry and Guy are in this together, and most likely D'Arblay as well. All we have to do now is find out who made Lily pregnant.'

'And exactly who killed her and how,' he added.

'Alyssa – Hooper here.'

I was in the middle of convincing Jack to come with me

to Upwood House when I stopped to answer my phone. 'You found something new?' I asked.

'Yeah. I printed off a membership form for the CRP then I rang the membership secretary, a Michael Morrison, and asked if I could come to their next meeting, but he said I had to fill in the form and join first. We got into a long conversation.'

'Cool, Hooper, but can you speed it up? I'm in a hurry.'

'I'm getting there. I asked what I got for my hundred and fifty quid membership – a card, a badge, whatever. He said no, no card or badge. But listen to this, Alyssa – all members are invited to wear a special ring.'

'Two bands of interlocked gold,' I said with total, heart-stopping certainty.

'With the initials CRP engraved on them,' Hooper confirmed. 'I guess it's their form of the freemasons' secret handshake, so that members can recognize each other . . . Alyssa, are you still there?'

'Yeah, thanks, Hooper. Thanks for that.'

'Where are you now?'

'In the stable yard with Jack. We're going to sneak out and follow Harry. He's meeting Chris Cooke at Upwood House – you know the place?'

'Over by the abbey – yeah.'

'I'm officially grounded so don't tell anyone.'

'I won't. Call me if you're in trouble, though.'

'We will. Bye.'

Jack waited for me to finish talking. 'So we're sneaking out?' he said edgily.

'We have to!' I frowned and bit my bottom lip. 'Listen, Jack – you don't have to come if you don't want to . . .'

'Alyssa!'

'Yeah, sorry.' I was amazed how easily I still slipped back into sulky-child mode. 'But we do have to go. We can't come this far and back out now.'

'I know, but I'm slower than you at taking it all in – Harry, Guy, Chris Cooke and now D'Arblay.'

'Definitely D'Arblay,' I said. He wore a CRP ring on the third finger of his right hand.

'OK – Tom's party,' I said to Jack.

We took two bikes and cycled as fast as we could past the lake and through the wood, across the stream and out on to the back lane with not more than two hours of daylight left on this overcast winter's day.

'That was ages ago,' Jack replied. 'I thought you'd remembered everything already.'

'There's always more.'

We pedalled fast through the Bottoms and only slowed down when we turned up on to Meredith Lane, heading for Upper Chartsey and beyond that Hereward Ridge. My lungs were close to bursting so I had to speak in fits and starts.

You had to be brain dead to live in chocolate-box Chartsey, Tom had told me the first time I'd met him while I kept my eyes glued on Jack and Jayden in the corner of the room.

This was before Lily had thrown herself at him.

But that had been a whole hour into the party. What

had happened before that? 'Alex and Micky were part of the Ainslee Comp gang who gate-crashed with Jayden,' I told Jack. 'That's right – isn't it?'

He nodded and we cycled on.

'But I didn't really notice them because I was on edge about meeting everyone. I only really paid attention to the people from St Jude's who I already knew.'

'Me, Zara, Luke, Paige . . .' Jack said. 'Anyone else?'

'Harry. There was almost a fight between him and Jayden out in the hall.'

I'd seen it through the door – Jayden rushing up to Harry, ready to head butt him, Alex and Micky stepping in to stop him. The music had been loud, but I could still work out what they were saying.

'What did Harry do?' Jack asked.

'He threw a punch at Jayden as soon as his back was turned. He looked like he wanted to knock him dead. Then the front door opened and that was when Lily arrived.'

I stepped forward to say hi, told her she looked cool in her shiny top.

'Thanks, Alyssa.' She slurred my name, couldn't focus as she tottered across the hallway and ran into Harry – literally smack into him. It took a full three seconds for her to register and recognize him.

'You're pissed again,' he sneered as she fell sideways against the hall stand.

'Better pissed than a wanker like you, Harry.'

I was convinced he'd have punched her too if Jayden hadn't pulled free from Micky and Alex, and stepped in between them.

'Ah, sweet!' Harry laughed. 'Look at this, the ex-boyfriend still has "feelings" for you, Lil.'

'Wanker,' she muttered. 'Everyone knows what a tosser you are, Harry Embsay.' She was out of her head on drugs and alcohol, but she still had enough focus to want to hurt him. She hated him. She loathed him so much she wanted to destroy him.

He moved in so close that I couldn't hear what he said to her, but I had a crystal-clear picture of the way she glared at him and I would be able to re-run and lip-read his words as many times as I wanted.

'Don't drink when you're pregnant!'

He wasn't offering advice – he was tormenting her.

'Don't drink when you're pregnant.'

She crumpled and fell against Alex, who handed her on to Zara and told her to take Lily into the downstairs cloakroom while he and Micky steered Jayden into the lounge.

That was when Jayden cornered Jack, and I was left talking with Tom.

'So how come you live here?' I asked him, one eye on Jack and Jayden, the feral kid.

Tom called it la-la land and we'd chatted for a while then Lily escaped from the loo and targeted Tom. 'There you are!' she cried, kissing him full on the lips and swamping him in an octopus embrace to make Jayden jealous.

And after that the 'Don't drink when you're pregnant' episode out in the hallway had completely slipped from my eidetic memory, until right here, right now.

chapter seventeen

Defying all orders and advice, I was out of the school grounds and cycling with Jack along Hereward Ridge until Upwood House was in sight.

'How could Harry have known Lily was . . . ?' Jack asked, braking hard.

'Pregnant?' I finished the sentence. 'He couldn't have – not unless she'd chosen to tell him he was the daddy.'

It was the evidence I needed to fill two empty pages in Lily's diary – two yawning blank days for Harry to move in on Lily and take what he wanted. My heart bled when I imagined the details. A big house in the country, lots of land, rows of stables. But no, Lily hated horses and the great outdoors so it didn't happen in the Kellys' stable yard or in the grounds. It had to have been in the house, probably on the day he and Guy arrived. Maybe his room had been along the landing from hers.

'Pissed again,' he would have sneered as she'd stumbled up to bed. He would have grabbed her and shoved her into his room.

She would have been manic and angry, pushing him away. He wouldn't have listened. Lily was drunk and no one would believe her if she accused him later. Anyway, if anyone challenged him, he would say she'd been willing, the sex was consensual.

But I always said that was impossible. I knew Lily and I knew Harry. Just no way!

'This is the deep shit Guy was talking about back in the stable,' Jack decided. 'He was telling Harry, "You got yourself into this mess in the first place, now sort it."'

'We'd better keep moving.' I took a left fork on the bridleway and cycle path, down from the ridge towards the neat and spacious grounds of Upwood House. Dark green clipped yews stood in rows beneath the graceful silver branches of ancient beech trees. I only stopped when we reached a sign advertising opening hours and entrance costs.

'Harry said Chris Cooke was working with a guy called Audley,' Jack reminded me. 'Who the hell is he?'

'Charles Audley, 204 Bristol Road – Chairman of Ainslee CRP.' I had Hooper to thank for this nugget of information – intense, serious Hooper who never asked for anything but was always there. 'Look over the far side of the car park – see the white truck?'

Jack nodded and we were so busy reading the green lettering down the side – Green Shoots – C. P. Audley, Landscape Gardener – that we didn't notice a thickset guy in his forties carrying a sack of garden waste down some stone steps. It was only when he tipped the dead leaves into the back of the truck that we saw him.

He'd already spotted us so it was too late to duck out of sight. 'The house is closed,' he called helpfully.

'OK, thanks!' Jack turned away while I stared at Audley to discover whether or not he was wearing the CRP ring.

'How far did you cycle?' Audley asked, striding across the car park. He looked less friendly than he sounded, with his shaved head and deep frown marks between dark eyebrows. And, yes, he was wearing the ring.

'Not far,' I told him, swinging my bike round to follow Jack.

'You're not from St Jude's, by any chance?' Audley's head was to one side, his bottom jaw jutted out – attentive and ready to break out into aggression.

'No!' As usual my reply was too fast and an octave too high. I must teach myself not to misjudge my lies like this – role play and rehearse until I grew more convincing.

'Yeah, St Jude's,' Audley contradicted, as if my one short negative had told him everything he needed to know. 'You're Alyssa Stephens.'

I launched myself back along the track, not quick enough to stop the CRP chairman from cutting across in front of me. He grasped my handlebars, swung the front end of the bike sideways and knocked me clean off. As I sprawled on the floor, I saw Jack brake and turn round, riding his bike straight at Audley, who had time to sidestep and let Jack veer off the track smack into the upright post of a visitor-information notice board. I heard the impact – was helpless as Audley dragged him off his bike and punched him.

Jack fought back. He's strong and gave as good as he got. I scrambled to my feet, yelling for Audley to stop, but my shouts only brought Chris Cooke and Harry racing down the stone steps – the last thing we needed. Chris piled in to help his Green Shoots boss, taking turns to trade blows with Jack while Harry grabbed me round the waist and threw me back on to the ground face down, stamping his foot into the small of my back.

Audley and Chris together were too much for Jack. They used fists and then feet, kicking at him and forcing him across the car park until they had him backed up against the flat-back truck.

I tried to roll away from Harry and crawl free, but he only ground me down harder with his boot. Just able to turn my head, I saw Audley seize a garden spade from the back of his truck and swing it at Jack's head. I heard the thud of impact, watched Jack go down and stay down. Not a flicker – nothing.

Oh God, let him not be dead!

Quickly Audley gave the order for Cooke to help him lift Jack into the truck. Together they raised him out of the dirt and tossed him like a limp scarecrow in among the dead leaves and clippings.

'Stay with Harry,' Audley told Cooke as he flung open the driver's door and climbed in. The engine choked into life then tyres crunched over gravel. Audley reversed the truck and swung it round towards the gate, passing within a metre of where I lay.

'Deal with her,' Audley yelled out of his window as he disappeared with Jack. 'Do whatever you have to do.'

Oh God, let him not be dead!

Twisting the upper half of my body, I used all my

strength to free my arms from under me and catch hold of Harry's ankle. He tried to kick me away, but I held on and toppled him. He swore as he crashed down on top of me.

Cooke laughed at him – a big insult and a mistake. This is Harry Embsay, remember.

Still swearing, Harry leaped to his feet to confront Cooke, giving me a chance finally to roll and heave myself up from the ground with gravel embedded in my bleeding palms and gasping for breath. I was up and off, lifting my bike as a shield to fend off Harry and Cooke, smashing it against their chests, dropping it and running on along the bridle path towards the old abbey. They were close behind, trampling through bushes, trying to cut me off. I veered away from the track, and half slipped, half ran down the steep hill towards the river. I could see it snaking through the valley, glinting in the last of the sun's rays. If I could just make it to the abbey ruins and find somewhere to hide . . .

I was down the hill, out of the cover of the oak trees and on to open grassland, deserted except for a scattering of cold, miserable sheep. I sprinted on towards the abbey.

Cooke and Harry hadn't gained on me until we were in the open, but then they seemed to pick up pace. Looking over my shoulder to check, I hit a dip in the ground and stumbled, picked myself up and changed direction.

'Split up. You go that way, I'll go this – we'll cut her off before she reaches the river, no problem,' Harry told Cooke.

That stubborn suffragette gene kicked in. Who did these guys think they were – saying they could sprint ahead and capture me in a pincer movement? No way! I can outrun you – watch me!

I flew over the rough grass, beat them to the water's edge and without pausing I sprang on to the first stepping stone. Harry crunched to a halt on the gravel bank and it was Cooke who followed me.

I hurried on as fast as I could across the worn, mossy stones – step then balance, step again. The river was deep after melted snow and rain, the current dangerous. I knew it, but I was dead set on not losing my balance. I fixed my sights on the far bank and kept on going.

Cooke came after me. I could hear his feet land with a splash and take off again. I was more sure footed and I spread out my arms to keep my balance – until I reached the middle of the river and the low sun suddenly dazzled me.

I paused to shield my eyes, heard Cooke lurch and splash. Now the sun was in his eyes too, blinding him. There was another splash – no yelling, no crying out as he lost his balance and fell into the water.

The dark brown current boiled to either side of the stepping stone. By the time I turned round, the black undertow had sucked Cooke below the surface. A few seconds later he resurfaced fifteen metres downstream – just his head and left arm. Frozen in horror, I saw the water spin him round, drag him down again then push him up to the surface twenty metres further away, in the deepest part of the river. His mouth opened and he gulped in air and water as the current twisted and pushed him on.

At last the water rolled the drowning man into a calmer section of the river – I could see him lying motionless and face down just under the rust-brown surface. The cold current toyed with Cooke. It turned him face upward and pulled him out of reach. His eyes were open – those grey eyes with dark lashes. Then the undertow caught him again. He was sucked down, turned and rolled among the reeds and weeds, down into the blackness.

'Now it's just you and me, Alyssa.' Harry had dragged me kicking and screaming back across the river, up the slope and into the abbey ruins and was enjoying this window of opportunity – a chance to gloat.

'Sadist!'

'Thanks.'

'It's not a compliment!' I lashed out with my right foot and landed a kick on his shin.

His grin faded and he got a tighter grip as he manhandled me towards the dark cloisters and threw me against a slimy stone pillar. 'You're an idiot,' he snarled. 'You're so far up your own arse – just like Paige and Lily. You girls don't see what's going on around you in the real world.'

I groaned as I slid to the ground and put my hands over my head to shield myself. 'I never liked you, Harry. I'd say that was a good call on my part.'

He smiled again as he kicked me, and I curled into a ball. The ground was cold and damp. I made a resolution to take whatever was coming in silence and clamped my mouth shut.

It was Harry who did the talking, squatting confidentially beside me, big, square hands clasped in front of him. 'I remember seeing you on the first day of term, Alyssa – the scared little newbie getting dropped off in the quad. Everyone clocked you – me, Luke, the two Jacks. Great legs, well in the running for the Pippa Middleton Rear of the Year. That seems like a long time ago.' He picked up a stone and turned it this way and that before tossing it carelessly against the nearest pillar. The stone landed with a light rattle that echoed down the row of cloisters. 'I bet you never in your wildest dreams thought you'd end up here.' He tossed another stone, which rattled and echoed. 'The problem is – you still think you're so fucking clever.'

Curled up in my foetal position, I didn't respond.

He shoved the side of his foot into my back. 'Hey, Alyssa – I'm talking to you. You think you're mega clever, remembering everything the way you do. But what would really have been smart would be to forget – you see what I'm saying?' He shoved again then leaned over and forced my arms down by my side, tutting then wincing when he saw my bloody hands. 'Ouch, I bet that hurts. Yeah, I warned D'Arblay what you were like – think bloodhound with a photographic memory, I said. That pretty much nails it. After the Lily thing he said to me to make sure you and Paige didn't get a chance to poke your snouts in. I said, that's Cooke's job – he's good at stuff like that. I lived too close to the action. I didn't want to draw attention to myself.'

'The Lily thing' – Harry was so casual and heartless that

I broke my resolution not to talk. 'She didn't deserve what you did to her. What did Lily ever do to you?'

'You mean Crazy Girl? She didn't have to *do* anything. She just didn't have the right parents. Come on – you're so clever you worked this out already, Alyssa. Comco is making an exposé of the CRP. We tell them to stop; they ignore us. That's why we had to kidnap Lily. Simple.'

'So go ahead – tell me exactly how you did it.'

He laughed in the semi darkness then stood up and yelled at the top of his voice. 'Is anybody there? . . . Nope, nobody. So I guess it won't hurt to let you into our little secret. How did we kidnap Lily? OK so I heard on the grapevine that she had to go home – you know what a small place St Jude's is, you can't take a shit without everyone finding out. I told Guy, who passed it on to D'Arblay. We never do anything without orders from him, by the way, even though he keeps his name out of – what do they call it – the public domain? He said, call Audley and Chris, tell them to wait for her at Ainslee Westgate. Me and Guy had to steer clear – he didn't want anyone from St Jude's involved. So it was Chris and actually a couple of other younger CRP guys – you might know them, yeah? One has a tattoo right here on his neck. They saw Lily get out of the taxi and made their move, end of story.'

'No, no, it couldn't have been that easy. Lily would have fought back.' In public, in the middle of a busy station forecourt – someone would have seen what was happening.

'You've heard of ketamine?' Harry asked, as if he was passing the time of day. 'Party drug of choice. It inhibits the central nervous system's receptors and an overdose leads to loss of feeling and paralysis. Perfect in this situation.'

'Cooke drugged Lily?'

'Yeah, there you go. Ketamine comes as a liquid in small pharmaceutical bottles – very handy. Administered by intramuscular injection as an emergency general anaesthetic – out in the field, in war zones and so on.'

'Don't tell me – Cooke got hold of it from the hospital pharmacy by using his dad's security pass?'

'Good again, Alyssa. I'm impressed. So Lily steps out of the cab and Chris goes up to her, syringe in hand and says hi, boyfriend to girlfriend as far as everyone around is concerned. She doesn't even see the needle coming. What people nearby see is a girl sinking into her boyfriend's arms. There are two other guys on hand – no one needs to bother offering any more help. They think that someone should tell her to cut back on the drink or the drugs, but stuff like this happens every day.'

'Where did Cooke take her?'

'Audley has a workshop where he stores his tools, out on an industrial estate on the edge of town. He and Chris drove her there, but by the time they locked her up the ketamine was wearing off and she woke up and grew crazy, started hammering at the door, using a spade, whatever she could lay her hands on to smash the store room window. They had to go back in and up the dosage.'

Harry stopped talking. I sat up and leaned against the pillar, covering my face with my hands.

'That wasn't part of the original plan,' he acknowledged

with a sigh, as if he cared. Then straight away he laughed at what might be interpreted as a sign of weakness. 'Lily goes down, out like a light, and Audley and Chris shit themselves, thinking this time they've killed her. Audley calls D'Arblay, who straight away moves the goalposts.

'D'Arblay!' I echoed. There he was, sitting at the heart of all this darkness, just as I'd suspected.

Harry didn't even pause. 'Robert Earle is out of the country, not responding to our demands, blah blah. We're not likely to get him to stop making the documentary, and even if Lily eventually comes round from the overdose we can't rely on being able to keep her quiet. She'll try to escape and then we're all up shit creek. To cut a long story short, D'Arblay says to bring her back to St Jude's and dump her in the lake, make it look like suicide.'

'In the Green Shoots truck?'

'Yeah. Audley is due to do some work in the grounds anyway. Nobody will pay any attention.'

'Were you there?'

'No, but I was watching from my window. It all went smoothly – hardly a splash as they slipped her into the water.'

I shuddered and tried to slough off the horror of what he was telling me. 'So you – you didn't kidnap her and you didn't kill her?'

He laughed out loud. 'Don't sound so surprised. Think of me as an angel compared with some of them.'

'Compared with D'Arblay?'

'Exactly.' Harry's legs got cramp so he stood up and

dragged me with him. 'This is how much of a perv D'Arblay is – he's the one who wanted the tooth.'

I groaned and put my arms across my chest.

'Cowboy up, Alyssa – this is by far the best bit. Guess what – D'Arblay managed to get hold of the five teeth from the other victims.'

'From the 1930s?'

'Yeah. It turns out that PC Plod back in those days never tracked them down and our neo-Nazi forefathers kept them in a little box as souvenirs. They got handed down from one generation to the next.'

'That's disgusting,' I muttered.

Harry grinned. 'D'Arblay waited four days until they dragged the body out of the lake and it was safely in the morgue, then he gave Chris another call and started to talk orthodontics with him – specifically the lower molar on the right-hand side. He's a man of tradition. He wanted that tooth and no one was going to stop him getting it.'

Shuddering again, I staggered away from Harry, down the dark cloisters.

'You realize why?' he asked, catching hold of me and raising me up after I tripped and fell.

Eleanor Bond, 1938. Plus four other victims – five ritualistic, symmetrical killings.

'You've stopped talking to me so I'll tell you anyway. D'Arblay tried to convince us that he wanted to follow a historical tradition, to walk in the footsteps of the great fascists of the 1930s. Personally I think that was bullshit.'

'So why do *you* think D'Arblay needed the tooth?'

'Like I said, the guy's a total perv. He made Chris sneak into the morgue and steal what he wanted partly because of the tradition but mostly because that's what he gets off on. And where do you think he keeps his collection of molars? No, it's too weird – you won't be able to guess.'

I pictured D'Arblay's office – the bookshelves behind his desk, the leather-bound books, memorabilia – shells, a statuette of a horse. 'They're in a silver box next to a small bronze statue,' I told Harry. 'It's locked with a tiny key that D'Arblay keeps on top of his desk so that every time he goes into his room he can unlock it, take out the teeth and gloat.'

'Wow, you really are pretty smart, Alyssa.' He sighed and stared at me as if he'd be sad to lose me. 'What a waste.'

I wasn't finished – not yet. 'So, as far as your personal involvement goes, Harry – it's no to Lily's kidnap and no to her killing – right?'

He held up both hands. 'Not me, not guilty.'

'But you attacked her at Paige's house – you're the baby's father.'

He croaked out another laugh. 'Is this really how you want to spend your last few minutes, Alyssa – raking up the sordid details?'

'Yes. I need to know.'

'Then who am I to disappoint you? No, m'lud – on the third count I also plead not guilty.'

I turned on him and shoved him off balance. I couldn't see his face – only the gleam of his teeth as he kept on laughing. 'You're a liar.'

'Why would I not tell you the truth? Who are you going to share this with before you die? Look around – do you see anyone?'

I used my bleeding, throbbing hands to slap his face and his chest. 'So who?'

He easily fought me off and pinned me against the cloister wall. 'Again – simple when you think about it. If it wasn't me, who else could it be?'

Oh God – only one other name flew into my mind with arrow-like precision. 'Guy Simons!'

'*Ker-ching!*' Harry said. 'Good job, Alyssa – you got there in the end.'

chapter eighteen

Disgusting, horrible, sick, revolting. I spat out all these adjectives into the echoing darkness.

'Don't waste your breath,' Harry told me.

Guy Simons – clean-cut sports teacher – turns out to be a closet fascist and rapist.

How did the guy live with himself after what he'd done to Lily? He'd closed the door on his crime, went around St Jude's showing you how to hold a tennis racket and execute a forehand drive, teaching the basics of dressage.

Shock made it feel like someone had rammed a core drill into my gut and scoured out all my organs.

'Come on – it's time,' Harry decided, as if he'd got nothing bigger in mind than a coffee in the Squinting Cat or a game of pool in Ainslee Leisure Centre.

I tried to resist as he clutched my arm and dragged me out of the cloisters down towards the river. 'Where are we going?'

'First, let's take a look at what happened to Chris, the daft sod.' He took a small torch from his pocket and shone it towards the water. The beam glinted and danced over the swift-running surface. 'The current's tricky just here. You get wide, shallow stretches then a few metres downstream it's all forced into narrow gorges – often less than three metres wide and more than ten metres deep – good for white-water rafting. See, this notice tells you to watch out.'

He shone the beam on a faded sign.

PUBLIC WARNING: DO NOT ATTEMPT TO USE THE STEPPING STONES. THIS STRETCH OF RIVER IS DANGEROUS AND HAS CLAIMED LIVES IN THE PAST.

'It's about to claim one more,' Harry muttered, meaning not Cooke but me. He was ready to give up his search, but then he spotted an object floating among the reeds maybe fifty metres downstream. 'Could be a log. There again it could be a corpse. Let's find out.'

I resisted again, kicking and scratching, but still weak. I got a shocking HD image inside my head of Harry eventually putting his square hands round my neck and choking me, forcing me under the water. 'Why are you doing this? What are you waiting for?' I yelled. 'Just get on with it!'

Harry dragged me along the bank until he could shine the beam directly on the floating object. 'Patience, Alyssa. Yep, that's Chris all right.'

Cooke lay half submerged, his face white, eyes still open. The water rocked him gently in a final, icy lullaby.

Harry waded in among the reeds, dragging me with him. 'What do we do – leave him there? Yeah, it's best if the cops find him for themselves. I'll say you went after Chris like a mother tiger, red in tooth and claw, accusing him of crazy stuff like killing Paige. The poor guy didn't stand a chance.

I was too far away to stop you picking up this big rock and hitting him on the back of the head.'

As he spoke, he acted it out, rolling Cooke face down, picking up a jagged rock and smashing it against his skull. 'Got to have injuries consistent with the story,' he explained.

I heard the impact of stone on skull, bent double and retched.

'You smacked him with the rock when he wasn't looking and he keeled over into the water. By the time I reached you, you'd come to your senses and realized what you'd done. You jumped in to drag him back to the bank but it was a bad stretch of river and the current grabbed hold of you and sucked you down.' He nodded and shone the beam on my face. 'What's wrong, Alyssa? Can you spot a loophole?'

I was still retching and pulling away, thinking, *If this is it, if this is really what's going to happen, just do it.*

The sky was black, the river rushed on.

Just do it!

It was so dark we didn't know anyone was there until a dog hurtled out of the cloisters and down the hill towards us. I didn't see it but I heard it, snarling as it came.

Harry just had time to swing his torch towards Bolt as the Staffie leaped chest-high and sank his teeth into Harry's shoulder. The torch dropped to the ground. I dived down, grabbed it and swung it along the bank towards the stepping stones. Jayden walked in our direction – *strolled* actually – with both hands in his jacket pockets, shoulders hunched against the cold. I half ran, half staggered to meet him, with the sweet chorus of Bolt's snarls and growls playing in the background.

Jayden didn't say anything. He took the torch from me and aimed it at Harry and Bolt. The guy was still standing, the dog hadn't let go and blood gushed from the shoulder wound. I groaned and retched.

'Call off the dog! Tell it to stop!' Harry screamed.

Jayden waited a while then glanced at me.

'Tell him to stop,' I pleaded.

'Down, Bolt!'

It was instantaneous. Bolt clicked out of killer mode into guard-dog duty, crouching low, ready to pounce again. Harry shook and bled. He had the river behind him and Bolt in front – there was nowhere for him to go.

'How come?' I groaned at Jayden.

'How come I'm here? Your friend, Hooper,' he drawled without taking his eyes off Bolt and Harry.

'He called you?'

'Hooper said to get my arse over to the Ridge, see what I could see.'

I took a deep breath to slow my racing heart. 'How much of the stuff in the cloisters did you hear?'

'All of it.'

'I thought I was going to die.'

'Not today,' Jayden promised, walking slowly towards Harry to take a look at the damage. 'That'll need stitches,' he remarked.

Bolt lay and growled, curling back his lip.

Then we heard vehicles approaching along the Hereward Ridge bridleway, looking for a route down into the valley. Blue and orange lights flashed as two police Land Rovers threaded between ash trees and bumped across the grass, followed by an unmarked white Range Rover. They arrived in a slow procession then deployed the vehicles so that their headlights were trained on me, Jayden, Bolt, Harry and Chris Cooke's floating corpse.

Inspector Cole stepped out of the first police car with the expressionless female sergeant from the interview room. She held open the back door and I saw Jack get out with Hooper. Hooper had to support Jack as they made their way towards me.

My heart stopped; my mind went blank. Jack broke away from Hooper, stood waiting for me in the white glare of headlights.

Heart and mind kicked back into action. Jack's alive! He's alive!

I ran, reached him and was shocked again by the damage to the side of his head, which was cut and bruised. Gingerly I put out my scraped and bleeding hand to stroke his cheek – the unbruised one. His skin was smooth and warm. 'You're OK?' I whispered.

He gave the faintest nod then reached out for me. I put my arms round him and pressed my face against his chest. He kissed the top of my head.

'What happened? How did you find me?' I asked.

'Hooper grabbed a bike and followed us to Upwood House,' Jack explained.

'Too late to see the action,' Hooper added, modestly underplaying his role. 'I'm afraid I'm no Bradley Wiggins.'

'And then?' I urged, arms still wrapped tight round my Jack.

'I did get there in time to see the Green Shoots truck speeding off. The driver must have seen me, but he didn't slow down to let me pass. In fact, he forced me into the ditch. I thought it didn't look good so I called Emily and asked her to find out anything she could – where Green Shoots was based, who ran it etcetera.

'Emily? Emily Archer?'

'Here I am,' said a breezy voice. The journalist had stepped out of the white Range Rover with D'Arblay and Guy Simons. She made a beeline for us while the bursar and Guy hung back. 'Give me an investigative job to do and I'm all over it like a rash. I was in Ainslee checking out the Green Shoots depot within thirty minutes of Hooper's call. One look at Audley double-padlocking the store and manically hammering boards over the broken window told me it was time to bring in the professionals.'

'The cops found Jack inside the store and arrested Audley.' When Emily had joined us, Hooper had faded into the background, but he stepped forward again now with a reminder. 'Jack still needs to go to hospital to get his head X-rayed.'

'I wanted to find you first,' said Jack, his lips still against my head.

'Jayden saved me,' I murmured, and we turned towards the river to watch the latest developments.

There were four uniforms plus Cole cagily circling Bolt and Harry until Cole told Jayden to call off his dog.

'Heel, Bolt,' Jayden said. The Staffie stood up and trotted stiff-legged over to Jayden – master and dog in unison.

This gave room for two uniforms to move in and put restraints on Harry.

'First stop, hospital,' one said when he took a look at Harry's injuries.

I hung on to Jack for a few seconds more, until I saw the restraints and felt some of the fear recede. There would be no hands round my neck, no watery death.

'Once I knew the police were on to it, my next job was to get back to St Jude's and inform the school,' Emily went on. 'I wanted to get their reaction.'

'And?' Taking a quick look at D'Arblay and Guy Simons, I saw they were still hanging back, quietly observing Harry's arrest.

'Let's just say it put a bomb under their backsides. Those two had jumped into D'Arblay's car and were collecting me at the gates before I had time to file my report.'

'You'll probably need to rewrite it anyway.' I watched from a distance as the cops bundled Harry towards a car. Harry resisted. Guy came forward to speak to him.

'We'll get you a good lawyer,' he promised, gripping his arm and speaking with quiet intensity. 'We can deal with this.'

Harry shook his bleeding head and groaned.

'Get him to the Queen Elizabeth,' Cole ordered.

Then Harry was manhandled into the Land Rover and

driven away while the remaining two cops waded into the reeds to recover Cooke's body.

It was only then that D'Arblay came forward. 'Thank you, Inspector. As Guy said, I'm sure we can sort out the details and get to the truth once things have calmed down.'

His words came out smooth and polished, bland as Saint Sam. But I could see that both he and Guy knew they were hanging on by a thread. Even so, D'Arblay would play out the game to its bitter end.

'Is it in order for me to drive Alyssa and the two Jacks back to St Jude's?' he asked Cole. 'We'll take good care of them until you're ready to interview them.'

I shook my head and tried to attract Cole's attention.

The inspector hesitated, glancing from D'Arblay to Guy then to Jayden who was standing with Bolt out of the glare of the headlight beams.

'Don't even think about taking my dog away from me,' Jayden muttered, quickly turning on his heel.

He and Bolt were halfway up the hill before I caught up with them. 'Stay!' I pleaded. 'I need you to back me up.'

He walked on. 'No, you don't.'

'You can see what's happening – D'Arblay's going to deny everything!'

Jayden kept on walking, tapping his forehead. 'Everything I need to know is safe in here so I'm through with this crap. I don't like cops. I won't talk to anyone until we get to court.'

'Please!'

'You talk to them, Alyssa. You're good at that.'

309

'You knew all along Harry was involved. You got there before any of the rest of us. Did Lily tell you?'

'No. You lot use your brains. I use gut instinct. The guy makes my skin crawl – always did.'

It was the last thing Jayden said before he and Bolt strode up into the abbey ruins out of sight and I ran back to Cole. 'Jayden saved my life.' The words tumbled out, my breathing was uneven. 'It's God's honest truth – I'd be dead without him.'

'We'll need a statement,' Cole decided.

'Don't send me with them,' I begged, pointing at D'Arblay and Guy Simons.

'You'll be quite safe,' D'Arblay promised as Jack and Hooper came to stand either side of me.

'But that's the point – I won't!'

'Alyssa, please!' The bursar's voice sharpened.

'No, Mr D'Arblay.' Cole drew me into the light. 'Let's hear what she has to say.'

I rushed ahead, my voice getting faster, higher. 'It doesn't end with Harry Embsay. There's more.'

'I take it he's the one who just tried to kill you?'

'Yes, but he didn't have anything to do with Lily or Paige. Them – D'Arblay and Guy Simons – they're the ones you need to arrest.'

'Inspector, this is ridiculous.' D'Arblay tried another desperate throw of the dice as Cole reacted by beckoning the two cops who were dealing with Cooke's corpse. 'Alyssa has a wild fantasy playing out inside her head. You can't believe what she's saying.'

Cole stonewalled him. 'I'll be the judge.'

'Obviously something extremely traumatic has gone on here. Surely the important thing is for us to get Alyssa safely back to school.'

'I said I'll be the judge. Go on, Alyssa.'

'They're all part of the Campaign for Racial Purity. Chris Cooke, Audley – the guy from Green Shoots, Harry Embsay and these two. They wear rings engraved with the group's initials.'

D'Arblay smiled thinly and held up his hands – look, no ring!

'They killed Lily because Comco wouldn't stop filming an exposé of their group.'

'How? Exactly how, Alyssa?' It was D'Arblay's final throw. You could picture two white dice rolling across a green baize table, coming up with double one, snake eyes – a killer combination.

But no – unlucky for him, Harry had given me the details and I had Jayden as my witness. 'They kidnapped Lily at Ainslee Westgate and drugged her with ketamine. They dumped her body in the lake.'

D'Arblay's face was still cold and calculating, but Guy's nerve snapped. He gave a short grunt of defeat then broke away and started to run up the hill. Cole's two men went after him and brought him down.

'How do we prove this?' Cole wanted to know. He was patient and respectful with me.

It all hinged on this moment – whether or not I could make the inspector do what I was about to tell him. 'Go to

D'Arblay's office, look on his bookshelves for a locked silver box.'

'What's inside the box?'

'Lily's tooth.' Two small words from me blew D'Arblay's world apart.

The police found D'Arblay's CRP ring in the box along with Lily's tooth and five others from the 1930s. Guy Simons wore his ring on a gold chain round his neck. They found traces of DNA from Harry Embsay on Lily's bag, which meant D'Arblay had given him the task of getting rid of it and Harry had hit on Tom Walsingham's house as a good enough dumping ground. He'd been too lazy and arrogant even to think it through.

Out on the periphery, Cole trawled through the membership of the local CRP branch, picking up the guy with the neck tattoo and his sidekick who mugged me at the train station.

After the Thursday night when D'Arblay was arrested, I didn't see him again – not until the trial seven months down the line. The magistrates didn't give any of them bail.

Jack's face needed five stitches. Harry got thirty-five. I hope they gave him minimal pain relief. He stayed in Queen Elizabeth's for three days, then they transferred him to the hospital wing at Bristol Prison to await trial.

It wasn't Emily Archer or any of the journos at the school gate who got the scoop. No – it was one of Comco's own reporters who went large with it on the front page of Friday's paper. *Race Hate Group Kills Lily Earle*.

Here's the relevant sequence of events – as we're all driving away from Ripley Abbey, Cole phones Dr Webb and tells him that there are vacancies for the post of bursar and head of PE – and the reason why, of course. Saint Sam is totally, one hundred per cent shocked, because it turns out he's been doing an ostrich, head-in-the-sand act right from the start. When he finally comes to his senses, he gets right on the phone to Robert Earle and breaks the news. Meerkat Man never misses an opportunity. He tells his people, run it on the front page tomorrow, 'Because if we don't someone else will.' A leopard doesn't change its spots.

And while we're with the Earles, I heard in the new year that Adam had signed his mother's release documents from the secure wing of her psychiatric hospital and Anna was in London again – not in the Berkeley Square house she'd shared with Robert, but in a quiet new apartment overlooking Regent's Park. Adam quit his job as Comco's director of digital media and plans to pour money into setting up a rival news organization using Anna's money. I only hope that in future they steer clear of conflicts with fascist and racists.

Anyway, they both wrote to me to say that thank you didn't come close to what they really wanted to say. No words did.

'Dearest Alyssa, What happened to Lily has broken my heart,' Anna wrote. 'I miss her every hour of every day. But there are crumbs of comfort to be found, the biggest of which is that you and Paige loved Lily enough to risk your own lives to get to the truth.'

I wrote back. I made a card out of one of Lily's small graphite sketches, a self-portrait that I'd drooled over at the time, and she'd signed it then left it on my pillow for me next morning. The sketch showed a glossy-haired Lily, looking up and smiling.

'Your daughter was amazing,' I wrote. 'I'd do it all again.'

'Lily Earle was amazing,' I told Emily Archer in an exclusive interview for her weekend supplement.

Emily recorded all my words. Her paper printed them without dodgy edits or additions – now there's a first.

'She had more energy, more life than anyone I've ever known. She lit up the room.'

'And Paige?' Emily asked.

I gave my new journalist friend a copy of the eulogy I'd spoken at Paige's funeral. In the first paragraph I covered the serious stuff – Paige's extraordinary talent, her courage, her openness. Then I took a risk. 'Paige's favourite perfume was Equus, otherwise marketed as Eau de Horse. She was the top stylista of the equine world and sales at Joules and Mountain Horse will now plummet.' Paige would have smiled along with most of the mourners – the ones who knew her best. 'She was magnificent. She was my friend.'

And so those of us left alive staggered on under the shadow of our grief to the end of term.

On the day before we packed our bags and left for our family Christmases, Jack and I took a walk along Hereward Ridge. It was calm and sunny on the shortest day of the year.

'You know one of my favourite things about you?' I asked as we went along hand in hand.

'My intellect?' he suggested.

'Nope.'

'My love of numbers?'

'Nope.'

'I give up.'

'I love it that you're taller than me, that I have to stand on my toes to kiss you. Plus I've always loved your quads.'

'Hm.'

'I know – shallow.'

'But cool,' he decided as we wandered between trees. 'You want to guess what's top of my I-love-Alyssa list?'

'My knowledge of Shakespeare?'

'Wrong.'

'My fascinating family history?'

He shook his head.

'My incredible memory?'

'Definitely not that.'

'OK, I give up.'

'It's a contest between your eyes and your hair. Some days I love your eyes better, some days it's your hair.'

'Shal-low!'

'But cool.' He kissed me on his favourite spot on the top of my head.

We came out of the trees and looked down towards the abbey. I spotted a brown dog chasing a stick. I saw Jayden lope down the hill to meet Bolt, pick up the stick and throw it again.

Then Ursula came through a gothic archway and ran to catch up. Jayden put his arm round her shoulders and they walked by the river.

Stick man and stick dog plus new stick girl. I hoped Lily would have drawn a smiley face in her diary. I reckon she would.